DEADLY

THREADS

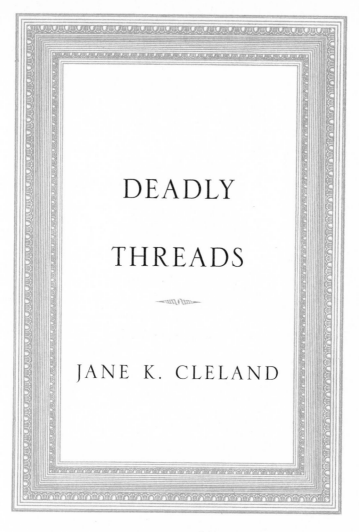

DEADLY

THREADS

JANE K. CLELAND

MINOTAUR BOOKS ❧ NEW YORK

DEADLY THREADS. Copyright © 2011 by Jane K. Cleland. All rights reserved. Printed in the United States of America. For information, address St. Martin's Press, 175 Fifth Avenue, New York, N.Y. 10010.

www.minotaurbooks.com

Library of Congress Cataloging-in-Publication Data

Cleland, Jane K.
    Deadly threads / Jane K. Cleland.—1st ed.
        p.   cm.
    ISBN 978-0-312-58656-0
    1. Prescott Josie (Fictitious character)—Fiction.   2. Murder—Investigation—Fiction.   3. Appraisers—Fiction.   4. New Hampshire—Fiction.   I. Title.
    PS3603.L4555D44   2011
    813'.6—dc22

                                                                    2010041091

First Edition: April 2011

10   9   8   7   6   5   4   3   2   1

Since I was a young girl, cats have been among my best friends. This is for Blackie, Stanley, Tiger, and Aubrey, love bunnies all… and Angela, love bunny #1. And, of course, for Joe.

AUTHOR'S NOTE

This is a work of fiction. All of the characters and events are imaginary. While there is a Seacoast Region in New Hampshire, there is no town called Rocky Point, and many other geographic liberties have been taken.

CHAPTER ONE

W ow! I can't believe it!" Gretchen said, her pretty green eyes fixed on her computer monitor. "That's Bobby Jordan." She lowered her voice to a near-whisper, and I knew the juicy part was coming. "Riley's not in the photo." She looked at me, her eyes round. "Bobby's holding Ruby Bowers's hand."

I knew I shouldn't look at the photograph. I didn't want to contribute to the already rampant rumors that Bobby and Riley Jordan's marriage was on the rocks. As I neatened a pile of antiques-themed magazines, tapping the bottom edges to square them up, I told myself to walk away, just walk away. Instead, I found myself rationalizing looking. The photo was, after all, on a public Web site, and I didn't see how taking a quick peek could do any harm. It wasn't as if I were peeping into someone's bedroom, after all. Curiosity and discretion warred inside me, and curiosity won.

The photo was just as Gretchen described.

I shrugged, feigning a lack of interest. "Maybe Riley's just out of the shot," I said.

"I suppose . . . or maybe she's in the ladies' room." Gretchen stared at the photo for a moment longer, then turned to face me. "Do you think they're . . ."

I didn't know how to respond.

Bobby Jordan was the founder of the trendy Rocky Point–based, blue-themed restaurant chain, and since he was as charismatic as he was handsome, his occasional TV appearances had opened a floodgate of work and social opportunities. Within a year, he'd become one of the most recognizable celebrity chefs in the world. He was also a former Olympic biathlon medal winner—and the grandson of Babs Miller, one of America's sweethearts, an Olympic figure skating champion in the 1930s and one of the first female graduates of Hitchens University. Bobby's flagship restaurant, the Blue Dolphin, was my favorite hangout.

Riley, his wife of seven years, was more reserved. She exuded ladylike elegance. If there had been a New Hampshire Best Dressed List, she'd have been at the top. She was also a serious collector of vintage clothing and had recently started a small consulting business advising museums and individuals on how to build their twentieth-century designer clothing collections. Her book, *Collecting Vintage Clothing,* had brought her instantaneous acclaim in the fashion world.

During my first year in Rocky Point, I'd heard Riley speak at the Rocky Point Woman's Club. Her topic had been "Letting Your Passion Drive Your Collecting." She'd focused on her own favorite collectibles, vintage clothing, specifically the sexy and glamorous gowns designed by Bob Mackie and the practical and stylish separates designed by Claire McCardell, the groundbreaking inventor of "ready-to-wear" fashion. I'd been transfixed. Not only had Riley's presentation been filled with insider stories, she'd been a terrific speaker: energetic, accessible, and informative. I could trace my fascination with vintage clothing to Riley's fun and inspiring program.

Bobby and Riley Jordan were a golden couple, and it was awful to think that their relationship was unraveling.

I looked at the photo again. Ruby Bowers was a bona fide A-list movie star. She was tall and ethereal, in her early thirties and single, and her comings and goings were constant fodder for the gossip magazines. I knew this because Gretchen, the first employee I'd hired when I opened Prescott's Antiques & Auctions six years earlier, had an addiction to celebrity gossip and chattered about her all the time. In this shot, Ruby was wearing Versace. Bobby's tux had been tailored by a pro.

It wasn't the first time Ruby's name had been connected to Bobby's. Lurid headlines in cheesy tabloids had become the norm. According to Riley there was nothing to it but a publicity stunt that seemed to be working. Ruby had started frequenting Bobby's New York City Blue Apple restaurant last fall, and he, a smart and ambitious businessman, had leveraged their burgeoning friendship into priceless publicity. Ditto for Ruby. Occasionally, Riley tagged along on their outings, but as Riley had explained to me over lunch a month earlier, whereas Bobby was in his element smiling for the paparazzi and waving to Ruby's fans, she hated being in the spotlight. Other rumors swirled around Bobby, too, and not just about his alleged affairs. One gossip column Gretchen had told me about speculated that his newfound fame had gone to his head, that with his jet-setting lifestyle and aggressive expansion plans, he was nearly broke.

I sighed, still staring at the photograph of Bobby, with his chiseled features facing the camera, his eyes alight with pleasure, and Ruby, larger than life and as magnificent as always, in her shimmering gold lamé gown, flashing a radiant, Botox-enhanced smile.

Gretchen was waiting for me to speak. I didn't want to add fuel to the already smoldering fire, and I didn't want the rumors to be true. Bobby and Riley were good customers and good friends. I liked them both—a lot. Plus, I'd been in grammar school when I'd learned that there was no upside to gossip.

I smiled at Gretchen and shrugged. "I'm sure their holding hands is completely innocent," I said. "Bobby's in chef-to-the-stars mode, so it makes sense he'd be hanging out with a movie star like Ruby Bowers at some tony Broadway opening party."

"Maybe," Gretchen said, gazing at the screen.

I could tell from her tone that she didn't for a minute believe it.

Neither did I.

Just last week, I'd asked my boyfriend, Ty Alverez—the former Rocky Point police chief and a current training manager for Homeland Security—what he thought about their alleged affair. He'd smiled at me, a private, just-for-me smile that started in his eyes.

"I think Bobby's insane to be messing around with an empty gown like Ruby," he said, "but that's because compared to you, she's nothing but a pretty face. I don't know what Bobby thinks of Riley. Maybe in his mind, Ruby's a hot ticket."

I'd leaned my head against Ty's shoulder and smiled, luxuriating in the knowledge that the man of my dreams wanted me above all others, including a gorgeous-to-the-max movie star.

I shook off the memory and picked up a copy of Riley's book from the stack on Gretchen's desk.

"How many copies did you get?" I asked Gretchen, consciously changing the subject.

"A dozen," she replied. "I figure that whatever doesn't sell at tomorrow's class will sell in the boutique. I thought I'd put up a display by the cash register."

"Good thinking!" I said, pleased at her initiative.

Gretchen had started as a receptionist when I'd opened Prescott's. She'd moved up to chief cashier and administrative manager, and in the last month, she'd taken on a major new responsibility—managing one of our two newest ventures, the small boutique we'd added called Prescott's Vintage Fashions. I'd opened it after I'd purchased the entire inventory of a Manhattan consignment shop. The owner, a woman named Lana whom I'd known since my days working in the city, had called last fall saying she wanted to retire and move to the Bahamas. She'd made me an offer I couldn't refuse, and overnight, we were in the vintage clothing business.

I was taking care of the other new undertaking myself—a workshop series. "Prescott's Antiques & Collectibles: How to Build a Great Vintage Clothing Collection." Tomorrow evening's class, the third in the series, was scheduled to cover shoes and handbags, and I'd invited Riley to co-facilitate. I was thrilled that she'd accepted my offer, and I hoped her book would sell like hotcakes.

"I wish I could take credit," Gretchen said, laughing, "but it was Ava's idea!" She nodded at Ava Marlow, our new intern, a graduate student at nearby Hitchens University.

"Kudos to Ava, then," I replied, smiling at her, then turning back to Gretchen, "but managing a team takes talent, too, so you get credit as well."

"Thanks!" Gretchen said, her expressive eyes sparkling at the compliment.

"Speaking of a team effort," Ava said, standing up and stretching, "cataloguing Prescott's incredible vintage clothing collection makes a girl hungry! I'm going to run over to Westil's Deli. Can I bring anyone anything?"

Ava, in her midtwenties, was a little taller than me, about five-three or so, with platinum blond hair styled in an angle-cut bob and intelligent, dark brown eyes. Not only was she smart and a quick learner, she was innately curious, a must-have quality for an antiques appraiser. She researched carefully, wrote well, and chatted with customers with ease. She also had a terrific work ethic. In addition to attending grad school full-time and interning part-time for us, she spent most of her weekends waitressing at the Blue Dolphin for extra money—and she sewed her own clothes to boot. Today she wore a dark orange raw silk sheath with a brown nubby silk jacket. Her only jewelry was a long, heavy silver link chain that disappeared under her dress. She looked like a million bucks. I was already formulating plans to offer her a full-time job when she graduated.

We all said no, thank you, we didn't want anything. She slipped in her iPod earphones and left, setting the wind chimes Gretchen had hung on the door shortly after we opened tinkling.

I watched as she strolled across the parking lot toward her car, then glanced into the woods, eager for signs of spring. It was only April, too early to realistically expect warm days in New Hampshire, but I was tired of what had been an especially bitter winter. This year's snowfall had shattered all previous records. Adding insult to injury, forecasters were predicting that an overnight storm would add at least another dusting.

"Look!" I said, pointing to a spot near the street. "The forsythia is about to bloom! I see dots of yellow."

"Finally!" Gretchen said, marking the end of her lunch hour by closing the Web site where she'd found Bobby and Ruby's photo. She joined me at the window. "Well, would you look at that?" She pointed to a scruffy-looking silvery gray and beige long-haired cat sauntering through the parking lot. An innate caretaker, she frowned as she watched the cat meander toward our building. "Do you think he's lost? He must be, poor thing. There are no houses nearby."

"Lost or homeless," I said. "Can you tell if he's wearing a collar?" From his sturdy physique, I thought the cat was probably a male.

"No," she said, following his progress until he passed out of sight, heading, it seemed, for the tag sale venue.

"I'll go see," she said.

"I'll come with you."

The cat was sitting behind a bush near the corner of the building. As we approached, he came to meet us. Without hesitation, he rubbed up against my blue-jean-clad leg and mewed, then walked to Gretchen and mewed again. Little tufts of fur grew on the tips of his ears and in between his paw pads. His tail was as bushy as a squirrel's.

"No collar," I said. The cat looked up at me. "He needs a good brushing, but he's very handsome, isn't he?"

"Yes." She watched him for a moment. "He seems friendly. Maybe I'll put out a little bowl of water for him in case he's thirsty."

"Okay—and why don't you ask Eric if he's seen him around?" I suggested. Among Eric's responsibilities as facilities manager was caring for the grounds. "Also, you could call the animal shelter and see if anyone's reported a handsome silver-colored long-haired cat missing."

"Good idea," she agreed.

Inside again, I watched as Gretchen made the calls. Eric had never seen the cat before, and no one had reported him missing.

"He's just a little wanderer," I said.

"I'm sorry to bother you, Josie." Sasha, my chief appraiser, said as Gretchen stepped outside with the water bowl. "Do you have a minute?"

Sasha was quiet and self-effacing most of the time. Only when talking about antiques and art did she become animated and confident.

I zigzagged around a welter of ladies' handbags, purses, and totes covering most of the floor from her desk clear across the room to the guest table. I recognized a black caviar leather Chanel shoulder bag in a quilt pattern, a bamboo-handled patent leather Gucci handbag, and a red-and-white-striped Capezio tote.

If Sasha could authenticate them, and they were in as good shape as they appeared to be, some of them were real finds. The Chanel would sell for around four hundred dollars, and the Gucci would fetch almost a thousand. The Capezio wasn't rare, but it would thrill someone who had just the right outfit to match. Probably it would sell for around fifty dollars. To a stranger, the jumble of bags might appear haphazardly arranged, but knowing Sasha as I did, I was certain there was a method to her madness.

"We found this beautiful Pucci purse at the bottom of one of the boxes," she said, holding it up. "I thought you might want to add it to tomorrow's examples."

"Wow!" The psychedelic pink and orange swirl-patterned purse nearly glowed, the colors were so effervescent. It looked to be in new or near-new condition. "Gotta love the sixties! Too bad we don't have the go-go boots to go with it!"

"I remember go-go boots!" our grandmotherly receptionist, Cara, exclaimed. Cara wore her wavy white hair short. With her round cheerful face and rosy complexion, both the color and the style suited her. "I had a pair! I loved those boots."

"I bet you looked great in them," I said. To Sasha, I remarked, "It's in terrific condition, isn't it?"

"Yes. I doubt it's ever been used. I'm thinking it's worth between five and six hundred dollars."

"What's worth that much?" Gretchen asked as she stepped back inside.

"This Pucci purse," Sasha replied.

"We were wishing we had some go-go boots," I added. "It would have been fun to show the pairing at tomorrow's workshop."

"I guess you'll just have to make do with those gorgeous Christian Dior pumps!" Gretchen said, pointing to the workshop handouts that sat on her desk next to Riley's book.

The cover photo showed the open-toe Dior pumps. They were classically styled with see-through heavy-duty plastic uppers, embellished with navy blue leather trim. Even from a photo, you could tell that they were beautifully crafted.

"You're right—we'll just have to power through somehow," I said, smiling.

"While we're on the subject of gorgeous accessories, I have a question," Gretchen said. "How come these shoes are more than double the price of those Italian turquoise suede and copper metallic ones? They're beautiful, too."

"Good question," Sasha said, in her element. "The Italian shoes are lovely and well constructed, and they're unusual, all of which add value, but the brand isn't as famous or as desirable as Dior. Also, the Diors are made primarily of plastic, a perishable material. Over the years it dries out and cracks."

Gretchen nodded. "Got it! Supply and demand. So the Italian pumps appraise at four hundred dollars, while the Diors go for nearly nine hundred."

"The way of the world," Sasha said.

"And the bane of an antiques dealer's existence!" I remarked, thinking that I didn't need to add what we all knew—it was way harder to find good-quality antiques than it was to sell them. I swept my arm toward the various bags and purses littering the floor. "What's your plan for all of this?"

"If they're on the floor, they're in our database. I've asked Eric to move them all to the warehouse. I'm just trying to create a basic inventory at this point."

"Sounds smart," I replied. I pushed open the door to the warehouse, thinking how lucky Prescott's was to have Sasha at the antiques appraisal reins.

My footsteps echoed as I walked across the cavernous concrete space en route to my private office on the mezzanine level. No one was working at the tables that ranged around the perimeter, so the lighting was dim. Orderly shelves of inventory covered half the space. Most of the other half was cordoned off, separating the various lots of consignment goods waiting for appraising or sale.

I hoped the rumors about Bobby and other women weren't true. Why, I wondered, not for the first time, do people risk everything for a moment or two of transitory pleasure? It made no sense to me, but I knew enough about the world to know that sense wasn't what drove people to cheat.

Riley was loyal, rich, supportive, and fun, but she was also highly private. You always hear how it's the quiet ones who do the most damage if and when they lose it, and Riley was one of the most self-contained people I knew. I had a bad feeling. If Bobby was seeing Ruby, there was a chance he was playing with fire. If I were Bobby, and if the rumors were true, I'd be looking over my shoulder for sure.

CHAPTER TWO

A t noon the next day, while I was reviewing my accountant's quarterly report, Gretchen called up, bubbling with good news.

Yesterday, after the weatherman had upped his prediction from a coating of snow to eight inches, Gretchen had come up to my office, her eyes clouded with worry.

"I don't know what to do about that cat," she'd said. "I called all the vets in town. No one has reported him missing."

"And it's supposed to snow tonight."

"Exactly. The problem is that none of us can adopt him. Between people who have allergies, like Sasha's roommate, people who have dogs who don't like cats, like Cara, and people who aren't home enough to care for him, like you—well, that idea just isn't going to work." She paused for a moment. "He seems so sweet . . . I was wondering . . . what would you think about . . . well, what would you think about his living here?"

I couldn't possibly have resisted the appeal in her eyes even if I'd wanted to, which I didn't. I'd happily agreed to welcome him to Prescott's—if he got an all-clear from a vet.

Before I had time to turn around, she'd made an appointment with Cara's vet, gratefully accepted the check I'd handed her to cover the expenses, and whisked him away. He'd gotten his shots and a flea bath, and had stayed at the animal hospital overnight pending the results of his blood work. With his tests back from the lab, the vet declared him—a two-ish-year-old neutered male—to be in perfect health. He was, it seemed, a

Maine Coon, a very desirable breed, known for its friendly personality and for fetching like a dog. His coloring, we were told, was called chinchilla.

Gretchen's voice on the phone was peppy and full of joy. She said she'd stop by a pet store to load up on supplies, then pick him up. I invited her upstairs for another check.

About ten of two, I went downstairs to greet the cat. Gretchen wasn't back yet, but the office was bustling. Ava was just leaving for lunch as Fred, my other appraiser and a night owl, was arriving for work, grumbling about Big Brother. He'd been caught by Portsmouth's newly installed red-light camera. As he was warning us about it, Gretchen pushed open the door, letting in the bright sunshine and a mild breeze. We'd only gotten a dusting of snow after all, and today it was in the mid-sixties, a perfect spring day.

"Come on in," she called to someone behind her.

Gretchen moved out of the way and lowered the cat's carry case to the floor as Riley Jordan stepped into the office, car keys in one hand and a Louis Vuitton Neverfull tote bag in the other.

"Welcome!" I said to her, smiling. "It goes without saying that we're delighted to see you, but you do realize you're hours early for the workshop, don't you?"

Riley's caramel-colored eyes met mine. She didn't reply, and from her blank stare, I wondered if she'd even heard me. Her auburn hair fell in soft waves to her shoulders. Her Burberry trench coat was buttoned to the neck. Folds of her matching scarf peeked out from under the coat's collar. Her brown leather knee-high boots gleamed. Appearance-wise, she looked as put together as always, but her eyes told another tale. She took a few steps toward Sasha's desk, then stopped. She seemed to be in shock and fearful, as if she'd just seen a ghost.

"Are you okay?" I asked softly, no longer feeling any inclination to joke around.

Riley inhaled as if it were work. She placed her tote bag on the floor, brushed her hair out of eyes, took a deep breath, and smiled, barely. "I'm fine, thanks, Josie . . . just a little tired. I was driving by, so I thought I'd pop in rather than call. By any chance, are you free for lunch tomorrow?"

"Tomorrow," I repeated, thinking aloud. "Wednesday." I turned to Cara. "Do I have any appointments?"

She double-clicked to open our calendar program. "No," she said. "You're available."

"Lunch sounds great," I said, smiling at Riley. "Is twelve-thirty good? Shall we meet at the Blue Dolphin?"

"No," she answered sharply. She seemed to register my surprised reaction, because she smiled again, another wan effort. "I'm in the mood for Italian. Is Gino's all right? You know it, don't you? On Route One?"

"Sure," I said, curious why she didn't want to have lunch at her husband's restaurant. "Gino's is fine."

She glanced at her watch. "Thanks, Josie. I've got to run. I'll see you at six-thirty tonight." As she turned to leave, she noticed her books sitting on Gretchen's desk. This time, her smile seemed sincere. "How lovely! You have my book!"

"Absolutely!" I said. "We'll be selling them tonight and in the shop."

"Thank you," she said, sounding genuinely pleased. She waved good-bye to us all and left.

"She doesn't look well, does she?" Gretchen said.

"I thought she looked drawn," Cara said. "Maybe she's coming down with a cold."

I watched Riley cross the parking lot. Her shoulders were bowed. Her feet dragged. *Something's wrong*, I thought. *She looks as if she has the weight of the world on her shoulders. The kind of weight that comes from a heavy heart, not a head cold.*

"I'm sure she's fine," I said, wanting to nip pointless gossip in the bud. I smiled and looked at the cat's carry case. "What have you there?"

"Prescott's new cat!" Gretchen exclaimed, immediately distracted. "Everyone . . . gather around to meet our new resident!"

"Go ahead and call Eric," I said to Cara.

Eric, in his twenties, was tall and twig-thin, with a serious demeanor. He'd worked for Prescott's since his junior year in high school, joining us as a full-timer as soon as he'd graduated.

A minute later, Sasha, Fred, Cara, Eric, and I stood in a loose circle as Gretchen unzipped the end flap of the carrier. Sasha smiled shyly. Fred leaned back, his arms crossed, reserving judgment. Cara smiled welcomingly. Eric stood a step away, half-frowning, a die-hard dog person trying hard to keep an open mind.

A silvery face poked out of the opening. He looked at us, one at a time.

"He's very good-looking," Cara said.

The cat stepped out and sniffed around. He seemed mildly curious and totally at ease. As he ambled around checking us out, greeting us one by one, rubbing our legs, stretching leisurely by lowering first his front half, then his rear half, I found myself wishing that I handled change half as well as he did.

"What are we going to call him?" Fred asked.

I'd recruited Fred from New York City about five years earlier, and despite his big-city sophistication, he seemed content to live in small-town New Hampshire. He was one of the few New Hampshire men I knew who routinely wore suits. His were Italian made, and he wore them with starched white shirts and skinny black ties. His glasses were of-the-moment stylish—black, with small square frames. I preened myself on the hire. Fred was clever, savvy, and conscientious. As an added bonus, he and Sasha were a terrific team: No matter how much they argued about an appraisal, their disagreements were always professional, never personal. Plus, there was no backstabbing or one-upmanship; there was only mutual respect.

The cat's name was Hank. I didn't know how I knew that was his name—I just did.

"Hank," I said, keeping my eyes fixed on the cat's face. "His name is Hank."

I could feel everyone's eyes as they turned to look at me, then back to him.

"Why Hank?" Gretchen asked.

I smiled at her and shrugged. "I don't know . . . I guess he looks like a Hank."

After several seconds, Sasha said, "You're right. He does look like a Hank."

"Is he really a Henry?" Cara asked. "Are we calling him by his nickname?"

"No. He's a Hank, not a Henry," I replied.

"Yo, Hank," Fred said, shooting him a cool-kid-in-the-'hood grin. "It suits him. I like it."

"Come here, Hank," Gretchen said, scooping him up and carrying him toward the warehouse. "It's time to get you settled into your new home. That's a good boy."

Eric followed her, and I heard him say, "I put all his stuff by the side like you told me. I'll help you with the carpet."

Hank has his own carpet, I thought. I wondered what else Gretchen had bought him.

"Fred," Sasha said, "when you get a chance, would you look at one of the Bob Mackie labels for me? I'm having trouble authenticating it."

"Sure," he said. "What's the problem?"

"There are several different label styles," Sasha said as they headed into the warehouse, "and the differentiations aren't clearly defined."

The phone rang. Cara greeted the caller and began giving directions from Boston.

I started toward my office to resume reading my accountant's report but decided to go see how Hank's new quarters were coming along instead. Eric stood off to the side watching Hank with what looked to be forbearance.

"What do you think of him, Eric?" I asked.

"He's okay, I guess."

"Given that he's not a dog," I said, smiling.

"Exactly." He grinned. "He seems pretty smart, I'll give him that."

"He is *so* smart, aren't you, Hank," Gretchen cooed.

Hank rubbed up against her leg, and she scratched him under his chin. He raised his head to provide better access and closed his eyes.

"Would that we were all so easy to please," I said.

They'd laid a 9' × 12' forest green carpet in an empty area halfway along the left side of the warehouse. Hank's covered litter box sat on a medium-sized black rubber mat at one end. On the other end, a second, smaller black rubber mat held Hank's food and water bowls. Hank stood nearby, aloof but watchful.

"What do you think, Josie? Should we put his bed against the wall over here?"

"It looks like a good spot."

She moved the basket against the concrete wall, then reached into the pet store's shopping bag, extracted a small plastic package, and tore into it.

"He's such a good boy," she said, still cooing, "I got him a catnip mouse."

She shook it and a tinny bell sounded. Hank's expression changed from mildly engaged to engrossed. She tossed it toward him, and it landed about three feet from where he stood. He pounced on it, picked it up by its tail, shook it savagely, then brought it to me and dropped it at my feet.

"Look," I said, astonished. I met their eyes. "He brought me the mouse. The vet said he'd fetch, but I didn't really believe it."

I lobbed the little felt mouse twenty feet or so, and when it landed, it bounced a few times on the concrete. Hank took off like a shot and jumped on it, sending it skittering toward the wall. He batted it like a soccer player running a ball downfield, then picked it up by the tail again and pranced back, dropping it at my feet a second time.

"Wow," I said, petting his whiskers. "You're a very clever boy."

He nuzzled my hand, purring, then yawned and strolled to his bed. I watched as he curled up on his pillow, his eyes half closed, ready for a nap.

"Isn't that something?" I said. "He went from flying through the air to attack a mouse to napping in a minute and a half."

Gretchen giggled. "I think it only took a minute."

Eric smiled. "It'll be good to have him around."

I gave Hank one last look. "Sleep tight, Hank," I said. "Welcome home."

I left them there and went upstairs. The next time I came down, about an hour later, I took another peek at Hank. He was solidly asleep, looking for all the world like a miniature lion.

I spent the next two hours on the phone with a potential client from Santa Barbara, California. Marianne Simpson was interviewing antiques auction houses before narrowing her choices and requesting formal proposals from those that made the short list.

Mrs. Simpson explained that she'd spent most of her adult life traveling the world with her husband, an archaeologist. While he'd overseen digs for major universities and museums, she'd collected rare maps. Now that they were retired, she'd decided to sell her collection to fund their travel. When she'd called to make the appointment to talk to me, I'd allocated half an hour, ample time, I'd thought, to answer her questions and ask some of my own.

Mrs. Simpson had a different idea on how to vet auction houses. She wanted far more detail about our policies and procedures than the typical consignee. To my mind, she was smart and I was lucky. In my experience, the more potential customers know about auction house practices, the more likely they are to choose Prescott's. While it was a great opportunity for me to highlight our advantages, it required enormous concentration and sustained focus. Two hours is a long time.

"Thank you," she said at the end of our call. "I'm putting Prescott's on the short list."

Woo hoo! I thought, silently congratulating myself. Her collection included fourteen examples of seventeenth-century maps, including a world view by Melchior the Younger dating from 1630, which would, I knew, sell for close to six figures. I grabbed a pen and started writing notes. I couldn't stop thinking about the possibilities. Maybe, I thought, we could call the auction "A World View" and offer globes and astronomical devices in addition to the maps. I did some preliminary research on recent auctions of rare maps, then expanded my research to include auctions of related objects. As the proposal began coming together in my head, I found I couldn't write fast enough.

The next time I looked up it was three minutes to six.

I hurried down the stairs to check out the tag sale venue. The workshop was due to begin in half an hour, not much time if the room wasn't set properly. Eric had placed the chairs in a semicircle facing the central podium. A poster featuring a cross-section diagram of a shoe rested against the lower cubby. On either side, long tables stretched along the walls and were draped with tablecloths. I nodded, satisfied. The room was ready.

Back in the main office, everyone but Gretchen and Fred had left for the day. Fred was on the phone. I noticed the purses that had ranged on and around Sasha's desk were gone.

"Want to help me wheel the cart in?" I asked Gretchen.

"Sure," she said, standing up.

The cart, stocked with the designer and counterfeit hand-bags and shoes that Riley and I would be using at tonight's workshop, made a *cunkita-cunkita* sound as its rubberized wheels rolled along the concrete flooring. When we reached the tag sale room, Gretchen opened the door and I guided the cart in.

"Everything looks in order," I said. "Once you bring in the refreshments, I think we're good to go."

"I wonder where Riley went," she said.

"Riley? She's here already?"

"Uh-huh. She got here about four. She said her appointment ended earlier than she expected." Gretchen walked to the win-dow. "Her car's still here."

"I bet she got antsy. On a day like this, teasing us with warm sunshine, I know I'd have been seriously tempted to go for a walk."

"I did see a car leaving the lot about, oh, I don't know, about half an hour ago, I guess. Maybe a friend stopped by and they ran out for coffee."

"You think? If so, I hope she gets back soon."

We began placing the bags and shoes on the tables in the order Riley and I would be referring to them. I stepped back to consider the alignment.

"Why did she come in here?" I asked. "I mean, why didn't she just hang out in the office with you guys?"

"I offered, but she wasn't interested. I felt bad . . . I mean . . . she asked if she could hang out, and when I said of course, she went back to her car and got a book from the trunk. She said that if I didn't mind, she'd just like to sit quietly and read. I told her that was fine and brought her into the tag sale room. That was all right to do, wasn't it?"

"Absolutely. As long as she's happy, I'm happy." We contin-ued to arrange the examples. After a moment, I asked, "How did she seem?"

"About the same," Gretchen replied. She sighed, her ready empathy surfacing.

"I hope she's okay," I said, shaking my head.

Gretchen went to bring the tray of gingersnaps and the pitcher of lemonade while I finished up. I stepped back and scanned the tables. I nodded, pleased. The examples were appropriately balanced in terms of color, designer, and value.

"Okay, then," I said, "we're ready."

I left Gretchen there to greet the arriving students and returned to the front.

I took a guest chair and told Fred, "Wait until you hear about the consignment we've been invited to bid on."

"A Melchior the Younger," he repeated, after I explained the map project's scope. He pushed up his glasses. "That's about as rare as it gets."

I smiled, pleased at his enthusiasm. "Let's keep our fingers crossed!"

We agreed to meet first thing in the morning to discuss the proposal, and I turned my attention to my workshop notes. I was wrestling with how much detail to provide. Riley and I had agreed that we wanted to equip the students, most of whom were novices, with the knowledge they needed to build their collections wisely, but we didn't want to burden or bore them with minutiae. At the same time, we didn't want to leave them with the impression that determining value was easy.

I never wear a watch since it always seems to get in the way when I'm working, so I'd placed my cell phone on the podium. As the time crept toward six-thirty, I found myself glancing at it every minute or so.

Riley still hadn't returned.

At six twenty-five, I approached Becka Dowling, an English professor at Hitchens and one of Riley's oldest friends. She was standing near the window with Kenna Duffy, Bobby's book-keeper, chatting.

"You haven't heard from Riley, by any chance, have you?" I asked.

Kenna, reed-thin, with an olive complexion, angular features, and an easy smile, shook her head.

"No," Becka said. "Why? Isn't she here?" Becka was curvy, with fair, flawless skin and straight, blunt-cut, chin-length brown hair. She glanced at Riley's car. "I assumed she was somewhere out of sight getting ready for a grand entrance . . . no?"

"No. We think she might have gone for a walk. Maybe she lost track of time. It's so nice out, it would be easy to do."

"Except it's getting dark," Kenna said, gazing out the windows into the gathering dusk.

"Besides, Riley's early to everything," Becka added. She looked at her watch, then at me. "I mean *everything*. She'd be early for a root canal."

I didn't know what to do. "Let's give it a few more minutes," I said, forcing myself to smile.

As I joined a clutch of students oohing and ahhing over the Dior pumps, I recalled Riley's haunted demeanor and my earlier thought that something was wrong.

At six-forty I decided to start the class. Riley still hadn't returned. I kept glancing toward the parking lot expecting to see her trotting toward the door, embarrassed at having lost track of time.

"Everyone!" I called. "If you'd take a seat, we're just about ready to begin." I smiled, covering up my anxiety with a high-voltage welcome. "Tonight we're going to enter the world of vintage shoes and handbags! As you can see from the display, we have some beauties to discuss. I expect our guest speaker, Riley Jordan, to arrive any time. Meanwhile, I thought it might make sense for us to review some terminology." I held up the poster. "We put together this diagram of a shoe—you'll find it in your handout as Appendix One . . ."—I waited for everyone to find the place—"so that you can become familiar with industry jargon. By using the correct words, you'll be able to communicate with each other and with professionals with confidence. You see the heel, of course, and the upper. There's the tongue—" I broke off and smiled. "My arms are getting tired holding this. Give me a sec. I'm going to grab an easel."

I reached under the back display table where we stash supplies and touched what felt like skin. I recoiled, nearly toppling over, then squatted, took a deep breath, and slowly raised the tablecloth.

Riley Jordan lay on her back, her arms by her sides. Her features were distorted, her skin swollen and bluish purple. Her eyes stared sightlessly at the bottom of the table. *Maybe,* I thought, *she's still alive.* I knew the thought was irrational, even as it came to me. Her Burberry scarf was twisted around her neck, knotted, and pulled taut. I took a to-my-toenails breath, then tried to ease my finger into the knot, hoping to loosen the restraint, but the fabric was so tightly drawn, it cut into her neck like wire. Her mouth was open, as if she'd been screaming when she died. I closed my eyes, fighting waves of dizziness and nausea, and dropped the tablecloth. There was nothing I could do. Without question, Riley was dead.

CHAPTER THREE

J osie?" Gretchen asked, crouching beside me. She must have seen anguish in my eyes, because she added in a whisper, "What is it?"

"It's Riley," I whispered. "She's dead. Go into the warehouse and call nine-one-one."

Her eyes opened wide, and she started to say something, but she stopped when I shook my head.

"Go quietly," I said into her ear. "Go now."

Without another word, she stood up and hurried to the warehouse door.

I used my hands to push myself upright. Everyone in the class, eight women and two men, sat in varying stages of agitation, waiting for me to speak. Becka perched on the edge of her seat, her legs pulled under her, as if she were about to take off at a sprint. Kenna's grip on her purse was so tight her knuckles were white. A man stood up, then sat back down. I didn't want to tell them that Riley was dead. I didn't want to be the one to have to tell them.

"I have bad news," I said from the podium. "You just saw Gretchen leave." I looked down as I felt Hank rub my leg. He must have slipped into the room as Gretchen left. "I asked her to call the police. I'm afraid Riley's dead—murdered. Her corpse is under that table." Shock and horror registered on their faces. I stood silently, leaning against the podium, glad for its support. When their gasps and disbelieving murmurs had faded away,

I continued. "Obviously, we all need to stay here until the police arrive."

Gretchen came back in. "They're on their way," she said, her eyes moist.

I nodded. "Everyone, please stay seated. I'm certain the police would say that the less we move around, the better."

I walked to the outside door and stood there with my back to everyone. Tears welled in my eyes and spilled onto my cheeks. I was trembling. I wanted to call Ty, to hear his strong, deep voice. I wanted to curl up in a little ball and weep. I wanted to scream.

Someone had strangled Riley in my tag sale room. *Who could have wanted Riley dead?* I asked myself. *Riley, who wouldn't hurt a fly. Riley, who was generous and gracious.*

I recalled how distressed Riley had seemed when she'd stopped by to invite me to lunch. She'd acted shell-shocked. As I blinked away tears, I couldn't believe Riley was dead. I just couldn't believe it.

Poor Riley, I thought.

Chief Ellis Hunter, a former New York City homicide detective who'd taken on the Rocky Point police chief's job to see if Norman Rockwell had it right about small towns, had, over the year he'd been here, become a good friend. A widower, he was dating my neighbor, landlady, and best friend, Zoë Winterelli, and the four of us—Ellis and Zoë and Ty and me—spent a lot of time together. He was a friend, but there was nothing friendly in his demeanor now.

Standing just inside the room talking to Detective Claire Brownley, then informing everyone that we would be interviewed one at a time while the scientists began their investigation, he was all business. He explained that he and Detective Brownley would share the duty of conducting the initial interviews, then called me over.

"Is it on?" Ellis asked, pointing at the security camera mounted over the entry door.

"No."

"Why not?"

"We only keep them on during the tag sale—when we're setting up, running it, and breaking it down."

His brow wrinkled. "How come?"

I looked at my toes, embarrassed. "Money." I raised my eyes. "My security company charges by the hour—the more hours the cameras are on, the more manpower they need to monitor them and the more storage space is used on their computers. I didn't perceive the need for having cameras on in an empty room, or during events like tonight's workshop when there's just a few people here, and Gretchen or I are on-site all the time."

"But that's the door to the warehouse," he objected, pointing. "Shouldn't it always be monitored?"

"It's locked all the time, but it gets armed, and the camera facing it activated, when we set the night alarm."

He surveyed the doors and windows. "Do you use motion detectors?"

"No. It's totally impractical. We're in and out all the time."

"Keycards?"

I shook my head.

"Thanks, Josie," he said, dismissing me. "We'll get back to you in a minute."

I felt completely stupid. What was the point of having security cameras if I didn't turn them on? If I had, we'd already know who'd killed Riley. My eyes filled again and I swallowed twice, fighting to regain control. *Keycards,* I thought, *make a lot of sense.* We'd be able to track who entered or exited each door, and when.

I crossed the room to where Gretchen was standing, her eyes open wide, taking it all in.

"First thing in the morning," I whispered, "call Hale Alarms and get them in here to conduct a full security audit. I want to know vulnerabilities in the system and what they'd recommend we change. And I want all security cameras on, all the time."

She glanced up at the dormant camera. "Okay," she said.

I knew it was a classic case of closing the barn door after the horse escaped, but at least it was better than stubbornly leaving the door wide open.

I sat in a corner, watching the technicians work and stroking Hank. Hank somehow sensed that I was upset, and he was doing his best to comfort me. Gretchen was fussing about, offering coffee and lemonade and cookies. Kenna was trying hard to get permission to leave, explaining that she had young children and had to pick them up. Once the police learned they were at her mother's, and that her mom had no problem keeping them, even overnight, if necessary, they refused to let her leave. I could see in her eyes that she was impatient and annoyed. Becka, sitting beside her, looked stricken.

When my turn came, I answered Detective Brownley's questions as simply as I could. I recalled Max, my lawyer of choice when only a lawyer would do, telling me that when talking to the police, the shorter the answer, the better. In fact, he said, one-word answers were ideal.

Detective Brownley wore a navy blue pantsuit with a coral blouse. Her black hair was cut short and parted on the side. Her eyes were blue. Her skin was creamy white, and flawless. I'd first met her four or five years earlier, and I knew her to be honest and diligent, a winning combination.

"Josie, this is a preliminary interview," she explained. "Of course, I have your name and contact information. You haven't moved, have you?"

"No," I said.

"Okay, then, let's start with your relationship to the victim. How did you know Ms. Jordan?"

"We were friends. She was a customer, too."

"How did you meet her?" she asked.

I explained about hearing her speak at the Rocky Point Woman's Club luncheon.

She nodded, then asked, "When did you see her last?"

"About two o'clock today. She stopped in on her way to an appointment to invite me to lunch."

"Any special occasion for the lunch?"

"She didn't say."

"You said you're friends. Am I correct, then, in assuming that you've seen her socially before?" the detective asked.

"Yes. Several times."

She jotted a note. "When did you schedule the lunch for?"

"Tomorrow." I closed my eyes for a moment. *Poor Riley.*

"Who else did she talk to while she was here?"

"No one. I mean, she said hello to everyone, but I was the only person she talked to, specifically."

"So you'd say she was here for a minute or two?"

"That sounds about right."

"Did she tell you where she was going next? What appointment?"

"No."

"How did she seem?"

"Upset."

"In what way?"

I described her appearance and mannerisms and her snapping response when I'd suggested eating at the Blue Dolphin.

The detective nodded and made a note. "When did she return?" she asked. "Do you know?"

"Gretchen said around four. I didn't see her."

"Where were you?"

"Up in my office."

"I don't mean to upset you, but I need to ask a few questions about your finding the body."

"Okay," I said.

She asked me to explain how I came to discover the corpse, then asked, "What was your first thought?"

"That she was dead."

"Didn't a name come to you? Didn't you think, 'She's dead. So-and-so killed her'?"

"Not really."

"Who, Josie?"

I shook my head, staring at the ground, not wanting to meet her eyes.

"It's important, Josie," she said softly, "or I wouldn't ask."

I looked at her. Her eyes conveyed a hint of compassion, but mostly she looked determined.

I took in a breath. "I didn't have the thought that anyone in particular killed her. I just wondered if maybe Bobby was somehow responsible for her being so upset."

"Her husband."

I nodded.

"What made you wonder that?"

I explained about Gretchen finding the photo of Ruby and Bobby and the reports of Bobby's financial difficulties, then added, "I have no personal knowledge that Bobby was having an affair with anyone, let alone Ruby Bowers, nor do I know anything about his business. Riley dismissed the idea that he was playing around out of hand. In fact, she was very good-humored about it. She laughed at the gossip she read in magazines. Still, the photo was pretty damning." I lowered my voice as if I were revealing a secret, not describing a photograph that had been uploaded to a public Web site. "They were holding hands." I shrugged.

She nodded, then wrote for several seconds. "When did you last see Mr. Jordan?"

I thought back. "About a month ago. He came in and asked me to help him pick out a birthday present for Riley." I shook my head at the memory. "We got her a fabulous Bob Mackie gown, black with feathers and crystals. Mr. Mackie had originally designed it for Cher."

"Back to finding the body. I know you were stunned at seeing her strangled. Apparently the murder weapon is a scarf. Did you recognize it?"

I winced as the picture came back to me. "Yes. It was hers. She was wearing it this afternoon with a trench coat. The coat was under the table, too, kind of rolled up."

"How about her outfit? Had she changed clothes?"

"I didn't see what she was wearing earlier—just her coat and scarf and boots. Her boots were the same as before."

"She was also wearing gold knot earrings and a diamond wedding band. Were those the same as earlier?"

"Yes."

"Was anything missing?"

"Like what?"

Detective Brownley shrugged. "Like a shawl or a hat... anything?"

I considered the question for a moment. "No, not that I noticed."

"What else can you tell me that will help us?"

I shook my head slowly. "I have no idea."

"That's it for now, then," she said, sliding her notepad into her pocket.

I glanced around the room. "Have you learned anything?" I asked. "Anything at all that will help?"

"Everyone's being very cooperative," she said, revealing nothing at all. "We appreciate that—a lot."

At nine fifteen, after the police had scheduled appointments for Gretchen and me to stop in at the police station the next day, they allowed everyone to leave. Riley's car had been towed away, and they'd sealed the tag sale room as a crime scene. I called Ty from my private office. He'd already heard the news. Wes Smith, the incredibly plugged-in reporter for our local newspaper, the *Seacoast Star,* had posted a news flash report on the newspaper's Web site. In it, he promised more details for the morning online edition, and I knew what that meant. Wes would be hounding me for a quote.

"How are you holding up?" Ty asked.

"About like you'd expect. I'm pretty upset. Mad, too."

"Have you eaten?"

"No . . . I'm not hungry."

"Come home. You need to eat. I'll have something ready for you."

"Okay," I said. "Thank you, Ty."

Before I left, I read Wes's online article. He started by saying that rumors abounded that Bobby had been cheating on Riley for months, maybe years, but I already knew that. I hadn't heard that he and Riley were alleged to be growing apart. According to the article, Wes had spoken to several unnamed friends and associates who confirmed the story. As examples, Wes stated that while Bobby loved traveling the world, Riley didn't even own a passport, and while Bobby had wanted to relocate his company's headquarters to New York City to cement his role as a player in the celebrity world he'd just entered, Riley didn't like New York and had no intention of moving there. She'd wanted to stay close to home, to live where she'd always lived—in Rocky Point, New Hampshire. Wes also reported that while Bobby's money was all tied up in his business, Riley's fortune was in the $35 to $40 million range. *Yowzi!* I thought.

As I turned off my computer, I shook my head, impressed as always at Wes's abilities. Riley had only been dead for a few hours, yet Wes had nailed down relevant quotes and filled his story with prurient innuendo. I also had the thought that unless Riley had a very unusual will, Bobby was now a very rich man.

CHAPTER FOUR

W es called as I was driving home. He'd already left me two voice mail messages. Knowing him as I did, I knew what he wanted: inside information. I let this call go to voice mail, too. I just didn't have the emotional wherewithal tonight to deal with his relentless questioning. Talking with Wes was work. He'd prod and poke and peck away until I found myself reliving the evening's horror and revealing more than I intended. Tomorrow I would tell him what I knew, a necessary first step to getting information from him, but tonight I needed Ty's tender care, not Wes's bludgeoning. I was just about running on empty.

I pulled into the driveway, relieved to be home. Ty must have been on the lookout for me. He had the porch light on and the front door open before I turned off the engine. I waved at him, then sat for a moment, overwhelmed with surging and conflicting emotions. I still couldn't believe Riley was dead. I was grief-struck. I'd valued her friendship and had been looking forward to getting to know her even better as the years went on. I also couldn't believe someone had killed her in *my* tag sale venue, of all places. It felt like a personal affront, and I was outraged. I was also scared—a killer had entered my building, and left. Was it someone I knew? Terror, shock, sorrow, and anger raged inside me, leaving me emotionally battered and physically exhausted.

"Hey," I called to Ty as I stepped out of the car.

"Hey," he said. "How you doin'?"

I shrugged and walked up the path. Ty was tall, over six feet, and fit. His hair was short and dark brown. His complexion was dark, too, even darker now than before he took the job with Homeland Security, a testament to the frequent training exercises he conducted outdoors. He was smart and sexy and caring and funny. I adored him.

"I feel miserable," I said, tears stinging my eyes. "Sad. Angry. Frightened. Shocked. Really shocked."

"Makes sense."

He hung my coat on the hook by the door and watched as I exchanged my work boots for pink fuzzy slippers.

"I want to take a bath," I said. "A very hot, very bubbly bath."

"Before or after you eat?"

"Were you able to find anything?" I pressed my fingers against my forehead. I didn't have a headache, but a faint throbbing behind my eyes made me think that I might be getting one. I couldn't remember if there was any food in the house.

He said, "We're set. I borrowed salad stuff from Zoë and got a pizza out of the freezer. I added basil."

I touched his cheek. "Thank you."

He smiled. "You're welcome. All I need is ten minutes' notice. Before or after the bath?"

"After."

"Zoë sends love and says if she can do anything, call."

"She's such a doll."

"Do you want a drink?"

"Are you kidding me? I want two. I'm thinking I ought to have a Cherry Blossom."

"Why?"

"It's a happy spring drink."

"You're a very whimsical girl, you know that, right?"

"Whimsical. I like that."

Ty brought me the frothy pink drink in a chilled plastic martini glass just as I was settling into the tub.

"This defines decadence," I said.

"No. That would involve champagne, rose petals, strawberries, and chocolate." He waved it aside. "Another day."

"Date," I said, smiling.

I leaned back, resting the glass on the tub's edge, and closed my eyes to let the hot soak work its magic. After a while, I opened my eyes and sipped the drink until the glass was empty. Downstairs, wrapped in my toasty-warm pink chenille robe, I sat at the round kitchen table and watched as Ty poured me a refill. He dropped his empty Copperhook bottle into the recycling bin and pulled another from the fridge.

"Want to make the dressing?" he asked.

"Sure," I said.

I whisked a cup of my mom's Dijon vinaigrette, a recipe I knew by heart.

We didn't eat until after ten thirty, but it didn't feel too late. It felt just right. After dinner, watching as Ty cleaned up, I realized my brain was more than half focused on the question of who'd killed Riley, and I was certain I'd have trouble sleeping. I was wrong. Much to my amazement, by eleven thirty, I was dead asleep.

Ellis, Chief Hunter, called at seven thirty the next morning just as I was pouring my second cup of coffee. Ty had already left for a day trip to Medford, Massachusetts.

Ellis apologized for the early call, explaining that he wanted to fill me in on what would be happening that day at Prescott's.

"The technicians plan on taking another look at the tag sale room first thing this morning," he said. "It'll be off-limits for the foreseeable future, certainly for today, and maybe longer. I know that's a hardship for you. I'm sorry for it—but the technicians need to take whatever time they need."

"I understand. To tell you the truth, I've already decided to cancel this week's tag sale. It would just feel creepy to go ahead with it. Creepy and disrespectful."

"Understood. When does your staff get in?"

"Nine, more or less. At least, Gretchen and Cara are in by nine. Fred usually comes in later, sometimes as late as noon or one or even later. Ava planned on working today from ten to three, if I'm remembering right. Eric usually starts about eight. His girlfriend is a teacher, so he's up and about early."

"Can you call Fred and Ava and ask them to get in by nine, too? I need to talk to everyone who spoke to Ms. Jordan yesterday, and I'd like to do it as a group discussion."

"I'll call them as soon as we're done talking," I said.

"Thanks, Josie." He cleared his throat. "One more question. Have you spoken to that reporter? Wes Smith?"

My heart skipped a beat. Ellis had, in the past, asked me to talk to Wes, to pass along information that he'd hoped Wes would publish without attributing it to a police source. Ellis's avowed goal had been to generate leads and tips and suggestions from the community, and maybe that's all he was up to. I'd wondered at the time if he was trying a diversion, to get Wes focused on my tips in the hope that he wouldn't notice other lines of investigation. From what I'd been able to tell, whatever Ellis's strategy had been, it had worked. He'd gotten helpful leads from the community, and Wes hadn't tripped him up.

"He called me, but I haven't called him back," I said.

He paused. "Okay, thanks, Josie. I'll see you soon."

I didn't know what Ellis had up his sleeve this time around, but I sure as shooting knew he'd be pulling something out from under his cuff.

Cara, Ava, Gretchen, Sasha, and Fred sat at their desks. Eric, Ellis, and I sat in a loose circle around the guest table.

Ellis scanned our faces. He was a big man, tall and fit, with regular features and an appealing smile. He had a short, ragged dark red scar near his right eye. He wore a brown and tan tweed jacket, brown slacks, and an ivory shirt with a brown-and-gold-striped tie.

"First off," he said, "I'd like to hear about any interactions you had with Ms. Jordan yesterday. Let's go around the room. If someone seems to be forgetting something, don't wait, jump right in."

Cara, Sasha, and Fred reported that they'd said hello and chatted about little nothings, like the odd April weather, snowing one minute, then mild the next, and nothing else.

"I ran into her in the parking lot at lunchtime," Ava said. "We talked for a minute about clothes. I admired the Claire McCardell jacket she was wearing—I mean, wow, it was so gorgeous! I told her that since I design and make most of my own clothes, I'm always on the lookout for inspiration, and I often find it by looking at McCardell's designs. Riley said McCardell was one of her all-time favorite designers."

"That's when I came up," Gretchen said. "You were saying how some designers use things like bows not as closure devices, but as decorations on shoes and handbags and to create or adorn jewelry, but that McCardell never did."

"Yes, that's exactly right," Ava agreed, nodding. "Riley said it was an example of staying true to your design ethos. McCardell believed that form had to follow function."

"Riley was incredible, wasn't she?" Gretchen said sadly. "She knew so much, and was so generous with her knowledge."

"Thank you," Ellis said. "Eric? How about you?"

Eric said he hadn't spoken to Riley at all. "I mean, not even when I went into the tag sale room to arrange the chairs. She was reading. She just looked up and smiled."

"When was that?" the chief asked.

"About five thirty."

"When did you leave work for the day?"

"Right after that. I normally work eight to four, but what with sweeping out the new boutique and starting to polish the Fallor estate furniture, I got behind schedule." He looked down as if he expected to be criticized for poor time management. "I was late setting up."

I made a mental note to get him a temporary helper right away, while we assessed whether we needed to add a new permanent position.

"And you, Josie?" Ellis asked.

"Riley and I scheduled lunch. She was pleased we had her book in stock. She said she was on her way to an appointment. That's it. I didn't see her when she came back."

"Gretchen?" he asked, turning toward her.

"Ava was on her way out to lunch when I was on my way in with Hank, our new cat. The three of us chatted for a minute, then Ava left and Riley and I came in. I heard Riley and Josie make the lunch date, and she talked about her book, just like Josie said. That was it for then. When Riley returned about four, she said her appointment had ended early, and she asked if she could sit somewhere and read. I said of course, and she went back out to her car. When she came in, she had a book with her, a Nero Wolfe mystery. I took her into the tag sale room, unlocked the outside door, and asked if she wanted any coffee or cookies or anything, and she said she didn't." She shrugged. "That's it."

"Why did you unlock the door?"

"For students who come early and in case Riley wanted to stretch her legs or something."

"Did you check on her later?" Ellis asked.

"No" she replied sadly.

"What time did you see that car?" I asked her.

"What car?" Ellis asked before Gretchen could answer.

"A car leaving the parking lot," Gretchen said. "I wouldn't have thought about it at all except that when Josie and I wheeled the samples into the tag sale room and Riley wasn't there, it occurred to me that maybe a friend had stopped by and she and Riley had gone out for coffee."

"Couldn't it have been a customer leaving, or a vendor?"

"Sure, except there hadn't been anyone here."

He nodded. "When was that?" he asked.

She pursed her lips, thinking. "About five thirty or quarter to six, I think . . . somewhere in there. I'm sorry I can't be more exact."

"Was the room set up?"

"Yes."

Ellis turned to Eric. "And you were done with the setup by five thirty?"

Eric looked nervous, as if he wished he didn't have to commit to a specific time. "I think so."

Ellis nodded again, then turned to Gretchen. "What kind of car was it?"

"I don't know. I only saw a flash of silver, and I only saw it for a second."

"Do you have a sense of the shape of the car?" he asked, his tone patient, almost uncurious.

She shook her head. "Not really."

"Keep thinking about it. Something may come back to you."

"Okay," she said. "I'm sorry."

"You're doing fine," he told her, smiling. He took us all in with a sweeping glance. "What impression did you have of Riley? Did you notice anything unusual about her appearance or manner?"

"She seemed troubled," Cara said without hesitation. "Several of us commented on it."

"In what way?" Ellis asked.

"Her expression . . . and the way she nearly bit Josie's nose off when she suggested they have lunch at the Blue Dolphin."

Ellis confirmed that Gretchen and I shared Cara's opinion, then turned to Ava. "How about you?" he asked.

"I didn't know her well, so I'm not sure I would have noticed a difference in her manner. When I ran into her in the parking lot, she seemed fine—a little tired, maybe."

He asked if anyone had socialized with Riley outside of work. No one had except me. He told me he'd get the details about our relationship later in the morning. He also asked if anyone had any idea who killed her, but no one had, or at least, no one voiced an opinion. He thanked us as he handed out his business cards.

"If you think of anything, even something that seems inconsequential or minor, give me a call. Rumors are good, too. We're looking for leads, and the schoolyard rules about tattling don't apply. If you think of something, tell me."

We all promised we would.

"And I'll see you, Josie, at ten, and you, Gretchen, at tenthirty, at the station house, right?" he asked.

We confirmed the appointments and then I walked him through the warehouse to the tag sale room, where the technicians were standing with their backs to us, talking. I paused before opening the door, my hand on the knob, and turned to face him.

"I know you talked to everyone last night. Did anyone in the class see anything?"

"Why would you think they might?" he countered.

"I wouldn't. I was just curious."

"Everyone was cooperative, which doesn't always happen." He smiled at me, then glanced at the doorknob. I got the hint and opened the door. Before entering, he called to a technician. "May I come in?"

"Yeah," one of the men replied. "We're almost done."

He smiled at me again and nodded good-bye.

I stood for a moment watching through the window, thinking that Ellis was more adept at tactfully avoiding answering questions than anyone I'd ever met, even Detective Brownley.

I kept my ten o'clock appointment at the Rocky Point police station and was led directly into Interrogation Room One, a dreary space with an old metal table in the center and a human-sized cage in the corner.

Ellis sat across from me, thanked me for coming in, and turned on the video recorder, the department's standard operating procedure.

After reciting routine information about the date and time, my name, and the reason for the interview, he asked several questions about Riley, including how we met and what she was like. I repeated what I'd told Detective Brownley the day before.

"Did she ever talk to you about the gossip surrounding her husband?" he asked.

"A little. She said she and Bobby got a good laugh at the gossip sheets." I shook my head, saddened as I recalled how her attitude had shifted in recent weeks. "That was at first. About a month ago, things changed. Riley and I were having lunch, and she seemed . . . I don't know . . . off. I asked her if anything was wrong. She said that to tell the truth, she was fed up with all the gossip magazines asking her to comment on Bobby's relationship with Ruby Bowers. She said there was nothing to it, and she just wished the media would let it—and her—alone." I looked at Ellis directly. "Riley said that Bobby's spending a lot of time with Ruby was just a publicity stunt, that he was milking her for all she was worth." I shook my head. "I told her that was kind of icky."

"Icky?" Ellis repeated.

"Yes. Icky. Riley said that it wasn't icky at all since Ruby was doing exactly the same thing for exactly the same reason. By letting the paparazzi think there was something going on, they each got more media coverage than they would have without the ploy. I understood and couldn't really argue. That's how it works, you know? I mean, forget the ethics of trying to manipulate the press and just evaluate the tactics—to me, it definitely makes it less icky knowing they were in it together, but it's still pretty icky."

"Did she ever talk about Bobby and other women besides Ruby?"

"No," I replied.

"What about the Blue restaurant business? Did Riley discuss it?"

"Not really. At some point, she mentioned that she'd invested in Bobby's business. She was excited that his expansion was going so well. I didn't think anything about it. I mean, along with everyone else in town, I knew she was well-off— you know that her grandfather founded the Marshall Soup Company, right?—so it just seemed natural that she'd put money into his restaurants."

"Did she ever mention any concerns she had about the business?"

"She didn't like it that Bobby traveled so much, if that's what you're asking. I mean, she knew he needed to travel for business, but I got the impression that she wished he was a little less into the celebrity chef see-and-be-seen thing."

"What gave you that impression?"

I looked away, recalling her frank comments, then turned back to Ellis. "It wasn't an impression—she said so."

He nodded. "What other concerns did she express?"

"Bobby talked about relocating to New York City, and she didn't want to go."

He nodded again. "What else?"

"That's it."

"Why do you think she wanted to have lunch with you?"

I shrugged. "We were friends. She didn't need a special reason."

"So you don't think the timing meant anything?"

I recalled her frazzled deportment. "I don't know."

Ellis pecked away at me for several more minutes, asking for details I didn't have about Riley and Bobby's relationship and Bobby's business. Then he thanked me and told me he'd be in touch.

When I left at ten thirty-five, Gretchen was just getting started.

Wes called again as I was getting settled at my desk, and this time I took the call.

"Why didn't you call me back?" he asked, sounding hurt, skipping saying hello, as usual.

"Hi, Wes. How are you?"

"Good, good. Didn't you get my messages?"

I swiveled to face my old maple tree. Lawn-green clusters of small leaves seemed to have appeared overnight.

"I didn't want to talk about it, Wes. I was pretty upset. I still am."

"We need to meet. I have questions—and I have an info bomb."

I didn't hesitate. I could only tell Wes a little about Riley, but Wes could tell me a lot about the investigation. If he had information, I wanted it. "Okay," I said. "Fifteen minutes. At our dune."

I told Cara I was leaving and was out the door in nothing flat.

CHAPTER FIVE

I stood on the shifting sand watching the tide roll in. The April sun was bright, but weak. It was sixty-six degrees, way above average, and it felt downright balmy. The ocean was calm, the water midnight blue and glittering with golden sparkles. The beach was thick with bottle-green ribbons of seaweed and littered with pebbles and rocks and shells and driftwood.

I heard the rumbling of Wes's old car and turned in time to see him jerk to a stop and jump out. He looked good, still a little pudgy, as if he never exercised, but less so than the last time I'd seen him. More surprising, he appeared to have color in his face. His normally pasty white complexion was definitely less ashen than I'd come to expect.

"You look great, Wes! Do you have a tan?" I asked as he scampered toward the top.

"Not really," he said, and from his tone, I could tell he was embarrassed.

While Wes and I weren't close like buddies, I wasn't worried that he'd find my curiosity impertinent. I suspected he thought of me like an older sister. I knew I thought of him as a younger brother, half annoying and half a really good guy I trusted and cared about.

"Did you go on vacation?" I asked.

"Sort of. I went to see my grandmother in Florida. She just moved to Boynton Beach, so I went down for a few days to help her settle in."

"That's sweet, Wes."

His cheeks reddened. "Finding a corpse in your tag sale room," he said, changing the subject, "that must have been a shockeroonie and a half! What did she look like when you found her?"

I closed my eyes, appalled at Wes's sledgehammer tactics. I knew it wasn't that Wes didn't care. It was that bad news sold newspapers.

"She looked dead."

"Josie!" he whined. "I need details."

I opened my eyes. Talking to Wes often left me pummeled, and I could feel the assault beginning. I could walk away, but I knew I wouldn't. Curiosity was my stock-in-trade, but sometimes it felt like a besetting sin.

"You can't quote me," I said.

"Josie!"

"Promise, Wes, or I won't tell you anything," I said, knowing he'd agree now as he had in the past. He had no choice. I was one of his most important sources, and he knew I knew it. This little dance we did was all for show, reiterating ground rules we both knew by heart. I spoke openly to him, occasionally going on the record, often providing background information and photos, and in return, he answered my questions.

"I promise," he said, sighing loudly, communicating his frustration.

"She was on her back, her hands by her side." My voice cracked. I took in a deep breath, then described her skin tone, the twisted scarf, and her expression. "It was awful, Wes. Horrible."

"Was her clothing ripped? Was there any sign that she fought with her killer?"

"No," I said, talking quickly, wanting to get it over with. "Her jacket was buttoned properly. Little bits of her burgundy silk blouse showed. Her skirt was brown, to the knee. She wore knee-high brown leather boots. They were zipped up."

"Good stuff, Josie. Was the skirt rumpled? You know, like someone roughed her up?"

"God, no, Wes!" I exclaimed, appalled at his question. "It was smoothed out."

"Someone killed her, rolled her under the table, then straightened out her clothes? Doesn't that strike you as bizarre?"

"Now that you mention it . . . maybe. It is odd, isn't it? You'd think the murderer would just want to get away, wouldn't you?"

"Yeah. Why would someone bother?" Wes asked.

I thought about his question. "Because they cared about her and knew how much she cared about clothes and her appearance."

"Nah. That doesn't sound likely."

"Maybe smoothing out her skirt was done without thinking. Perhaps whoever killed her is neat."

He nodded, pausing for a moment. "Did you hear about Bobby?" he asked.

"No, what about him?" I asked, thinking that Bobby was as much a clotheshorse as Riley had ever been.

"He was at the police station most of the night."

I swallowed hard. "Why?"

"Why do you think?" Wes chuckled. "From all accounts, when it came to women, he was a busy boy."

"That's all gossip, Wes. Riley didn't believe Bobby was cheating on her."

"You talked about it with her?" Wes asked, his tone shifting from casual chat to all business. "What did she say?"

I looked out over the ocean as I repeated what I'd told the police, that Riley was more irritated by the gossip reporters than the gossip itself, and that Bobby's cynical manipulation of the press was, if true, icky.

"Whether Bobby was playing the press or not, didn't Riley get suspicious when mentions of other women started showing up? I mean, no matter who I talk to, speculation about Bobby and other women—note the plural—comes up."

"I have no idea, Wes. Can't you confirm the reports?" I asked, hating to ask but wanting to know.

"I'm working on it. One claim looks pretty damning. According to a waitress at his New York City flagship restaurant, Blue Apple—her name is Tamara Mitchell—she and Bobby had an affair that lasted for months. She said it was really hot, and she has the text messages to prove it. I'm waiting to see them before writing anything."

"How did you find her?" I asked.

"Tamara had been reading about Ruby for months, but didn't believe there was anything to it. She told me that when Bobby ended their relationship, he said he wanted to try to make his marriage work, and she believed him. Then yesterday, she saw a TV spot speculating that Bobby and Ruby's relationship was the real deal, and that Bobby had asked Riley for a divorce, not the other way around. She got completely bent out of shape thinking that Bobby dumped her for Ruby. She couldn't reach the show's producer—how stupid are they to keep the producer under wraps? Jeesh! So she called me."

"What an awful situation! I just hate thinking about it, Wes. I like Bobby!"

"Yeah, everybody does. Maybe Tamara thinking that Bobby was that into her is just her imagination. You know how that goes. Girls can make a romance out of nothing. Like, you say, 'Hi, how ya doin'?' and the next thing you know you're in a relationship."

"Well, Wes Smith, you hound dog, you. Have you been holding out on me? Who is she?"

"As if," he said, grinning. "I read a lot, that's all. So what do you think—is it true about Bobby and Ruby?"

"I have no idea. What do their friends say?" I asked, certain that Wes would have already tracked several of them down.

"Ruby's friends say no comment, not like I've spoken to them, but I've spoken to her publicist, who tells me to forget it, that no one knows anything because there's nothing to know.

She says it's all an attempt to ruin Ruby's reputation as a wholesome girl next door. I never pictured Ruby that way, but whatever. I mean, I think of her as pretty glamorous, you know? I guess girls next door can be glamorous, why not? Anyway, until Bobby started trying to build his man-about-town rep, he and Riley were a pretty private couple, especially considering how rich and famous they were. I mean, they aren't members of any clubs. Bobby doesn't hang out with his former Olympic buddies. They didn't do things with their neighbors. It's not like they were recluses or anything, just they didn't socialize much. Mostly, they worked. Riley was pretty involved in local charities—she was on the New England Museum of Design board of directors, for instance. I spoke to one of Riley's oldest friends, Becka Dowling, and Bobby's bookkeeper, Kenna Duffy. You know them both from your workshop, right?"

"Yes. What did they say?"

"Becka insists it's all hype, that Bobby was as devoted to Riley as Riley was to him. Kenna says she's been hearing rumors about Bobby and other women for years, but she's never seen Bobby cross the line with anyone, including herself."

"Let's hope that's the truth of the matter."

"While I'm waiting for Tamara to talk to her lawyer about whether it's okay to show me Bobby's text messages, I'm checking phone records. By the way, I think Tamara is lying when she says she's checking with her lawyer to make sure she's not breaking any laws in turning over the texts. I think she's sending out feelers hoping to sell her story to a junky tabloid instead of giving it to a bona fide journalist for free." He shrugged. "By looking at the phone records, I'll be able to track how often Bobby and Ruby speak, although if they're friends, you know, innocent friends, they still might call each other a lot. I'm going to talk to everyone who works at the Blue Dolphin, too, not just Kenna. Can you think of anything else I should check or anyone else I should talk to?"

"No. I'm pleased to report that I have no idea how one

confirms or disproves rumors about sex," I said. "So what's your 'info bomb'?" I grimaced as I quoted his colorful word choice. Wes had a communication style all his own.

His eyes were gleaming. "Bobby's infidelities—if there are any—might have had nothing to do with Riley's murder. It's possible that she was killed over money. You know that Riley inherited a fortune, right?"

"Sure, from her grandfather," I said, thinking how much I loved Marshall's chicken noodle soup.

"You know she was an investor in the Blue restaurants?"

"Yes."

"It seems that Riley sent an e-mail from her BlackBerry to Quinn Steiner, her financial adviser, asking him to audit the Blue restaurant chain's finances. That was around noon on the day she died. If Quinn looked into things right away and found problems, and if Riley confronted Bobby, there you go. Motive up the kazoo."

"What kind of problems?" I asked.

"According to my police source, she used the term 'financial improprieties' in the e-mail. She asked Quinn to check out whether Bobby was padding expenses to make profits look smaller and transferring money overseas to hide assets. Details are sketchy, but I gather that Riley thought Bobby might have been trying to rook his chief investor—herself."

"Wow—this sounds very serious, Wes. Does Kenna know anything about it?"

"She says she doesn't. She also says that she didn't do anything illegal, period, and if Bobby did, she doesn't know anything about it. Do you think she might have been involved? What do you know about her?"

"Kenna? I can't imagine her doing anything even a little shady. She's a peach, Wes. Very sweet. During our first class when I was talking about frauds and knockoffs and how hard it can be to tell the real McCoy from a fake, she was shocked."

"You mean, she's gullible, so if Bobby told her to send money to some account somewhere, it wouldn't occur to her to question it?"

"No, not exactly. I think you're right in how she'd react to instructions, but wrong to label her as gullible. I think she's very literal. She takes things at face value. She trusts easily. Let me give you an example. One of the other students, Marlee, told this story about how stupid she felt after she bought a bag she was told was a Prada from one of those online auction sites for twenty dollars. Turns out it was a phony, no surprise. Prada bags start in the hundreds and go up from there into the thousands. To Marlee, it was a learning experience, but Kenna had a different take on it. Marlee asked herself how she could have been such an easy mark. Kenna was upset on Marlee's behalf. She said it's not your fault, how could you possibly have known, and so on. I thought it was an interesting exchange, and revealing. Marlee took it as a lesson to smarten up. Kenna took it like a victim."

"Gotcha," he said. "Let me make a note." He extracted a smudged, much-used piece of lined paper from an inside pocket and jotted something down. When he was done, he added, "Chief Hunter's talking to the Portsmouth Police, too, to see if they know anything."

"How come?" I asked.

"Part professional courtesy, I guess, because Bobby's business is in Portsmouth, and part hoping to pick up some scuttlebutt. From what I heard, he didn't." He slipped the paper back in his pocket. "On a new subject, I know the tech guys spent hours at your place, and that Chief Hunter talked to your staff this morning. Did you get any hints about what the police are thinking?"

"No," I said, awed yet again at the depth and breadth of Wes's contacts. From police and bankers to clerks at utilities and credit bureaus, Wes found ways to stay abreast of investigations and access private data. He seemed to have his fingers in everyone's pies.

"Anything else for me?" he asked.

"No."

"Okay, then. See ya!" he said.

I stayed on the dune and watched Wes hustle toward the street, then turned back to face the ocean. As I reviewed Wes's observations about Bobby and other women and what Riley had deemed "financial improprieties," I barely noticed the frothy tide and glittering sun-specks. Bobby, it seemed, didn't just have one motive to kill Riley. He had two.

CHAPTER SIX

When I got back to Prescott's, Gretchen was behind her desk. She reported that Detective Brownley had shown her photos of an array of cars, but she hadn't recognized any of them as the one she'd seen leaving the parking lot, and that Hale Alarms would begin the security audit within the next few days. I thanked her and asked her to work with Eric to get him a helper.

"He needs someone right away, so call the temp agency, okay? Then let's figure out where his time is going so we can design a permanent part- or full-time position if we need to."

"I'll get right on it," she said.

I went to peek into the tag sale room. The technicians were gone, but the police seal was intact. My stomach clenched at the sight of the yellow and black tape, and I stood for several seconds, trying to picture what the scientists might have found. Fingerprints, maybe. Fibers. Hair. I shook my head. It was useless. Hundreds of people were in and out of the room every week. We kept it clean, but we didn't sterilize it. I went back to the office and asked Cara when they'd left.

"About fifteen minutes ago," she said. "They said that they might be back later and reminded me that none of us was to enter the room until they said it was all right."

I nodded and announced that I'd decided to cancel this week's tag sale. I asked Cara to call the part-timers scheduled to work the event and change our regular recurring newspaper ad to one offering our condolences to Riley's family. I asked

Gretchen to send a media release to the *Seacoast Star* and the area's TV and radio stations. We talked for a while about the wording, finally deciding to keep it informational and matter-of-fact, and not to mention Riley at all.

"Speaking of the media," I said, "Cara, would you ask Eric to come into the office? I want to talk to all of you."

When Eric arrived, he looked like a schoolboy who'd been called to the principal's office. Naturally self-effacing, Eric always presumed he was guilty of something until he was proven innocent. I smiled to reassure him.

"May I have your attention for a minute?" I called to the room.

Sasha looked worried and began twirling a strand of her mud-brown hair. Gretchen seemed keyed up, hoping I was about to make a major announcement. She wasn't the least bit ghoulish, but she sure loved the drama of crises. Ava was rubbing her neck through her turtleneck sweater as if her muscles were knotted and she was trying to ease the tension. Cara was frowning a little, braced for bad news. Fred was leaning back in his chair, his eyes narrowed, watchful and relaxed. Only Hank was oblivious. He lay on his tummy on a guest chair, half hanging off the cushion, fast asleep.

"I know that you're all as sick about what happened as I am," I said. "Riley was a wonderful woman, a valued customer, and a good friend. We are, of course, cooperating fully with the police. It is up to you whether you talk to the press or not. If you decide to do so, please make it clear that you're speaking only for yourself, not Prescott's." I paused to look at them, to ensure they got the message that I was serious. "Everyone reacts to stress differently, just as everyone grieves differently. If you need time off, take it. For me, it's important to keep working. Any questions?"

No one had any. Gretchen shook her head. So did Cara, then Ava. No one spoke.

"So Fred, if you're okay with carrying on, I'd love to hear

what you learned about the *Le Petit Echo de la Mode* magazine covers."

Gretchen filled Eric in about our plans to cancel the tag sale.

"Your timing's perfect," Fred said to me. "I was just about to tell Sasha and Ava about Dr. Walker and the magazines."

We'd found 147 magazine covers mixed in with Lana's shop's vintage clothing inventory, all from the French magazine *Le Petit Echo de la Mode,* which in English means "a small review of fashion." All were from the first half of the twentieth century, and I had high hopes that the magazines were a real find.

I swung a guest chair around so I could join their conversation. The scraping sound woke Hank up, and he stretched.

"Sorry, baby," I said, reaching over to give him a little bottom pat. He yawned and curled onto his side, slipping back into sleep.

"Dr. Walker is a curator at the New England Museum of Design," Fred explained to Ava. "He's one of the consultants we call about anything to do with vintage clothing, textiles, and costume design." Fred turned toward me. "From what he said when I met with him, I gathered he was a pretty big Riley Jordan fan. He sent you his regards."

I nodded at Fred, acknowledging the message, but I didn't reply. I didn't want to talk about Riley anymore, not now. I didn't want to sink back into melancholy.

"So," I said, forcing myself to smile, "are the magazine covers genuine?"

"Yes," he said dismissively, pushing up his glasses, "but even back then, the magazine had a circulation in the hundreds of thousands, so none is rare." Fred was an antiques snob, so to him, anything mass-produced was, by definition, unworthy.

I turned to Ava. "What do you think, Ava? Fred says they're real, but not rare. How would you price them?" I asked, knowing that thinking through the process was one of the best ways for an appraiser-in-training to hone her skills.

Ava lowered her eyes to study the cover on top of the pile. It dated from the mid-1940s. The color illustration showed two attractive women, one standing, one seated. The woman standing wore a red plaid dress, a red beret, and gray gloves. The other woman wore gloves, too, but hers were red. She also wore a beret, gray with gold trim. Her dress was a solid dove gray.

Ava raised her eyes to Fred. "When was the magazine first published?" she asked.

"Eighteen seventy-nine," he replied.

"I know we market magazine covers as art prints, and that at the tag sale they go for twenty dollars each, but I'm thinking these might be worth less. If you look along the left side of this one, for instance, you can see there's a red-brown blemish at the corner."

"Foxing," I said, nodding. "Good catch." I turned to Fred. "Fred?"

"It's definitely a flaw," he told Ava, "but if you consider the spot in context, in other words, the age of the magazine and the fact that a lot of hands have held it over the years, you know what, it's no big deal. The foxed area is relatively small, and since it doesn't affect readability or mar the artwork, I'd call it minor."

"What do you think, Sasha?" I asked.

"I agree. There are no tears, rips, or chips, and no uneven yellowing. In setting the price, I wouldn't deduct anything for condition."

Ava nodded, her mind fully engaged. As always, she was a sponge, soaking up information. She lowered her gaze to the cover again, thinking. I could almost see the wheels turning.

"If Dr. Walker says that the magazine covers have no historical value," Ava said, thinking aloud, "the fact the cover was *cut off,* destroying the magazine, must not affect the value, is that right?"

"Clearly, removing the covers ruins the value of the magazine," Fred said, "but it doesn't tell us anything about the value of the cover itself. All we can infer is that at some point someone either wanted the artwork or knew, or thought they knew, that the cover would sell for more on its own than it would if it were attached to the magazine."

"I'm thinking that we should use the same checklist that we use for appraising everything—rarity, scarcity, condition, past price trends, current popularity, and association."

"Wow!" I said. "You already memorized our checklist? I'm impressed."

Ava smiled. "It's just so fascinating."

"That's what I like to hear! So, Ava, what do you think? How much are the covers worth?"

She sighed and made a face. "I don't know."

"No problem—that's how you learn. Fred?"

"Properly trimmed, nicely matted, and encased in plastic sleeves—about twenty bucks each. Same as all the other art prints we have in stock."

"Got it!" Ava said, smiling and nodding.

"Which to someone who loves vintage fashion will be a bargain and a half," I said, smiling.

I left them talking about how many covers to display at any one time, an age-old merchandizing conundrum with no clear answer. It was a treat to see Fred and Sasha helping Ava learn the trade. I gave a final wave good-bye and entered the warehouse. Hank followed me, then trotted purposefully around a shelving unit, toward his corner. *He has an errand,* I thought.

Upstairs, I started reading a proposal from our database management company and was halfway through when Hank came up to me and rubbed against my leg.

"Are you a good boy, Hank?" I asked, reaching down to give him a little pat without taking my eyes from the proposal.

He made an odd mewling sound, part growl and part meow, and I looked at him.

"What is it, baby?"

He dropped a thumbnail-sized pearl rosette at my feet.

I picked it up. I'd never seen it before, nor anything like it.

What appeared to be perfectly matched round pearls were arranged in lines of three, forming petals that ranged around a larger center stone. The setting was silver metal. At first I thought it was a brooch, but it wasn't. From the set-in metal loop attached to the back, I could tell it was a button. There was engraving on the back as well, too small to read with the naked eye. It was distinctive, and if the stones really were pearls and the silver really was white gold or platinum, it might be valuable. In fact, if the pearls were natural and perfectly matched, and the silver was platinum, it might be close to extremely valuable.

"Where did you get this, Hank?"

He yawned.

As a company, we were neat and organized. Stray buttons weren't left around for a cat to find—it just didn't happen. Yet it had. I stared at Hank. Probably a customer had dropped it, we'd somehow missed it, and Hank, the little devil, had picked it up.

I walked downstairs to the main office, button in hand. "Does anyone recognize this?" I asked, displaying it in the palm of my hand. "Hank just dropped it at my feet."

No one did.

"It's unusual, isn't it?" Gretchen asked. "Do you think it fell off a garment from the vintage clothing collection?"

"Maybe. Or a customer dropped it. Are you certain you don't recognize it?"

"Yes. I'm sure I'd remember if I'd seen it." She brought up the database where we tracked our inventory, and I stood in back of her, looking over her shoulder. She entered "pearl button" in the keyword search box. Nothing came up.

"Try just the word 'button,'" I requested.

"Button" got fifteen hits, including three garments with fabric-covered buttons, two buttons made of wood, seven featuring rhinestones, one each studded with faux rubies and emeralds, and one button made of horsehair.

"Okay, then," I said. "It doesn't belong to us. Probably a customer dropped it. Cara, would you enter it in lost and found?"

While Cara got the listing ready, I borrowed Sasha's loupe and examined the button. The milky iridescent sheen of the stones glistened against the silver metal. I turned it over. The engraving on the back read: "Industria et Munus," and "EZK," and "Pt999."

"We might be able to trace it," I said. "What do you say, Ava? Want to take a crack at tracking down the owner?"

"Sure," she said, smiling. "Thanks."

"Take a look." I waited until she had the loupe in place. "Do you see where it says 'Pt999'? That means it's made of platinum, and that the platinum is almost a hundred percent pure. Until World War II, it was very common to use platinum in jewelry settings, so the button might be an antique."

She removed the loupe and examined the stones, stroking them. "These pearls are spectacular, aren't they? They're so satiny."

"Depending on what we learn from the engravings, we might want to verify the materials. An expert can tell if a stone is a pearl, and if so, whether it's natural or cultured."

"Cultured?" Ava asked.

"Man-made," I explained. "A person inserts a bead or something similar into an oyster, or one of the other mollusks that produce pearls, and the mollusk deposits layers of what's called nacre, or mother-of-pearl. That's the opalescent inner layer of some mollusk shells that gives a pearl its lustrous patina. A natural pearl occurs without man's intervention."

"Do you want me to show her the sun and tooth tests?" Sasha asked me.

Fred chortled.

Sasha turned to Ava. "Fred is laughing because those tests are very low-tech, but in spite of Fred's derision, both of them are fairly reliable ways to tell if a pearl is a fake."

"Oh, pa-leaze," Fred said, pushing up his glasses. "Neither test means squat."

"I didn't say they were infallible."

"That's putting it mildly."

"You're overstating it," Sasha argued. She turned to Ava. "Both tests are free, easy, and quick. If the results are encouraging, then you consult an expert." She picked up the button. "Do you see how the pearls are all the same size, or darn close? Ditto the color—they're all ivory and luminescent. They appear to be perfectly matched. Think about what that means—to find pearls in nature that are exactly the same size, shape, and color is an astonishing feat. 'Perfectly matched' doesn't mean identical, by the way. Nature rarely produces identical anythings. There are always minute differences. One way to gauge the likelihood that the pearls are, in fact, perfectly matched is by viewing them in the sun. If they appear identical under sunlight, probably they're fake. Come outside and I'll show you what I'm talking about."

I tagged along, eager to see Ava's astonishment if the pearls tested as genuine, or her understanding if they didn't.

We stood two paces from the front door in full sun. Sasha placed the button in the palm of her hand. "Inside, you saw that the pearls appeared to be identical." We stared at the button. "Do you see how there are, in fact, color variations?" She indicated one of the pearls, using her pinky nail as a pointer. "There's a distinct lavender hue to this one that wasn't visible inside." She pointed to the center stone. "This one is opalescent, with overtones of cream and peach and pink that are only visible when I move it a little to catch the light."

Ava nodded, her eyes big with wonder. "That's astonishing! Inside they looked indistinguishable. Here it's clear how different they are from one another. It's hard to believe it's the same button."

"Meaning it's likely the pearls are genuine," Sasha said. "Which brings us to the tooth test."

We went back inside.

Sasha tucked her hair behind her ear. "The tooth test is even simpler than the sun test. Since natural and cultured pearls are comprised of layers of nacre, they have a texture like sand, which you can feel when you rub the pearl against your teeth." She handed the button to Ava. "Want to try?"

"Sure," Ava said. She laughed a little, embarrassed. "Would it be all right if I washed it off first? I can't forget that this button spent time in Hank's mouth."

Sasha smiled. "Only with a soft cloth and water. Anything stronger may destroy the nacre, so more in-depth cleaning requires professional care."

"I'll just do a quickie against my sweater, okay?" Ava rubbed the button on her sleeve, then against her front teeth. "Oh, I can feel it plain as anything. There are little . . . I don't know what to call them . . . ruts."

"Exactly," Sasha said. She took the button and gently rubbed the center pearl against her front teeth. "Definitely. It feels gritty."

"On the other hand," Fred said, "many synthetic nacres are laced with a coarse compound, which when applied onto perfectly smooth beads replicates the feel of a real pearl. You could get that same gritty sensation from a glass bead that's never been within a mile of a mollusk."

"Of course," Sasha responded, "but in this case, we have no reason to think someone went to that much effort to create fake pearls to put in a platinum setting—it's not logical." She raised a hand to stop him from interjecting. "Yes, it happens." She met Ava's eyes. "For instance, someone who needs cash might replace the original pearls with good fakes."

"What's the bottom line, Ava?" Fred asked, leaning back. "Are they real?"

She smiled. "The button appears to be genuine," she said, stressing the words "appears to be." "We'd need an expert to validate the assumption."

"Well done, all of you," I said. "Now let's see if we can find the button's owner. I know you're leaving for the day soon, Ava. You can get going on it tomorrow. Cara will show you how our lost and found system works."

"Thanks, Josie," Ava said, smiling. "I'll do my best."

I was pleased that she was pleased. I had a good feeling about Ava. As my company grew, attracting a talented and dedicated staff that loved their work and that worked well together would be a key to success. I crossed my fingers that Ava would prove to be a keeper.

Halfway up the spiral stairs, a thought came to me like a clap of thunder on a sunny day, out of nowhere and loud enough to make you jump. I froze midstep. Hank had been in the tag sale room just after I'd discovered Riley's body. It was possible that a button—this button—had fallen off or been ripped off Riley's blouse or skirt. The pearl rosette button could be hers. Or, I thought, grasping the handrail to steady myself, the killer's.

CHAPTER SEVEN

I called down to Cara and asked her to be sure to wrap the button properly when she locked it up with the other lost and found items, then left an urgent message for Chief Hunter.

"Ellis," I said, "I know this is going to sound nuts—but was Riley missing a button? Give me a call and I'll explain."

I hadn't been back reading the proposal for more than a minute or two when Cara called up. Quinn Steiner, Riley's financial adviser, had stopped by and wondered if I had a minute to speak to him.

"Sure," I said and asked her to escort him up.

I'd never met Steiner before, but Riley had talked about him enough for me to have gotten a picture in my head. I expected him to dress conservatively and be old enough to be her father, and that's exactly how he looked. If he'd been an actor, he could have landed the part based on appearances alone. He was about sixty, with a determined chin, thin lips, gray hair, and brown eyes. He wore a navy blue suit with a pale blue shirt and a red and blue club tie. He looked like what he was—a trusted financial adviser.

As he stepped over the threshold, he thanked Cara. I came out from around my desk and extended my hand for a shake. His grip was firm and practiced.

"I'm sorry to bust in on you like this, but Bobby Jordan's in a heck of a hurry," he stated. "Do you have a moment to talk?"

"Of course," I said. "I'm glad to meet you. Riley said wonderful things about you." I led the way to the love seat. "Please, have a seat."

He perched on the edge of the yellow brocade love seat. I sat across from him on a matching Queen Anne wing chair. I waited for him to talk. His lips were pursed. He didn't look happy.

"Bobby plans on moving to New York almost immediately, and he wants to retain your services to appraise the furnishings and other items in his home. He plans on selling everything as soon as can be arranged. He's asked me to oversee the process."

I blinked at him. "You're kidding."

"I'm not."

"Riley just died."

"Yes," he said, shaking his head, "and she hasn't even been buried."

"Why is he doing this?"

"I don't know." He sat back and met my eyes. "I strongly suggested that he should wait for a while before making a decision this significant and encompassing, especially one that would be viewed by the world as, well, unbecoming at best, but he refused. I tried to convince him to wait at least until after the funeral, but he's insisting on pushing forward. He says that he can't stand being in their home without Riley and that he doesn't care about public perception." Quinn rested his forearms on his thighs as he leaned forward and met my eyes. "He says the only thing that's keeping him alive is his work, and his work is in New York City."

I nodded. "I can understand using work as a coping mechanism. I'd feel the same in his situation. Well, then . . . sure. I mean, if that's what he wants, of course I'm glad to help."

Quinn opened his briefcase and extracted a thick folder. "Thank you. Riley gave me the appraisal documents you had her sign last year when you appraised that jardiniere and pedestal."

He was reading from the top sheet of paper. "Riley asked you to handle the transaction for her friend Rita Owen. From what I gather, Ms. Owen decided not to sell. Is that correct?"

"Actually, I don't think Ms. Owen ever intended to sell," I said, recalling Riley's kindness to one of her long-deceased mother's friends. "Riley asked me to appraise the object as her Christmas present."

According to Riley, Rita Owen had been white-hot curious about the cloisonné jardiniere and pedestal. Black, with a multicolored floral pattern, the object had been in her family for generations. Rita, a charming woman with short gray hair, had been tickled pink to learn the object, primarily because of the unusual pedestal, was worth upwards of ten thousand dollars, and I'd been struck once again by Riley's thoughtfulness.

"Understood. The consignment terms detailed in the document—are they standard?"

"Yes."

"Very good. They're fine with us. As soon as you prepare a new set of papers, Bobby will sign them."

"This is all happening so quickly. Do you want me to take a crack at trying to convince Bobby to take a breath first before he makes such major changes?"

Quinn paused, thinking, then leaned back and shook his head. "No—at this point, it would be inappropriate. He's not a child, after all, and, of course, he has a point when he says that he needs to get back to work—and that his work is now in New York City. He opened an office there about six months ago."

"Really?" I asked, taken aback. "Riley hadn't said a word to me about it."

"No. She was very resistant to the idea of moving. When I talked to him about delaying his move, he made the point that his second New York City restaurant is set to open in June, and that he travels internationally frequently—no easy feat from New Hampshire." Quinn looked at me straight on. "Riley didn't want to move, yet from Bobby's perspective . . . well, let's just say that running his complex and far-flung business operations from a one-man office in the Blue Dolphin has become increasingly challenging."

I nodded, not envying the dilemma they'd faced. Bobby could have expanded his headquarters in New Hampshire, but he didn't want to. He was more than enjoying his newfound, big-city celebrity. Now, with Riley gone, he had no one to think about but himself, and despite his grief, or maybe because of it, he wanted to get on with his life.

I closed my eyes for a moment as a nightmarish memory came to me. When I'd worked at Frisco's, the venerable New York City antiques auction house, a plum of a job I'd landed right out of college, I'd lived my dream. Then I'd caught on to a scheme my boss, a man who'd been my mentor, a man I'd admired to the skies, had initiated. He, along with the heads of two other famous antiques auction houses, had conspired to fix commission rates. Because I'd been raised that black and white really did exist—and gray, too, of course, but not when it came to ethics—I'd felt I had no choice. I turned him in. I was the whistle-blower. I'd expected to be praised for my integrity. Instead I'd been shunned as if I were contaminated.

Everything about those long lonely months had been awful. I'd lost most of my work friends as they distanced themselves from me in a desperate scramble to save their own jobs. The media had hunted me like hyenas. Worse, just after the trial was over, my dad had been murdered, and only a few weeks after that, my boyfriend, Rick the Cretin, had dumped me, saying I wasn't snapping out of it quickly enough, that I'd turned into a real downer. A day later, without warning, Frisco's acting president, a nerdy nothing of a man named Jamey, had called me into his corner office. I stood on the thick maroon carpet beside dark, heavy furniture, expecting a thank-you on behalf of the board of directors. Instead, he fired me, saying that because I wasn't a team player, he had to let me go. My company credit cards and ID were taken from me then and there by a security guard who'd been stationed outside Jamey's door. Jamey must have pushed a button built into his desk or stepped on one, because he didn't use the phone or raise his voice, yet seconds later, this tall white-haired man loomed over me with his hand out. Another man escorted me back to my cubicle and watched as I packed up my desk. The two of them, one in front of me and other behind me, walked me down to Human Resources, where a young woman handed me a yellow envelope labeled EXIT PACKET.

Yellow, I'd thought, *how appropriate.* I'd refused to sign any of the documents she'd handed me, and four minutes later I was on the street.

I started walking south to my apartment in Turtle Bay, feeling as if I'd fallen down a rabbit hole. Everything was upside down. Nothing made sense. I had no way of coping because I had no context. One day I had the world on a string. The next day I was on the street, alone, a pariah.

That was the darkest period of my life, bar none. After a month of soul-wrenching despondency, I recalled something my dad had told me years earlier. *If you feel as if you're at the end of your rope, tie a knot and hang on, and if you can't hang on, move on.* I decided it was time to move on. The next morning, I'd awakened full of energy, eager to research starting my own business. Within three months, I'd relocated to New Hampshire to start a new life.

My plan had worked. I'd found the business challenges and opportunities, the love, the friends, and the community I'd sought. Maybe Bobby's plan would work, too. Perhaps getting back to work as soon as he could would help him cope with losing Riley, just as opening a business in New Hampshire had helped me overcome the losses I'd endured. Certainly, it wasn't my place to judge.

"Please tell Bobby I understand," I told Quinn, opening my eyes.

Quinn extracted a standard-sized envelope from the folder.

"I'll pass on your message, but I'm sure you'll be able to tell him yourself. He hasn't left yet." He handed me the envelope. "Here's a letter he signed authorizing you and your staff to enter the Jordans' home and remove any objects you deem appropriate, and a key to the front door. Bobby tells me he only sets the alarm when he's going out of town."

I glanced through the authorization. "This is fine. If you'd like, I can print out the contracts and sign them now."

"Thank you," he said. He sighed and closed his briefcase. "I guess we ought to do it."

As we walked toward the front office, Quinn remarked, "I've known Riley since the day she was born. My wife and I were good friends with her parents."

"It sounds like she was more than just a client to you," I said.

"Very much so."

"I'm sorry for your loss."

He pressed his lips together. Men like Quinn did not break down in front of strangers.

Gretchen faxed Bobby the forms about fifteen minutes later. Five minutes after that, he faxed them back, and I'd officially been hired.

Ellis returned my call as I was driving to the Jordans' house to begin the appraisal. I explained how Hank had fetched the button, then told him that while I had no reason to think it came from a garment worn by Riley or the killer, I had no reason to think it hadn't.

The button, he said, wasn't from Riley's clothing. "I'd like to have the tech guys give it a once-over."

"Sure," I said, "except lots of us have touched it, including Hank."

"Still."

"No problem. Do you want me to bring it over?"

"No, thanks. We'll pick it up."

I told him I'd let Cara know someone from the police was coming, and he thanked me again.

When I called in, I spoke to Gretchen and asked her to take close-up photos from all angles before the police showed up so that Ava could begin researching the button even though we wouldn't have it in hand.

I changed my mind about going straight to the Jordans' house, and instead I took exit 7 off the interstate and wove my way through the city streets to the Blue Dolphin. I wanted to talk to Bobby, to look him in the eye and tell him how sorry I was about Riley.

Frieda, the longtime hostess, greeted me like a pal.

"Hey, Josie," she said, smiling.

"I was wondering if Bobby was around."

Frieda's smile faded. "Yeah, he is. Heck of a thing, isn't it?"

"Worse that that."

"Yeah. He's in his office in the back. You know the way, don't you?"

"I do. Is it all right for me to go on my own?"

"Oh, sure. You know Bobby—he always maintains an open-door policy."

"Thanks," I said.

I walked through the dining room on wide-plank oak flooring. After centuries of being scrubbed and polished, the wood had mellowed to a rich golden brown. The walls were painted antique white, with colonial blue trim. Blue and white French country-themed toile curtains hung at the windows, a nod to New Hampshire's strong French heritage. Several diners sat at tables laid with crisp white cloths, glistening silver flatware, and sparkling cut crystal. Crystal wall sconces, chandeliers, and table lamps cast a warm golden glow throughout the room. The Blue Dolphin's main dining room epitomized elegance.

I turned left and passed into a small passageway. A heavy

fire door labeled EMERGENCY EXIT ONLY was at the end. I passed the restrooms, a room marked PRIVATE that I knew contained the restaurant's impressive wine collection, and then an open door on the left. Kenna sat at her desk, frowning at her computer monitor. A guest chair was covered by a stack of three-ring binders. An old-fashioned four-foot-high cast-iron safe stood in back of her. There was no artwork on the walls, no photos of her kids on her desk, nothing to add warmth or personality to the space. To Kenna, an office was where you went to do a job, not a home away from home. It was messy and unwelcoming, not a place I would have liked to work.

Kenna looked up. "Hi, Josie," she said.

"Sorry to disturb you. I just wanted to offer my sympathy to Bobby."

She nodded. "He should be in his office."

"Thanks. How are you holding up?"

She shrugged. "Did you hear that Bobby's moving to New York?"

"Yeah. Does that put you out of a job?"

She shook her head. "No. Bobby's accountant, Quinn Steiner, has always been my direct report, so things will be pretty much the same for me."

"I hate change," I said, smiling a little.

She smiled back and nodded. "Me, too."

"Well, I'd better go. I'll see you at class next week, okay?"

"You bet."

Bobby's office was on the right, just before the emergency exit. The door was open, and I looked in. Bobby was seated behind his desk facing me. A woman sat across from him with her back to me. I couldn't see her face. She had dark brown chin-length hair.

"I'm sorry to disturb you," I said. "I was told to come on back." The woman turned as soon as I began speaking. It was Becka, and she was crying. I didn't know what to say.

"Hi, Josie," Bobby said, standing. "Come on in."

Becka turned away. I saw that she was clutching a crumpled tissue. She gulped, and I heard her breathe in deeply.

He looked in her direction, then at me. From his expression, I could tell that something was worrying him. He seemed guarded and tense.

"Becka and I were just finalizing plans for Riley's funeral," he said. "The service will be this Friday at St. Patrick's in Rocky Point. At ten."

"I'll be there," I said. After a short pause, I added, "I stopped by to tell you how heartbroken I am, Bobby. I'm really, really sorry for your loss. Riley was a special woman and a good friend." I turned to include Becka in my comments. "My condolences to you, too, Becka. I know you and Riley were close."

"Thank you," she said, her voice so low I could barely hear it.

Bobby dragged up a chair up for me, and I perched on the edge. He looked and moved like an athlete, fit and lithe, with a broad chest and narrow waist and strong, angular features. He coloring showed his Nordic heritage—his hair was blond, his skin pale, and his eyes cerulean blue. He wore khakis and a crisply pressed yellow oxford shirt with the cuffs rolled up two turns.

The charisma the gossip magazines wrote about was real, and was as apparent today as ever. Simply being in his presence, I could feel it, and having been around him dozens of times, I knew that it wasn't a manipulative technique he turned on or off at will; it was intrinsic to who he was. Today, though, he seemed on edge and somber, but those emotions alone wouldn't account for the change that I was finding so disturbing—they were the effect, not the cause. I sensed he was hiding something, or trying to. Maybe, I thought, it was simply that I'd walked in on a private conversation.

"I appreciate it, Josie," he said. "To tell you the truth, I'm still adjusting to the fact that she's really, really gone. It's hard to fathom."

"I can only imagine. Is there anything I can do to help?" I asked.

"Just with the appraisal. You got the forms, right? I faxed them over to you."

"Yes. Actually, I'm on my way to your house now to start the process." I stood up. "I'll keep you posted." I looked down at Becka, still worrying her tissue. "I'll see you soon, Becka," I said, just for something to say.

She nodded and tried to smile, but failed. She looked away again.

Bobby came around his desk, offering a hand, and when we shook, he placed his left hand on top of mine and squeezed. He walked me into the hallway. "It's quicker to the parking lot if you go this way," he said, pushing the silver bar on the fire door just outside his office. "It's not armed."

I found myself in the alley that ran behind the restaurant, standing on cobblestones and facing the Piscataqua River. Too narrow for vehicle traffic, the alley was used for deliveries wheeled in by hand and, during the summer, for outdoor riverfront seating. Bobby had divided the area into sections by strategically placing rectangular copper tubs of boxwoods, tall willowy grasses, and seasonal flowers. I could see Maine across the water.

"I'm really sorry, Bobby," I said.

He nodded, his expression solemn. "Thanks, Josie," he replied and stepped back.

The door latched shut. I turned toward the river and watched the choppy, fast-moving water swirl toward the ocean. On the Maine side, I spotted several trees sporting red buds.

Something was up with Bobby; I didn't know what. I couldn't explain how I knew that any more than I could explain how I knew when it was going to snow long before the first flakes begin to fall. It was as if the atmosphere gave off a certain scent and I could smell it. Here, today, I'd caught a whiff of trouble.

CHAPTER EIGHT

Seeing the Jordans' sprawling oceanfront home, and knowing that it would soon be sold, brought tears to my eyes. Ty and I had attended cocktail parties and summer barbecues there, and, one superhot August Sunday, a pool party. The house, a mansion really, was more than beautiful, it was substantial and historical. It had been home to Riley's family for generations. Riley's death marked the end of an era.

The wood siding had weathered to a soft taupe. The mansard roof was dark brown. The shutters were white. Tall grasses edged the small lawn. Because the house had been oriented to face the ocean, from the street, it looked plain, but from the beach, the porches and walls of windows were spectacular.

I stepped onto the driveway, hoisted my video recorder bag onto my shoulder, and circled the house to the front door. When I'd climbed the six steps to the covered wraparound porch, I lowered my bag and stood for a moment admiring the view. Far out to sea, whitecaps dotted the dark blue water, and close in, the waves were peaking at two, maybe two and a half feet. A storm was blowing in from the east. Off to the right a fenced-in pool area abutted the sand.

Inside, I decided to start at the top and work my way down, so I climbed the wide central staircase to the second floor, pausing on the landing halfway up. French doors opened onto a covered porch. I stepped outside, and after watching the waves roll toward shore for a minute, I sat on a teak Adirondack rocker.

With each undulating motion, I felt myself relax another notch. Thin wisps of thunder-gray fog appeared near the horizon, and the clouds thickened until the sun was completely blocked. The crashing grew thunderous, and windswept froth dotted the dark blue water. After a while longer, I went back inside.

I walked from room to room until I located the access point to the attic. A hinged door set into the ceiling of a small sewing room opened downward. I tugged on the dangling string, and a built-in collapsible ladder unfolded automatically.

I climbed the steps and found myself in an unfinished space. Beams and slats crisscrossed to a peaked roof. Pink insulation was stuffed in every void. There were three windows, one on either end and a round, decorative one positioned high in the wall overlooking the ocean. With the clouds growing denser by the minute, barely any light seeped in. A single row of uncovered 60-watt lightbulbs suspended from a strand of thick wire stretched the length of the space. I flipped the light switch. The bulbs cast overlapping circles of soft white light.

The only object in the entire space was a brass-studded leather trunk. I measured it, then turned on the camera and described what I saw, as per Prescott's protocol.

"This trunk is four feet three inches long, three feet eight inches deep, and three and a half feet high," I said, zooming in for a close-up. "It's covered in stiff dark brown leather. There are multiple splits, cracks, and worn spots. The leather is affixed to the frame with what appear to be brass fittings, specifically, brass straps and hobnails. A single handle is centered on the lid. An escutcheon surrounds the keyhole. There is no key."

I lowered the camera and tried to raise the lid, but the trunk was locked. I hoisted it to assess its weight. It was heavy, but not leaden. I guesstimated that it weighed fifty pounds or so, but how much of that was the trunk itself and how much was the contents, I had no way of gauging. As I lifted it, I heard the contents shift, but not rattle. Probably, I thought, it was filled with clothes.

As I walked from room to room, I annotated all the furniture, as well as all functional and decorative items, from bedside lamps and quilts to carpets and paintings.

In the central hall, I memorialized a spectacular moon-faced grandfather clock, positioned to hide the upstairs zone security alarm panel; a mahogany side table; and a pair of four-foot-high goldfish vases, probably Ming Dynasty.

Riley's walk-in closet was neat and well lit and paneled in cedar. The walls gave off a fresh woodsy scent. Clothing was organized by garment type, then color, so dresses hung in one section, skirts in another, and slacks in a third. Within each section, clothes were positioned from dark to light. Noticing a variety of sizes, from two to six, I decided to record the whole and have Sasha come back to inventory the items piece by piece. When I reached the evening gown section, I paused. A breathtaking Mainbocher peach and ivory satin dress featuring the French designer's hallmark corset lacing caught my eye. The satin was thick and soft. In the dress section, a suede colorblock empire Bonnie Cashin day dress in muted shades of cocoa brown, clay, and sunlit gold caught my eye. The suede was butter-soft, and the colors were true to nature and pure. I forced myself to move on. Left to my druthers, I'd happily spend the day, maybe the week, examining the garments, but I didn't have the time to allow myself the luxury.

I headed downstairs and continued on.

Nearly two hours later, I stood in the living room, taking a final glance around. I was just about done with my initial walkthrough. I only had the kitchen and pantry to go.

We'd need to research everything, but from my initial assessment, I knew that Bobby was looking at making some serious money. Almost all the furnishings appeared to be genuine antiques. The standard definition held that an object had to be more than a hundred years old in order to be called an antique. Some dealers used fifty years as their standard, but I'd decided years ago that Prescott's would use the more conservative metric. Some of the pieces were especially impressive and would,

I was certain, command top dollar. The bookshelves in the library, for example, featured a custom-made ladder that slid along a brass railing. The ladder's feet had a clever push-down, pop-up locking mechanism. Overall, every object had been designed and fabricated with creative vision, quality materials, and master craftsmanship. I'd be surprised if Bobby didn't net more than a million dollars from the furniture alone.

I sighed. When I appraised estates I always felt a little melancholy, but when the person who'd died was old and had lived a full and rich life, it didn't feel like a tragedy. This felt different. Here, Riley was everywhere I looked. I saw more than furnishings; I saw Riley's taste and her heritage. Change was inevitable, I knew, but that didn't mean it wasn't sad. What had taken more than a hundred years to amass would take less than a day to dismantle.

I'd finished with the closet and kitchen and was in the butler's pantry, recording the stacks of Minton china, drawers filled with Lunt sterling flatware, and cupboards stocked with Waterford cut-crystal glasses and bowls when the phone rang, startling me.

I pushed through the swinging door to the kitchen and approached the built-in desk. A phone number glowed on the combination telephone/answering machine's LED display. The area code read 310—Los Angeles. The answering machine clicked on. Two seconds later, Ruby Bowers began speaking. I lowered my video camera to the floor, found a pen and pad in a desk drawer, and wrote the number down and tucked it in my pocket.

"Bobby?" she said. "I thought you said you'd be there . . . Bobby? Are you there?" I could hear her breathing. When she spoke again, her tone was different. Lower. Huskier. Sexier. "You make me crazy, Bobby, you know that, right? Call me, baby."

I stared at the machine, unable to move. *It's true,* I thought, sick at the idea. *Riley isn't even buried, and Ruby's leaving Bobby a come-hither message.*

A car door slammed, jerking me out of my reverie. I ran to the front and peeked out the window. Bobby was walking up the path to the door. I dashed back into the kitchen, scooped up my video bag, and hightailed it for the front door. I didn't want to be there when Bobby discovered Ruby's message. If I kept my cool, maybe he'd think I'd been upstairs and out of earshot when the call came in.

I had the door open as he approached the porch.

"Hi, Bobby," I said, astonished and relieved at how normal I sounded. "I was just leaving."

"How did it go?" he asked.

"Good. I did my first go-over. There are some real treasures here, that's for sure."

"What happens next?"

"Some of my staff will come back to examine things in more detail and pack objects up. One thing—there's a trunk in the attic. Do you have the key? It's probably made of brass."

"A trunk?" He frowned, concentrating. "Oh, that would be my grandmother's. Riley went through it not that long ago, so she must have had a key. She told me there were some scrapbooks in there. Sorry, but I don't know where it is."

"Okay, well, if you find it, now you know what it goes to. If you don't, and if you want me to include the trunk and/or the contents in the sale, I can try some skeleton keys, and if that doesn't work, we can arrange for a replacement to be made."

"There's no point in my keeping it, so if I can't find the key, I'll take you up on that offer."

"Is it all right for me to send a team in first thing tomorrow morning?" I asked. "Around nine?"

"Sure. That'll work." He smiled at me. "I appreciate your help, Josie, and your speediness, too. I know this isn't easy for any of us."

"You're welcome, Bobby. And you're right. This is very hard." I shifted the video bag strap to better distribute its weight. "Okay, then. 'Bye for now."

I quick-stepped my way out the door, then ran for my car, tossing the case onto the front seat. As I began backing down the driveway, I glanced back at the house. Bobby was standing at a living room window, holding a sheer panel aside, watching me. Our eyes met, and I began breathing quickly, too quickly, as if I'd just finished a wind sprint. I waved, then took off. It wasn't until I pulled onto the interstate that I began to breathe normally.

Ick, I thought, recalling Ruby's message. *Double ick.*

As soon as I was out of sight of the Jordans' house, I rolled to a stop and called Ellis. His cell phone went to voice mail, so I called the station house. Cathy, the Rocky Point police civilian admin, answered on the second ring.

"Hi, Cathy," I said. "It's Josie, Josie Prescott. I need to speak to Chief Hunter."

"He's in a meeting, Josie. Can I take a message?"

I bit my lower lip, thinking. "It's pretty important. Could you slip him a note and ask if he can take my call? Tell him it will only take a minute."

"Sure. I'll put you on hold, okay?"

A few minutes later, Ellis was on the line.

"I'm sorry to disturb you," I said, "but I thought this was important." I repeated what had happened, then dug the paper out of my pants pocket and read off the number Ruby had called from.

"Thank you, Josie. You did the right thing to call. Talk to you soon."

He hung up.

I gazed into the trees that lined both sides of the street. About half of them showed some sign of life, soft green leaves or red buds. I thought about calling Wes and telling him about Ruby's call, too, but decided not to. I couldn't think of her message without shuddering. I'd had a duty to tell the police. I didn't have a duty to tell Wes.

I called Ty and told him about the call. When I was finished, he said he agreed with my analysis—"ick" summarized it well. He asked if I wanted to go out to dinner. I did.

"Yes," I said. "Someplace romantic."

"Not, I suspect, the Blue Dolphin."

I sighed. "I hate that one of my favorite places feels sullied."

"Sullied?" he repeated.

"Sullied was one of my mother's favorite words."

"It's a very good word. When all is said and done, the Blue Dolphin may be unsullied. In the meantime, I'll find us a good place."

"Thank you."

"I love you, Josie."

"I love you, too," I said, smiling.

CHAPTER NINE

T
he next morning, I was in the front office, leaning against Gretchen's desk, explaining the parameters of the Jordan appraisal to Sasha, Fred, and Eric, when Fred yawned.

He pushed up his glasses. "Sorry," he murmured.

"No problem," I said, smiling. "I know eight thirty feels like the crack of dawn to you."

"It *is* the crack of dawn." He glanced at Eric. "Support me here, buddy. Wouldn't you prefer to start work at noon?"

Eric grinned. "No comment."

"Moving on," I said, still smiling, "Sasha has the letter authorizing you to pack up anything and everything. For this first trip, focus on the antiques and collectibles that will require the most work to appraise: the vintage clothing collection and any decorative objects or paintings you think are worth researching, for example. We'll do the furniture next trip. Don't take anything Bobby might need while he's still living there, like his clothes, the kitchen utensils, TVs, and so on. Record and document everything as usual. Any questions?"

"Sounds clear," Sasha said.

"Good. Keep me posted."

"Can we stop for coffee en route?" Fred asked as they marched out.

I watched them drive off. It still hadn't rained, but it felt as if it might any minute. The clouds had thickened into a solid gray mass. With any luck, the storm would hold off until they got back. Eric had taken tarps, so nothing would be damaged if they had to work in the rain, but it was messy, nasty work schlepping valuable objects in bad weather.

Hank mewed, and I squatted to say hello. "How are you this morning?" He nuzzled my hand with his head.

The phone rang. I glanced at the clock. It was eight fifty.

"Prescott's. This is Josie. May I help you?" I asked, using our standard greeting.

"Hi, Josie. It's Max."

Max Bixby, my lawyer, was a solid-as-granite ally I'd known since I'd first moved to town. Having him in my life, as a friend to call on when needed, had made every aspect of settling into a new community easier.

"I'm calling on behalf of a client," he said. "Riley Jordan. Do you have any time this morning? I'd like to stop by and go over something with you."

"Sure," I replied, mystified. "Anytime."

"I'm on my way."

I stared at the receiver for a moment before returning it to its cradle. Apparently Riley and I had shared more than a love of vintage fashion. We'd shared a lawyer, too.

While I waited for Max, I sat at the guest table and read Wes's lead article in the *Seacoast Star*. His headline read:

WHY KILL RILEY?
Was It Greed or Lust?

Wes kept to the facts but laced his narrative with innuendo, suggesting that Riley might have been killed to cover up an underlying crime or sin like fraud or theft or infidelity. In a sidebar titled WHAT GRETCHEN BROCK ALMOST SAW, he reported that Gretchen might have seen the killer drive away in a silver car. *Leave it to Wes,* I thought, *to make a gossipy mountain out of an innocuous molehill.*

I'd just set aside the paper when Hank began mewing again; he wanted access to the warehouse. I pushed open the door and watched for a moment as he trotted toward his corner, then turned as the wind chimes jangled. Cara, Gretchen, and Ava arrived together, chattering about some TV show they'd all watched the evening before.

"Can you believe Wes's article?" Gretchen said, pointing to the newspaper I'd left on the guest table. "Three people have already called to ask me about that stupid silver car!" She giggled, then covered her mouth with her hand. "I don't mean to laugh over something as awful as Riley's murder, but Wes is absurd! He makes me sound like the star witness."

"Well, dear," Cara said, "you do have a role in the investigation. Not only did you give the police an important clue, but memories frequently surface—usually when you least expect it."

"I guess." From her tone, it was clear she was unconvinced. She hung up her coat, then asked, "Anything for me right now, Josie?"

"No. Nothing special. Max will be here any minute. Sasha, Fred, and Eric are en route to the Jordans' to pack up some of the collections." I pushed open the warehouse door. "And Hank is awake."

Max sat across from me. It was good to see him, and I told him so. He was tall and thin, about my age, maybe a few years older. He always wore tweed jackets and bow ties. Today, both were olive green.

"Riley was with me for several hours on the day she was killed," he said. "During our time together, she signed a new will and established a foundation. It's the foundation that brings me here today. The Riley Jordan Fashion Education Foundation's purpose is to fund initiatives that promote fashion preservation and education. The foundation will be funded through Riley's substantial assets, including debts to be collected from her husband." He reached into his briefcase and extracted a one-page document. He glanced at it, then handed it to me. "You can see here that she drafted a list of sample projects: a museum exhibit focusing on specific designers or design themes, scientific research into textile preservation or green methodologies, and scholarships for students interested in a career in fashion."

"This is terrific, Max. Really wonderful."

"Yes." He shifted position and paused for a moment. "She hoped you'd help."

"Me? In what way?"

"She named you as the foundation's trustee."

"What?" I asked, stunned.

Max nodded. "She said she trusted you and your judgment completely."

I opened my mouth, then closed it again. I was speechless. I was flattered beyond measure, yet amazed that she hadn't hinted that such a plan was in the works. I didn't know where to begin thinking about this news.

"This is quite a compliment," I said. "I don't know what to say, Max. Is it as big a job as it sounds?"

He rubbed his nose for a moment, then said, "Yes, although it's left to your discretion how big to make it. She allocated ten million dollars cash to the foundation. She's owed another two million, give or take, from Bobby, which I hope to collect immediately, so you have twelve million dollars at your disposal. Invested conservatively, and allowing for some reinvestment of capital to ensure the foundation stays ahead of inflation, it should provide an annual after-tax income of close to half a million dollars. That's a significant sum to be responsible for handing out."

"It's huge. Should I accept the trusteeship?"

"Since I'm not here advising you, I can't venture an opinion. Before you decide, though, there's more information you should consider. Riley set up a separate fund to pay the trustee a generous stipend and to fund a part-time employee, someone to handle the paperwork and winnow down applications, that sort of thing." He handed me another document detailing the amounts. "I'm sure you'll want some time to think it over."

I was about to agree with his statement when I realized that really there was nothing to think about. There was no way I could refuse. All I could do was try to honor Riley's vision. "I don't need to think about it. I accept." I shook my head, thinking about Riley. "She stopped by the day she was killed and asked me to go to lunch the next day," I said. "This must have been why."

He nodded, standing. "Probably." He picked up his briefcase. "She also arranged to pay me for consulting services going forward. Whatever support you need, Josie, Riley wanted to be certain that you had it. You don't need to think twice about calling on me."

"Amazing," I said as we walked to the door. "She thought of everything."

"And then some."

"What else did her will provide? Can you tell me?"

"Yes. I filed for probate yesterday afternoon, so it's public information. The only other beneficiaries named are the New England Museum of Design, whose costume department will receive Riley's extensive vintage clothing collection, the Sisters of Repose, a local convent, which will receive a generous cash bequest, and the New Hampshire chapter of CHF, which will receive the residue of the estate. Do you know them? Children's Hope Foundation? They help children with disabilities get whatever they need to succeed at school and in life, from wheelchairs to scholarships to in-home nursing care. CHF is Riley's chief beneficiary."

Two thoughts came to me simultaneously. One was that

while I'd known Riley was private, I'd had no idea how private. I hadn't had a clue that she was involved with CHF. The other thought was that she must have been unbelievably angry at Bobby. It's no easy task disinheriting a spouse.

"I know CHF well," I said, pushing my thoughts aside. "I support them, too. They do God's work, that's for sure. I had no idea Riley was involved with them."

"She didn't like to talk about it, but she'd been a major donor of theirs for many years." Max shook his head. "She was quite a woman. She told me she thought it was hard enough being a child in today's fast-paced world, let alone a child with a disability. The least she could do, she said, was make sure they got the best education and supplies that money could buy. I've already spoken to the board of directors. Her bequest is so large they'll be able to build a new research center on their campus. They've been trying to fund it for years, hoping to attract world-class scientists. Now they'll be able to. Which means that Riley's bequest isn't just good for the children, it's good for science, and it's good for New Hampshire."

"What a legacy," I said as I led the way down the spiral stairs. "I'm glad to know about the vintage clothing. I've already begun an appraisal on Bobby's behalf."

"Yes, you'll need to segregate her possessions."

"Shall I consult Bobby on who owns what?"

"That sounds like a good place to start. Once you have the two lists—his and hers—please show them to me."

"All right," I said.

For no apparent reason, when we were halfway across the warehouse, while I was thinking how unutterably sad this situation was, I stumbled and nearly fell. Max grasped my arm to steady me. Inexplicably, I began to cry.

"Oh, Max," I whispered, tears streaming down my cheeks. I covered my face with my hands. "I can't believe she's gone."

Max gave my arm a gentle squeeze, then released me. He stood next to me until I regained a modicum of composure.

Standing in the middle of the warehouse, waiting for my tears to stop, I realized I was exhausted. I felt as weak as if I'd been filled with helium and someone had pulled the plug.

"Sorry," I said, embarrassed, wiping my cheeks with the side of my hand.

"Don't be silly, Josie. You have nothing to apologize for. Your reaction is normal."

We continued walking toward the front office.

"Riley was right to choose you, you know," he said. "You'll do a great job."

Cara buzzed up at ten. Chief Hunter, she said, wanted to talk to me.

I took the call, and we had a one-minute conversation. No surprise, the technicians had found nothing useful on or about the pearl rosette button. He said he'd have someone run it back to us. I thanked him and went downstairs to let Ava know it was en route.

When I stepped into the office, I found Ava reading something on her computer monitor, Cara on the phone, and Gretchen on her knees near the photocopier.

"I don't know, Hank," Gretchen said. "I just don't know."

Hank sat nearby watching her. Her long copper-colored hair had fallen forward, blocking her face.

"Are you okay?" I asked.

She looked over her shoulder, brushing her hair aside. "I'm fine. It's Hank. He's upset. He batted his mouse under the copy machine. I can see it, but I can't reach it."

I looked at Hank. He didn't look upset. He looked curious. I glanced around the room for a tool and spotted an old wooden yardstick leaning against the wall near Sasha's desk. I handed it to her. "Try this."

"Good idea!" She swept the yardstick under the machine,

and the mouse shot out. "What a relief," she said, standing up and holding the mouse over her head like a trophy. "Now I can rest, knowing the man of the house will have access to his favorite toy." She spoke to Hank as she replaced the yardstick. "You can thank Josie, Hank. It was her idea!"

"Maybe we should get him more mice."

"Another good idea!" She tossed the mouse toward him, and he leapt on it and batted it toward the wall.

We watched him awhile longer, and then she turned to me.

"May I ask a favor? Would you mind if I left a little early today?"

"Of course not," I replied. I didn't want to pry, but I let my curiosity show in my eyes.

She laughed. "Jack is talking to his boss to see if he can get out early, too. If so, great—but regardless . . . he's taking me to Boston tonight for a special dinner. It's our two-year anniversary. We'll be staying overnight at the Ritz."

"The Ritz! Sweet! Has it been two years already?"

She blushed happily. "Not quite, but today's the one-year anniversary of when we knew we loved each other."

"That's completely charming." I smiled, thrilled on her behalf.

Gretchen was smart, beautiful, and kind. When she'd been single, I hadn't been able to understand why men didn't trip over themselves trying to get her attention, yet before she'd met Jack, she'd endured a long, lonely dry spell. Jack seemed perfect for her. He was a chemist, more reserved than Gretchen, but just as smart and just as giving. He was also head over heels in love with her. I loved watching him watch her, adoration patent in his gaze.

"Do you want to take tomorrow off, too?"

"Yes," she said, rolling her eyes. "Who wouldn't? But we can't. Jack has a client meeting he can't miss at eleven, so we have to get back." She giggled. "I may be in a little late, though."

"That's fine, just keep us posted." I turned to Ava. "Ava, the police are bringing back the button. Cara will log it into the lost and found system, then it's all yours."

"Did they find out anything from it?" she asked.

"No. Too many of us handled it."

She nodded. "I'll do my best to trace it. Maybe looking at it will inspire me. So far, I haven't gotten anywhere."

"All you can do is try," I said.

As I walked back to my office, I thought about Wes's article. He hadn't written anything about the New York City waitress, Tamara, and I wondered whether he hadn't been able to validate her story or whether he was still trying. *Was It Greed or Lust?* Wes had asked in his headline. *Or,* I asked myself, *was it both?*

Wes called about eleven. "I got a real bazooka. *Major.*"

"Tell me."

"Not on the phone," he said, lowering his voice conspiratorially. "At our dune in fifteen, okay?"

"Okay."

"See ya!" he said and hung up.

Wes's language was often colorful, but in my experience, he never overstated anything. If he said he had a bazooka, he did.

CHAPTER TEN

W es brought me a mini Coke, one of the old-fashioned glass bottles I hadn't seen in forever. He used a tool from his Swiss Army knife to pop the cap.

"Thanks," I said. "I didn't even know these little bottles still existed."

"I got them at the Rocky Point Gun and Rod Club. Do you know that place? Pretty fancy."

The Rocky Point Gun and Rod Club was a private country club, very old-school, with a dress code that included jackets and ties for men and closed-toe shoes for women anytime they were inside the building.

"Why were you there?" I asked. Wes's eyes were fiery bright, a sure sign he thought he was onto something.

"I was checking alibis. Quinn Steiner, Riley's financial adviser, was scheduled to meet a client there for a drink at about the time Riley was killed, but I can't nail it down. I think he was late, or maybe a no-show, but the bartender doesn't remember, and the person he met won't talk to me."

"You think Quinn might have killed Riley?" I asked, bewildered. It seemed bizarre. "Why?"

"I check out everything and everyone," he said with a certain haughtiness, as if I should have known that. His tone returned to normal. "With Quinn, there was a huge red flag. He's insisting that the e-mail Riley sent at noon the day she died asking him to look into the Blue restaurants' finances was a false alarm. When he met with her later that afternoon, he said he told her that his last full audit of the restaurant found nothing wrong, and since then, he's only noted what he called minor examples of sloppy bookkeeping. A few expenses were miscoded, for instance, so some categories looked too high while others appeared too low. He says the bottom line is that he found no evidence that anyone was intentionally padding expenses or improperly transferring money. Period."

"Why do you think he's lying?" I asked.

"I don't, but what if he is? Maybe he's doing the miscoding himself to muck up the works and hide that he's the one skimming cash. He has access to the books, right? He can do anything he wants. If Riley caught on and threatened him with exposure—not only would he lose two important clients, Riley and the Blue restaurant chain, but he might get charged with a crime. Murders have been committed for less."

I opened my mouth to argue that Wes was speculating based on nothing tangible, but he interrupted me before I could begin.

"I know, I know. At this point, it's all conjecture—but you've got to start somewhere, right? And money is one of the most common motives for murder."

"Fair enough," I acknowledged, wondering as I turned to face the choppy water if this information accounted for Wes's evident excitement. Ragged lines of white froth rose and fell from the shoreline all the way to the horizon. "What does Kenna say?"

"First off, she denies being a sloppy bookkeeper, but who'd admit being a screwup, you know? She says she doesn't know anything about anything and that if there's been any hanky-panky, someone else did it, and she doesn't know who. What do you think?"

"I have no idea. How could I?"

"You knew Riley."

I felt my brow wrinkle as I considered his comment. "I don't know if that's true, Wes. She played things pretty close to her vest."

"Which means she had secrets."

"For sure she had secrets," I agreed, thinking of her work with CHF, "but that doesn't make them *guilty* secrets."

"True," Wes agreed, sounding disappointed. "So . . . here's another shocker—Riley spent hours at her lawyer's office on the day she died. Do you know why?"

Max had said Riley's will had been filed for probate, so I felt comfortable filling Wes in. I explained about the foundation and her other bequests.

"Interesting," Wes said. "She must have been completely pissed at Bobby, huh?"

"I had the same thought," I said.

I recalled Ruby's seductive tone and edgy message. If Riley had learned that Bobby was unfaithful, she might have gone straight to her lawyer and told him to draft a will so her husband would get nothing. I would.

"I think I know why," Wes added.

I looked at Wes. The fire-hot excitement I'd seen in his eyes earlier flared up again. Quinn and his alibi had been the warm-up act. Here was the main event.

"I spoke to everyone at the Blue Dolphin," he said, "but no one knows anything. Or at least, if they do, they're not telling me."

"Which makes sense," I commented. "Bobby's their boss, and only a fool bites the hand that feeds you."

"Unless someone hates him or envies him or something," Wes said. "Not one of his employees has anything negative to say about him, though. Actually, they seem to like and admire him. It's weird."

"Why is that weird?" I asked.

Wes snorted. "How many people do you know who like their boss?"

I swallowed hard, wondering if my staff faked the easy cama-raderie we shared. *No,* I thought. *We really are a good team, hard-working and genuinely fond of one another.* I hoped I was right.

"Some," I replied, aiming for a neutral tone.

"Whatever. Even if people try to lie, I have lots of sources, and I usually get the truth in the end."

I could believe it. Wes was the most persistent person I knew. Except for myself.

"Have you heard anything about any other women?" he asked.

"Where are you with Tamara?" I asked, using the artful technique I'd learned from Wes: If you don't want to answer a question, ask one. "Has she agreed to talk to you?"

"Not yet. She thinks my paper ought to pay for her story. As if. I'm still trying to convince her. How about you? What have you heard?"

I hesitated.

"I won't quote you, Josie," he said, "and I won't print anything unless I verify it, so it's not gossip."

I nodded. I trusted him, and the reality was that I wanted to know about Ruby and Bobby's relationship, and Wes was my best source. I took a deep breath and told him about Ruby's call.

As I spoke, Wes jotted notes on his old piece of lined paper, nodding and grinning. It was clear he hadn't already heard about the call from his police source.

"Bonzo stuff, Josie!"

Bonzo, I repeated silently.

"What number did she call from?" he asked. "Did you see?"

I gave him the number, thinking how much Riley would hate it that I was talking to a reporter. She'd been so private, she'd hate the media attention her death was garnering.

As he wrote it down, a gust of wind blew through me. I shivered and rubbed my arms. The temperature was dropping, and the air was thick with moisture.

"Won't it be something if it turns out she called from her own phone? Then we'd have it nailed down for sure." He reached into his jacket pocket and extracted a small photograph. "Look at this."

No wonder Wes had called it a bazooka—the photo showed Bobby midstride in an ornate rotunda, smiling. He was holding Becka's hand and leading her through the crowd. He wore a tux. She wore a low-cut, shimmering burgundy evening gown. She was smiling, too.

"Where was this taken?" I asked. "And when?"

He slipped the photo back into his pocket and chuckled. "Cool, huh? I got him dead to rights on this one! It was taken last month at some museum fund-raiser in New York."

"I didn't see Riley in the picture."

"Bingo," Wes said, grinning.

Was it possible, I asked myself, that Becka and Bobby were having an affair? I was incredulous. Becka was Riley's oldest friend. You hear about that kind of betrayal all the time, but I still couldn't imagine it.

Once, when I was in college, a bunch of us had spent most of a late-night get-together talking about this sort of thing— stealing your friends' boyfriends. A girl from my dorm named Noreen told us about her uncle, her mother's brother. He'd fallen in love with his sister-in-law, his wife's sister, and she'd fallen in love with him. He'd gotten divorced from one sister and married the other one. That had been thirty years earlier. The rest of the family had never spoken to either of them again, but occasional reports drifted back that they were doing well. They'd moved from New York to Tampa and had two kids, cousins she'd never met.

"What does Becka say about it?" I asked.

"Nothing. Not to me, at least. I passed the photo on to the police, so probably she'll be talking turkey soon."

"Where did you get it?"

"From a source," he said, dismissing my question.

"Have you asked Bobby about it?"

"Not yet. I want to nail down all my facts first. That's why your giving me the scoop about Ruby's call is so great."

Was it possible that in addition to sleeping with a Hollywood movie star, Bobby was also cavorting with his wife's best friend? If it was true that Bobby's restaurant business needed Riley's funding, that meant that on some level, she was paying for his flings. I shuddered, partially from the raw dampness that hung over the beach like a shroud and partially from disgust. From where I sat, Bobby was lucky to be alive.

By the time I got back to the office, the rain that had been in the air for days had started up. Fred, Sasha, and Eric had returned with a load of Bobby's possessions, managing, they said, to time it just right. Two minutes after they returned, it began to pour.

"Obviously," I said, smiling, shaking off my umbrella, "you're living right."

"Obviously," Fred said.

From the gleam in his eye, I got his unspoken point. "You're thinking that I got caught in the rain, so that must mean I'm not living right."

He flipped up his hands. "I'd never say that to my boss."

"No," I responded, chuckling, "but you'd sure as shootin' think it!"

Gretchen, Ava, and Cara laughed. One corner of Fred's mouth lifted.

I slid my umbrella into the blue and white porcelain holder we kept near the front door and asked, "Where's Sasha?"

"In the warehouse," Fred said. "She couldn't wait to get started."

I found Sasha in a roped-off area on the right. She'd already begun cataloguing Riley's vintage clothing collection. Six free-standing racks and two shelving units had been wheeled over to accommodate it.

"Hey, Sasha," I said as I walked up. "What do you think so far?"

"Impressive," she said without hesitation. "Riley had impeccable taste, both design- and investment-wise. Look at this." She held up a pale pink and silver lamé evening gown with a pale pink silk net overskirt. The bodice was draped and fitted, while the skirt swirled and fluttered.

"Wow! Is that a Madeleine Vionnet?"

Madeleine Vionnet was credited with changing the way women dressed by creating garments that highlighted their actual shapes, unenhanced by padding or corsets, and that flowed and moved. In the 1920s, her ideas were avant-garde to the extreme.

"Yes. Couture. Look at the stitching."

I examined the minute, perfectly aligned stitches that ran in one unbroken line along the hem. "Amazing. She was called the 'queen of the bias cut,' right?"

Sasha nodded. "A reviewer coined that term after she introduced the technique. Her designs created quite a stir in the twenties."

"It's almost ninety years old," I said, looking at the gown, "and I'd wear it today."

"You'd be in style, too," Sasha said, hanging the Vionnet on the nearest rack. She flipped through several hangers, then extracted a full-length black rayon sequined dress with a matching cape and displayed it for me. "This is a Hattie Carnegie."

"It's spectacular." The sequins, each one hand-sewn, formed floral patterns that covered the dress from neckline to hem. I scanned the racks. "When I went through the house, I didn't find receipts or any kind of inventory of the collection, which, knowing how organized Riley was, seems odd. Maybe it's on her computer. I'll ask the police."

"It would be a huge help if there were provenance info available, that's for sure."

I flipped through a few more garments. "Riley was really something," I remarked. "I just learned that she bequeathed her entire collection to the New England Museum of Design."

"So generations of fashion lovers will be able to enjoy the collection. That's wonderful!"

We chatted for a moment longer about Riley, then discussed how best to package the delicate garments for transport to the museum when the appraisal was finished.

"I'll be in my office if you need me."

As I climbed the stairs, I recalled something my mother had told me before she'd died. I'd been thirteen.

"My thighs are chunky," I'd groused.

"Your thighs are lovely," she'd responded. "You're athletic, so you're muscular. That's very different from chunky."

I'd sighed heavily, unconvinced. "What if I grow up ugly?" I'd asked, bravely revealing my true concern. "Boys won't like me."

"You're cute as a bug, Josie, so I don't think there's any danger that boys won't like you. Even if you decide that you don't like your looks, you can take a lesson from Wallis Simpson, who went on to become the Duchess of Windsor. She was known as the best-dressed woman of her generation. She once said, 'I'm nothing to look at, so the only thing I can do is dress better than anyone else.' You have wonderful taste, Josie. The lesson is that when you dress well, people perceive that you care about yourself, and they gravitate toward you."

"Oh, Mom," I whispered now, missing her so deeply it felt like someone was pricking my heart. Missing her was nothing new. I missed her every day. She'd been infinitely kind and un-waveringly supportive. She'd never dismissed the fears I'd con-fided to her, not once; instead, she'd helped me cope.

Upstairs, I called the Rocky Point police station and asked for Ellis. Cathy told me she'd find him and asked if I'd hold on.

While I was waited, I glanced out the window. Through the pounding rain, I could just make out newly sprouted crocuses and daffodils. Soon their yellow and purple blossoms would dot the forest edge.

"April showers," I said aloud, then booted up my computer.

Ava had sent an e-mail saying she'd had no luck tracing the button and had given it back to Cara. I shrugged as I read it. Finding the owner had been a long shot at best.

My mind drifted to Wes's revelations, and I found myself wondering again where he had found the photo showing Becka and Bobby holding hands. I Googled "museum fund-raiser," "Bobby Jordan," "New York City," and "March" and got 4,278 hits. Scanning the list, I saw that Bobby had attended at least three museum galas in March, and his appearances all got huge play in the press.

Cathy came on the line. "Josie?" she said. "Sorry for the delay. Chief Hunter will be right with you."

"Thanks, Cathy."

I clicked through to the first site on the list, the Museum of Natural History. Their newsletter featured a photo of Bobby standing with a group of men. Everyone was laughing. The Museum of the City of New York's fund-raising page had a photo of Bobby posing with the mayor. On the New York Craft Museum's "Happenings" page, I found the photo Wes had shown me.

The caption explained that Bobby's New York City restaurant, the Blue Apple, had catered the gala. They'd uploaded a dozen photos of the event, including one that featured a wider-angle view of the same moment—Bobby leading Becka by the hand through the crowd. Riley was nowhere to be seen.

I brought up Bobby's restaurant's site. He had a page devoted to "Honors and Events" filled with shots showcasing his glamorous life. In one photo, he stood under a gilt dome in a gorgeous rotunda toasting an unseen photographer or someone standing behind the photographer. In a second, he stood next to Ruby under a glinting crystal chandelier. In a third, he was seated at a banquet table with his arm around Riley. Another shot showed Bobby wearing a white linen suit standing on a beach with his back to the camera gazing out over a tranquil turquoise sea. The photos from the Museum of Natural History and the Museum of the City of New York were posted, but not the one from the New York Craft Museum, which made sense. If Bobby was having an affair with Becka, of course he wouldn't post the image. If he wasn't having an affair, he wouldn't post it anyway because of how it might appear to his adoring crowds—or maybe because of how it would appear to Riley or Ruby or both of them. I was certain Bobby would agree that perception matters as much as reality, and sometimes more.

I clicked over to the museum's site again and stared at the photo of him and Becka holding hands.

"Josie?" Chief Hunter said, breaking into my ruminations.

"Hi, there," I said, feeling guilty, like a voyeur. I clicked on the corner x and closed the Web site.

"Sorry to keep you waiting. What can I do for you?"

"I have a question about whether you've found an inventory of Riley's vintage clothing collection. I didn't see anything on paper when I went through the house, so I got to thinking that maybe she computerized her records."

"Let me see . . . I have a list of computer files here."

I heard papers rustling, then silence.

"This looks like it," he said after a minute. "There's a spreadsheet called 'Vintage Clothes.' Let me take a look at it. If it's what it sounds like, I'll e-mail it to you."

I thanked him and was ready to end the call when he asked what we'd learned about the rosette button.

"Nothing," I said.

"Not a surprise, I guess. I'd like to come back and talk to everyone again. How's tomorrow afternoon?"

"Sure," I said, "but why?"

"Routine follow-up," he said, as vague as ever.

Once, when Ty had been the Rocky Point police chief, before he joined Homeland Security, he'd explained that when you're out of leads, you only have two options. You can either find new people to talk to or ask the same people new questions. I wondered if Ellis's "routine follow-up" was really an effort to generate fresh leads.

We set a time, and I called Cara and asked her to let everyone know.

I considered the work that was piling up on my desk. I needed to finish my accountant's quarterly report, and I needed to review a list of utilitarian and decorative antique fireplace objects Fred was recommending be included in an auction called Fire Starter, scheduled for next September, but I didn't want to do either. I wanted to think more about Riley and why she'd been killed in my tag sale room. No new thoughts came to me, and after a moment, I sighed and reached for my accountant's report.

I was deep in his analysis of revenue sources when Cara called up. Becka was on the phone. She wanted to know if she could stop by and see me. My curiosity fired up. Two images came to me: Becka holding Bobby's hand in New York City and her sitting, crying, in his New Hampshire office.

"Sure," I said, "tell her I'll be here all afternoon."

Ten minutes later, I had a delayed reaction to one of the photos on Bobby's Web site. I brought up the page again and scrolled down to the beach shot. Riley had e-mailed Quinn questioning whether Bobby's international money transfers were on the up-and-up, and here was Bobby at what was obviously a distant beach. Even in the dead of summer, New Hampshire beaches never looked like that. Our sand was taupe and rocky, our ocean water dark and foreboding. Bobby stood on sand that matched the white of his suit and looked as soft as satin. The water was deep turquoise, and calm. Maybe he was in Florida or Hawaii,

I thought, but it was just as likely that he was somewhere overseas.

The caption gave no information. It read, "Here's Bobby doing a site inspection. Look for new Blue restaurants everywhere!"

I called Wes.

CHAPTER ELEVEN

Becka had aged in the day since I'd seen her. Thin worry lines seemed to have appeared at the corners of her eyes and mouth overnight. She sat on the edge of the wing chair. Her eyes were rimmed in red.

"I'm sorry to barge in on you like this," she said, "but I'm pretty upset." She paused, her eyes watering. She swallowed and took in a deep breath. "Have you seen today's paper?"

"The *Seacoast Star*? Yes."

"It said Gretchen saw the killer's car. Is that true?"

I could sense the prayer inherent in her question. She wanted Riley's killer caught, and the car might provide a clue. I hated it that I had to be the one to dash her hopes. "Not really, I'm afraid. She saw a glimpse of silver, nothing else. No driver or anything."

She sighed and looked down at her hands, then up at my face. "Riley was like a sister to me. I can't stand not knowing who did this to her. From what I can tell, that's the police's best hope of catching him. What do you think? Is there anything I can do to help Gretchen remember more? I could ask her questions, or show her shapes of cars, or maybe hire a hypnotist. I have to do *something*."

"I understand. The police already showed her photos of cars, though, and nothing looked familiar. I don't think there's anything that she forgot, Becka. I think she just didn't see very much."

Becka shook her head. "Then it's hopeless."

"What's happened, Becka? When I saw you yesterday, you were upset, but not like this."

She didn't answer right away. I waited, watching her watch me. She looked down again.

"Bobby drives a silver Lexus," she whispered.

She thinks Bobby killed Riley, I realized with a jolt.

"Have you told the police?" I asked.

She shook her head. "They told me." She looked up at me. "Chief Hunter asked me to come in for an interview, and I did. That was today." She took a deep breath and closed her eyes for a moment. When she opened them, she asked, "Could I trouble you for a glass of water?"

"Of course." I reached down to the side of my desk where I kept a supply of bottled water. I opened one and handed it to her. "Here," I said.

She accepted the bottle with a murmured thank-you and sipped.

"Would you like a cup of coffee or tea or a Coke? We have lemonade, too."

She asked for coffee, and I passed on the message to Gretchen.

"Chief Hunter showed me the article," she said. "As soon as I read it, I thought of Bobby. I didn't say anything to the chief except that I had no idea who killed Riley, which I don't, but then he asked. He looked at me and said that he knew how much Riley had meant to me, how close we'd been, and surely if I knew something I'd tell him." She gulped and clamped her jaw closed.

Before I could respond, the click-clack of Gretchen's heels announced her approach. Becka turned toward the window, shielding her tear-stained face from view. Gretchen walked in and placed a silver tray on the butler's table.

"I brought some cookies, too," Gretchen said, casting an anxious glance in Becka's direction. When Becka didn't comment, her expression grew grave.

"Thanks, Gretchen," I said, jerking my head toward the

door to indicate that we needed privacy. She nodded and scooted out. I waited a few more seconds, but Becka didn't look up. I poured coffee from the Lenox pot. "Here you go. I'll let you help yourself to cream and sugar."

"Thank you, Josie," she said without changing position.

After about a minute, I said, "What did you say when Chief Hunter asked you to tell him anything you knew?"

Becka turned to me. "I told him I would." She seemed to notice the coffee for the first time and reached for her cup. "I thought I didn't know anything. Then he asked who Riley knew who drove a silver car and I told him—Bobby." She poured cream and stirred her cup as if she were in a trance, then raised her eyes to mine again. "I'm so afraid."

"Of what?" I asked her softly.

She held the coffee cup in front of her like a chalice and stared into it as if it held the answers of the ages. When she spoke again, her voice was muted. "I don't know."

"Do you think Bobby killed Riley?"

"No," she said too quickly. "He wouldn't do such a thing. He *couldn't*. I know him. I've known him for ten years. He loved her."

I nodded. "Do you think he was having an affair?"

Her eyes shot up and searched mine. "Maybe," she whispered. "Do you know anything?"

"Not for sure," I said, thinking that while I would have avoided gossiping in any event, I was telling the simple truth; Ruby's message was suggestive, not conclusive. Just as the photo of Becka holding hands with Bobby implied, but didn't prove, an intimate relationship.

"What do you think?" she asked.

I decided to answer her question openly. Doing so could do no harm, and with any luck, it might encourage her to answer in kind. "I think he may be seeing Ruby Bowers," I replied, alert for any signs of guilt or jealousy.

Her eyes remained fixed on mine. "I think so, too."

I nodded. "Did Riley know?"

She shook her head. "She would have told me."

I poured myself a cup of coffee, busywork, so I could ask a question without looking at her. "I saw a photo of you and Bobby at a museum gala in New York on the museum's Web site."

"What about it?"

"When was it?"

"Last month. Bobby's restaurant, Blue Apple, catered the gala."

I observed no guile in her expression and sensed no hesitation in her reply. "I didn't see Riley."

"She left early." She paused, frowning, then added, "What are you implying, Josie?"

"Nothing, really. Or rather, I'm not implying so much as asking. You and Bobby were holding hands."

"You don't think—" She stopped speaking for a moment, her frown deepening, and her lips thinning. When she spoke again, there was a definite chill in her tone. "Riley left early. She hated crowds. The party was in full swing, and more than a few people were getting rowdy, not Riley's cup of tea at all. About an hour later, Bobby and I decided to go. The crowd was thick, and it was hard to navigate. He said to hold on to him, he'd get us out of there, and he did. When we got back to the hotel, Bobby called up to the room, and Riley came down for a nightcap. It was nice, relaxed and pleasant. Then I went to my room and they went to theirs." She paused and looked at me searchingly. "You think I'm lying. I'm not. On my mother's eyes, I swear I never slept with Bobby."

"I didn't think you were lying, Becka. I figured it was something like that." I looked at Becka. She was watching me, gauging my reaction. "There's something I've been wondering. If Riley had discovered that Bobby was seeing Ruby, what would she have done?"

She leaned back in her chair. "She would have left him."

"How can you be so sure?"

"Because she said so. A friend of ours from college caught her boyfriend cheating and forgave him. Riley thought she was crazy. 'If he did it once, he'll do it again,' she said."

I nodded. "What a mess," I said.

"Completely." She sighed and stood up. "Thank you, Josie, for seeing me. I hope Gretchen remembers more about the car."

By the time we'd walked downstairs, her tears had dried up to nothing and she was able to chat about Riley's incredibly generous donation to the Children's Hope Foundation.

As I watched her drive away in her circa 1965 British racing green MG, I found myself thinking of my dad.

He rarely took photos, saying he wanted to live life, not record it. Photos, he said, show a moment frozen in time, nothing more. They don't provide context. You can't see what's out of the shot, what happened moments before or after the shot was taken, or what people are truly thinking or feeling. If you have memorable experiences, he said, you don't need photographs. As a result, I don't have many photos from my childhood, but it's never bothered me. Like my dad, I have the pictures in my head, and the joyous memories will stay with me forever.

By providing context, Becka helped me see that a photo that had appeared to be evidence of wrongdoing could possibly be evidence of something entirely different—good friends having fun.

It's just like appraising antiques, I thought. One of the most important lessons an appraiser needs to learn is that assumptions aren't facts.

I'd barely started a conversation with Fred about the upcoming fireplace accessories auction when Gretchen's boyfriend, Jack Stene, walked in the door.

Jack had just turned thirty. About five-eleven and well built, he had brown-black eyes and a friendly smile. Today he wore khakis and a button-down blue shirt. With his long sandy-brown hair tied into a ponytail, he looked more like a rocker dressed for court than the straight-arrow chemist I knew him to be.

"Aha!" I exclaimed. "You got out of work early and you're here to whisk Gretchen away."

"Would you mind?" he asked, grinning.

"Not a bit."

"Yea!" Gretchen exclaimed, clapping her hands. "We'll leave as soon as Cara's back from lunch."

"Go ahead," I said. "Fred and I will cover the phones."

"Are you sure?" Gretchen asked, sounding dubious.

"I wish I could help out," Ava said, "but I have a class."

"I'm perfectly capable of handling the phones," I said to Gretchen, smiling. "Go! That's an order."

Gretchen flashed a quick smile and ran into the warehouse to say a quick good-bye to Hank.

"I'm glad she's gone," Jack said to me in an undervoice. "Do you have a sec for a question?"

"Sure," I replied. "Do you want to run upstairs real quick?"

"No," he said, smiling at Ava. "You can keep a secret, right?"

"Absolutely," Ava said.

"I need some advice," Jack told me, his cheeks turning slightly pink. "About jewelers."

I smiled broadly. "Are you planning on making a purchase?" I asked. "Perhaps a ring?"

He grinned. "Yeah. I don't know a thing about good jewelry, so I need a recommendation for a reputable jeweler who won't mind teaching me the ropes."

"You're looking for Blackmore's Jewelers in Rocky Point. They've been in business, in the same location, for about a gazillion years. Still family owned and run. Mr. Blackmore is the real deal—knowledgeable and honest. Tell him I sent you, and tell him the truth about how ignorant you are. He'll take you under his wing and help you every step of the way."

"That's great, Josie. That's exactly what I was hoping for. Thanks so much."

"I'm really thrilled for you both," I said.

"Don't jinx me—she hasn't said yes yet."

"Fair point," I said. I knew, and he had to know, that there was zero chance Gretchen would turn him down, but I found his humility sweet.

"Wow," Ava said after they left, her eyes gleaming with vicarious pleasure. "Just like that, Gretchen's life is going to change forever."

Ava was right, I thought as I walked upstairs. Every big life decision has a ripple effect, affecting other aspects of your life, usually in unpredictable ways. Scary stuff, change.

Chief Hunter had e-mailed me Riley's spreadsheet. Riley had been as organized as I'd expected. The spreadsheet listed each garment, alphabetized by designer. Additional cells listed brief item descriptions and the date, place, and price of each purchase. Her collection totaled 214 garments.

I thanked him for sending it, forwarded it to Sasha and Gretchen, and printed out a copy for my own reference.

Wes called just as I was ready to leave for the day. Using his miraculous and mysterious sources, he'd already discovered that Bobby had traveled to Honduras twice in the last six months.

"Honduras?" I asked. "Why Honduras of all places?"

"Well, it's not like I know or anything," he replied, "but did you look at that beach? Jeez, why *wouldn't* someone go to Honduras if it looks like that?"

"Good point. Is he thinking of opening a restaurant there?"

"Looks that way. Are you ready for a shocker? Roatán Island

has some pretty high-end resorts, so I called around until I found where he stayed . . . and guess what?"

"I can't imagine. What?"

"He was with a woman both times. The *same* woman. The hotel staff called her Mrs. Jordan."

"So? Maybe he went with Riley." *Except,* I thought, *Riley didn't own a passport.*

"Nope. I e-mailed her photo."

My heart sank. *How could he?* "Who was it?"

"I don't know. I sent Ruby, Tamara, and Becka's photos, too."

"And?"

"It's none of them."

"What are you saying, Wes?"

He chuckled. "Bobby's been a very bad boy."

"Have you asked Bobby about any of this?"

"Not yet. I'm still gathering ammo. I've got lots of feelers out." He grinned devilishly. "Just you wait, though. I'll get him."

CHAPTER TWELVE

F riday dawned gray and damp. The rain had stopped, but it was foggy and cold, a fitting day for a funeral.

I went alone and sat in the last pew and hoped that no one would join me. I didn't want to talk. I wanted to listen to the service and think about Riley.

The church was crowded. I recognized many, but by no means all, of the people in attendance. Becka sat to Bobby's right, weeping. Bobby stared into the middle distance with seemingly stoic calm. A woman I'd never seen before, about Riley's age, sat on Bobby's left. Her head was bowed as if in prayer. I spotted Frieda, the Blue Dolphin hostess; Jimmy, the bartender; and several other employees I'd seen around the restaurant about halfway back. Kenna sat alone, off to the side. Quinn sat close to the front next to a kempt middle-aged woman, probably, I thought, his wife. She wore a gray suit. She whispered something to him, then skewed around as if she were looking for someone. When she turned, I saw that she was wearing three antique hat pins on her left lapel. She swiveled back to face the front. Dr. Walker, the fashion curator at the New England Museum of Design, sat not far from me. He caught my eye and nodded, his expression grave.

After it was over, I started to drive to work, then changed my mind. I wanted to be alone, to try to shake off the melancholy and ease the tension that had worsened during the service. I'd hoped for solace, and instead, I'd found myself becoming irritated and impatient. *Words,* I thought, *it was all just empty words.*

I wasn't ready for closure. I was ready for Riley's killer to be caught.

I drove to the beach, parked on the sandy shoulder, and changed from flats into rain boots. I clambered over the dunes and through the tall, winter-brittle grasses to the water's edge and set out walking, heading north.

With every step, my feet sank into the heavy, wet sand, and I stumbled on driftwood and rocks hidden by surf-pummeled mounds of sand and tangles of seaweed. After about twenty minutes, I felt the tension in my neck and shoulders start to ease, and by the time I got back to my car, faint tendrils of hope had replaced the leaden weight of despondency that had come on me like a fever. Riley's spirit would live on in her good works and in the memories of those of us who cared for her. I felt ready to get back to work, and I decided to spend part of the afternoon on her educational foundation. I needed to decide how best to use her largesse.

Back in my office, I reread the language of Riley's bequest establishing the foundation. She'd left it purposely vague. I decided a good place to start formulating plans was to talk to the people who knew her best, to get their take on how the foundation's focus should be narrowed. Before I could do that, I needed to come up with a list of questions to ask. I relegated that assignment to my mental to-do list, knowing part of my brain would be working on it full-time, and nodded, satisfied that I'd made a good start.

I surveyed the piles on my desk. Nothing appealed to me. I forced myself to read a proposal Gretchen had prepared recommending that we install new carpeting in the auction venue—I approved the expenditure—then gave up sitting in my office trying to concentrate on routine business matters. I felt too fragmented, as if most of my brain were otherwise occupied.

Wandering downstairs, I noticed that Fred was in the parking lot talking to an attractive silver-haired woman. They stood by her SUV's open hatch, evidently discussing something inside. I slipped on my jacket and went outside to join them.

"Hi, Josie. This is Florence Sheridan," Fred said as I approached. "She's considering selling her fire box."

The box, designed to hold fire-starting material, was roughly three feet long, two feet wide, and a foot high. It was made of maple and polished to a rich golden patina. Crude acorn shapes had been carved onto the front.

"One of my friends has consigned a few things to you for an upcoming auction," she said to me. She looked at Fred. "I've already forgotten its name, and you just told me!"

"Fire Starter," Fred said, smiling.

We already had some stellar objects in stock, including a spectacular eighteenth-century iron screen with forged metal peacock embellishments in perfect condition that Fred estimated would sell for several thousand dollars.

"That's right!" she said. "I don't use the box anymore, so I thought, well, maybe I'll consign it, too. When she told me that you offer free instant appraisals, I decided to come on down."

Word of mouth, I thought, the most valuable marketing tool I knew.

"One of the most unusual elements in this box is the joinery," Fred told me.

He stepped aside so I could take a closer look. The joinery was actually an entire system, obviously custom-crafted. All six pieces—the four sides, the top, and the bottom—slid into one another like pieces of a 3-D puzzle and were held in place by hammered metal rods and loops.

"Why do you think it's made that way?" Mrs. Sheridan asked.

"Probably for utility's sake," Fred said. "By sliding out these two rods, for example, you can see how the side panel lifts out. By tipping the box, I could empty the wood into a cubbyhole or bin without bending or lifting. This box was made by a smart carpenter."

She nodded. "That's exactly what we did. I bought it in Fair-field, Connecticut. Do you think it's an example of Connecti-cut River Valley furniture?"

"No," he said. "I mean, it might be eighteenth century, but that term—Connecticut River Valley furniture—that refers to finely crafted furniture. This is cleverly made, but the carpen-ter used pretty rudimentary techniques. I'd describe at as 'coun-try,' what some people call 'primitive.'"

Her blue eyes twinkled. "Which means it's of less value?"

Fred smiled. "I'm afraid so. Not all country furniture is less valuable than furniture made with professional-caliber cabinet-making techniques, of course, but this piece isn't signed or dated, so it's unlikely we can trace its provenance."

She nodded, then pointed to the acorns adorning the front panel. "A country carpenter tried his hand at carving, and didn't do so well, huh?"

"Well," Fred said diplomatically, "no one would call it fine workmanship, but it's an appropriate style for the object. I'd call it folk art. Acorns are commonly used to decorate furniture and other objects. You see them on cabinet doors, moldings, finials, gateposts, and so on. The acorn is a universal symbol of patience and endurance and well-earned bounty—you know that old say-ing, 'Great oaks from little acorns grow.'"

"I do indeed." She reached out and stroked the smoke-darkened wood. "So, break it to me gently. What's my beauti-ful box worth?"

Fred paused for a moment, his eyes fixed on the box. He pushed up his glasses. "What we have here is an antique of un-known period or origin in the style of utilitarian country furni-ture employing an unusual joinery system. It's in well-used condition, by which I mean, it's in the condition we'd expect a box to be in if it had been used every day for more than a hun-dred years. I'd want to do a little more research to see if we could trace the maker based on the carving style or joinery technique, but assuming we can't, I'd expect this box to sell at auction for around five hundred dollars."

Mrs. Sheridan smiled broadly. "Well, that's more than I expected! Five hundred dollars! That would let me take my entire family out for a special dinner."

"That's a fun idea! Where's your favorite place?" Fred asked.

"The Blue Dolphin," she said without hesitation. "I love it!"

Me, too, I thought, a fresh wave of sadness washing over me.

I left Fred directing her to drive around to the loading dock, explaining that he'd meet her there to unload the box. Inside, Cara and Sasha were both on the phone, so I just waved and headed straight into the warehouse. I thought I might finally be able to turn my full attention to work.

Halfway to the spiral staircase, I heard a rustling sound, a swish of what sounded like plastic fluttering in a breeze. *Hank,* I thought. *He's gotten into something.* I stopped to listen, to isolate the source of the sound.

"Hank?" I called. "Where are you, baby?"

He didn't mew in response, and I didn't hear the pitter-patter of his feet. I took a few steps, then paused again to listen.

"Hello!" I called. "Is anyone here?"

Silence, then a scrape, followed by soft sounds, footsteps maybe, then another rustle and another scrape.

Why isn't whoever's inside responding? I wondered. Maybe a small animal had snuck in, a squirrel, perhaps. I wasn't scared exactly, but it was eerie, standing there alone in a shadowy place, hearing odd, unfamiliar noises. I told myself not to be silly, that I was in my own building during working hours, that nothing could possibly be amiss. Still, as I started down the central aisle, I shivered as if a cold breeze had blown through the warehouse.

There were no windows, and the overhead lighting was dim, almost gloomy. It could have been any time of day or night. Row after row of freestanding shelving units stretched the width of the space. Objects slotted for the tag sale were shelved on the right; objects going to auction were housed on the left. In front of me, I could see the rear wall. As I walked, with my engineer boots clomping on the concrete and the sound echoing in the cavernous space, I looked from one side to the other, back and forth, peering down each row. Everything appeared normal.

"Hello!" I called again, louder this time.

No response. I paused, and for a moment, the quiet was absolute. Then I heard another rustle followed by another scrape.

Halfway down on the left, Hank's area came into view. He was in his basket, asleep. I frowned and stayed still, listening. The sounds were emanating from my right, somewhere diagonally in front of me. My view was blocked by the objects that filled the shelving units. I couldn't imagine what I was hearing. I took a deep breath and continued on, tiptoeing as best I could in my clunky boots, passing empty row after empty row.

I saw black boots and froze, gasping, then realized that I knew them—they were Ava's. I sidestepped through the row.

Ava was going through the racks containing Riley's clothing collection. What I'd heard was the sounds of research: plastic garment bags being raised and lowered, hangers sliding along metal rods, and zippers being pulled so she could examine labels. Her back was to me. As usual, she was listening to her iPod. No wonder she hadn't heard me calling. I stepped into her line of vision. She shrieked and jumped, pulling her right earplug from her ear. She pressed her hands to her chest as if to hold her heart in place.

"I'm so sorry!" I said, holding up a calming hand. "I didn't mean to startle you."

"It's okay," she said, trying to smile. "Wow! That sure got my heart going!"

"Sorry," I said again. "I couldn't imagine what I was hearing!" I pointed to the plastic-covered garments. "Little rustlings and tiny metallic sounds, and when I called, no one answered. It was pretty spooky!"

She held up the iPod wire. "Sorry about that. I was off in la-la land listening to music and falling in love with Riley's clothes."

I smiled. "I'm glad you were going through things. The faster you get up to speed, the better for us all."

"I'm really eager to help Sasha," she said.

She slid the last few pieces along the pole, finishing her survey, glancing at them one at a time, then shaking her head in astonishment. "Riley had incredible taste, didn't she?"

"Absolutely."

After ensuring that each garment hung an inch or so from the next to avoid wrinkling, we walked together toward the office. Sasha and Cara were still on the phone. Ava took her place behind her desk.

"One last question, Dr. Hutchinson. Where would I expect to find the word 'boutique'?" Sasha asked.

I didn't recognize the name.

"That's right, Mitch," Cara said. "We want to pick up with Sunday's paper."

I knew what that was about: Cara was confirming that we wanted our regular ads promoting the tag sale to resume on Sunday.

"What are you working on now?" I asked Ava.

She held up a catalogue from my former New York City employer, Frisco's, so I could see the cover. "I'm reading a vintage clothing catalogue from an auction that took place about two years ago."

"How does Riley's collection compare?"

She grinned. "It's way better."

"The museum will be pleased to hear that."

Ava resumed reading.

Sasha ended her call and turned to me. "Good news! I just

nailed down the Bob Mackie label question. The word 'boutique' appears *below* his signature."

"Is that what we have?" I hoped she'd say yes and confirm that we'd just taken a step toward authenticating some of the gowns in Riley's collection.

"Yes."

"Well done! Who's Dr. Hutchinson?" I asked.

"A professor at FIT," she replied.

A professor from the Fashion Institute of Technology was as credible a source as could possibly be found.

"Terrific," I said.

She looked down, her natural reaction to hearing praise.

I explained Max's request that we create a his and hers list of the Jordans' possessions, and her expression changed from embarrassed to engaged.

She jotted a few notes and nodded. "Do you think anything should be on the list besides her clothes, the knickknacks, and the tableware?"

"Assign everything that isn't specifically Bobby's to her list. Bobby will tell us if we're wrong."

She looked at me for a moment, maybe thinking I was going to add something, then said, "Will do."

I glanced around. Gretchen's desk was covered by paper. She always cleared her desk when she left for the day, so I knew she was still here. I hadn't seen her yet today.

"Do you know where Gretchen is?" I asked Ava.

"A customer came in for the boutique."

"Great! Anyone we know?"

"I don't think so."

"Even better—a new customer!"

"Becka and Kenna stopped by just as the customer came in," Sasha said, smiling, "asking about any new items and so on. Gretchen said she'd just put out a blue suede Adrienne Vittadini purse, and, well, need I say more? Kenna wanted to look at it. They're all in the boutique now."

"Excellent! Did Gretchen mention whether she had a good time in Boston?"

Ava grinned. "I believe the word she used was 'dreamy.'"

I smiled, but before I could reply, Gretchen pushed open the door and held it for Becka and Kenna. Kenna was holding a Prescott's shopping bag.

"The purse?" I asked.

"It's gorgeous!" Kenna said, extracting it from the bag to show me. "And only forty dollars—I can't believe it!"

I smiled, gratified that she was pleased. I turned to Gretchen. "We have a new customer, I understand."

She nodded. "A new customer who bought a Lanz dress—you remember it, don't you, Josie? The blue and red floral wrap-around?"

"Absolutely. That's a gorgeous dress."

"She said she'll be back!"

"Well done," I said and turned to Becka and Kenna. "How are you doing?"

"Good, good," Kenna said. "When I saw you the other day, you said the workshop was on for next week, but since we were driving by anyway, we thought we'd just stop in to confirm it. Gretchen tells me it's definite."

"It was a tough call," I said, "but we decided to resume the classes. We'll pick up where we left off, with handbags and shoes, which will extend the series one week."

"I'm glad," Becka said. "Riley would have hated to think it didn't continue."

"I think that's true," I said. I sighed. "I saw a woman at the funeral today wearing a cluster of antique hat pins arranged to look like a brooch. Do you know who she was?"

"That was Mrs. Steiner," Kenna said. "I noticed them, too. Amethysts, right? Didn't the arrangement look great? She often wears antique jewelry."

"It's a good example of repurposing antiques." I turned to Gretchen. "It got me thinking . . . how about asking Cara, Ava, and Sasha—three women of different ages and styles—to let us take their photos wearing three pins at a time? We can arrange them as Mrs. Steiner did, like a brooch. You could take their photos and display them next to a glass full of pins. People might have fun making their own arrangements."

"I love that idea!" Gretchen said. "I'll do it for the next tag sale—assuming my models agree to cooperate."

All three models seemed pleased to be included. Sasha smiled shyly. Ava grinned. Cara blushed.

After a two-second pause, Becka looked at Gretchen. "I read that article about what you almost saw in the *Seacoast Star*. Have you remembered anything else about the car?"

"No-o-o," Gretchen replied, yet from her tone and the way she stretched out the word, I got the impression that she might have remembered something. She shrugged. "It's funny. That woman just now . . . did you notice her car? She was driving a Volvo. It had a kind of boxy shape, and it made me realize that the car I saw wasn't boxy like that."

"If you thought the car wasn't boxy," Becka said, leaning in, pinning Gretchen with her fixed gaze, "you must have thought it was some other shape, like a van or a sports car."

Gretchen shook her head. "Nothing comes to me."

"I told you memories can come back," Cara said. "Just you wait."

Over the years, I'd observed how seriously Gretchen took her responsibilities. While I admired her attitude, I also worried that she stressed over things out of her control. She rarely cut herself a break. I was afraid that she'd misinterpret Cara's cheerful encouragement as an indictment that she wasn't doing her best.

"Sometimes they do," I said, "but sometimes they don't. Don't fret about it, Gretchen."

She sighed. "You're right," she said. "I'll try to remember. That's all I can do."

"What do you think?" Becka asked. "Should you call the

police? I know they already showed you pictures of cars, but maybe there's something else they can do to jog your memory."

Gretchen made a face. "It gives me a headache just to think about going through that again. After about a minute and a half, all the cars began to look alike. I'll wait until more memory comes back—if it does."

"That sounds smart," I said.

"If you stop trying to remember," Kenna said, "sometimes what you've forgotten just pops into your mind. That happens to me all the time, like when I misplace my keys."

The phone rang, and Cara answered, then put the call on hold. "It's Ty," she said.

"Excuse me," I said and ran upstairs to take the call in private. I was relieved I did. Ty had called to tell me he loved me, and I was glad to be able to tell him how much I loved him without feeling everyone's eyes on me.

When I got downstairs again, Fred was back behind his desk, frowning at his computer monitor, engrossed in whatever he was reading. Sasha was on the phone, talking to someone named Carl about Madeleine Vionnet's use of netting. Ava was still reading the Frisco's catalogue. Cara was entering customer contact information into our database. Gretchen was using Sasha's yardstick to retrieve Hank's mouse from under the photocopier again. Kenna was on her knees beside her, peering under the machine and directing her efforts. Becka stood with her back to us, looking out the window.

"Got it!" Gretchen said, scooping up the mouse as soon as it flew out.

"Well done!" Kenna said.

"I'm going to deliver it to him, the little devil," Gretchen said. "I'll be right back."

"We should get going," Kenna said to Becka.

Becka turned around and sighed, but she didn't pick up her purse or walk toward the door. She seemed lost in sorrow. She swayed for a moment, then leaned heavily against the wall.

Kenna's expression softened. "Are you okay, Becka?"

"I'll be fine. I just feel a little . . . I don't know."

"Would you like some water? Tea? Anything?" I asked, thinking she looked pale, wondering if she was going to faint.

"Water, please."

"I'll get it," Cara said, hurrying to the minifridge.

"There's nothing wrong . . . it's just . . . everything."

"Maybe you should sit down," I suggested.

Becka sank into one of the guest chairs and took in a deep breath. Kenna and I watched her until Cara returned with the water. She accepted the bottle with a quiet thank-you.

"What do you think happened?" Kenna asked her, concerned.

"I don't know," Becka said between sips. "Really, I'll be fine in a minute."

The phone rang and Cara reached across her desk to take the call. "Oh," she said, her eyes lighting on a sheaf of papers. She wiggled a stapled document out from under a paperweight and handed it to me. "I forgot to give this to you. It just came in."

"Thanks, Cara," I said, reaching across for it. I recognized the logo. It was a fax from the New England Museum of Design, time-stamped about half an hour earlier. I glanced through the cover letter. Dr. Walker wrote that he'd heard from Max Bixby that I was appraising Riley's vintage clothing collection, and he thought it might be helpful for me to have his old notes to refer to as I worked. I flipped through the pages. It was a printout of a word-processing document listing the vintage clothing and accessories Riley had intended to donate to the museum as of October 18, 1999.

There's been an ocean of water under that bridge since then, I thought.

The inventory was woefully out of date, but whoever had prepared it had been meticulous. It seemed to contain many more descriptive details than were included in the inventory the police had e-mailed me. A 1950's Tina Leser blue cashmere cardigan sweater was described as having a "floppy bow detail at the neck, owned by Babs Miller," for example, and a Bonnie

Cashin clutch bag was described as "coral-colored saddle leather w/ white saddle-stitching along edges and brass frame, bought at a York, Maine, flea market." I sat at Gretchen's desk and hunted around on her computer until I found her copy of the spreadsheet Chief Hunter had sent me. I wanted to confirm that I'd remembered correctly. I had; Riley's listing only included the basics of each item—a "Tina Leser blue cashmere cardigan sweater" and a "Bonnie Cashin orange clutch." Either Riley had decided to eliminate a lot of detail or someone else had prepared the earlier list.

Reading through Dr. Walker's inventory, I came to an unfamiliar object—a "Claire McCardell dove gray and lavender wool/flannel blend coat." I searched Riley's spreadsheet and found it listed. I turned toward Sasha. She felt my eyes on her, and she looked at me. Something in my expression caught her attention, and she asked Carl to hold on.

"Sorry to interrupt—have you seen a Claire McCardell dove gray and lavender wool/flannel blend coat in Riley's collection?" I asked.

"No." She rolled her chair toward me until she was close enough to see the spreadsheet on Gretchen's monitor. "No," Sasha repeated, sounding worried.

"That's okay," I said, smiling to reassure her. "Finish your call."

She nodded and rolled back to her desk.

Gretchen came back in the room. Noting I was sitting at her computer, she asked, "Is there anything I can find for you?"

"No, thanks," I replied, "I got it." I looked first at Becka, then Kenna. Becka looked better, less ashen. "By any chance, did Riley ever mention a Claire McCardell gray and lavender coat to you? It's listed on her inventory, but it wasn't in her closet with everything else. Did you ever see it or hear her talk about it?"

Kenna shook her head. "No, I don't think so."

"I seem to remember that coat," Becka said, her brow

furrowed as she dredged up the memory, "but I haven't seen it in years. Is it missing?"

"It's too early to call it missing. She might have taken it to the dry cleaner or something. Plus, there's a trunk in the attic that I haven't looked at yet. It may be in there."

"Don't tell me," Kenna said with a small smile. "It's locked and Bobby's lost the key?"

"He's famous for losing things, is he?" I asked, matching her smile.

"Infamous is closer!" she said, smiling and shaking her head. "He's a brilliant chef, but he'd be the first to admit that he's not the most organized person in the world when it comes to business."

"What will you do if he can't find it?" Becka asked.

"Try skeleton keys we keep on hand for just that purpose. If they don't work, I'll call in a locksmith. Either way, I'll be able to get it open today."

"Good," she said. She stood up and smiled at me, then Cara. "Thanks for the water. I feel much better." She turned to Kenna. "I'm ready if you are."

"You bet!"

They said good-byes all around and left, and I turned back to the fax. Dr. Walker described the coat as size two and fully lined with gray silk. Scanning the spreadsheet, I saw that many of Riley's earlier acquisitions were size two. Most of the latter ones were size four. Some were size six.

Sasha thanked Carl, hung up, then asked, "Is that coat missing?"

"I think it might be in a trunk in the attic. I'm going to call Bobby now and ask if he's found the key."

As I headed back upstairs to call Bobby, I wondered why Riley would have stored only one garment in the trunk. I needed to open it, pronto.

CHAPTER THIRTEEN

I reached Bobby on his cell phone, and we talked for a moment about the funeral service.

"I can't imagine what you're going through," I said.

"I'm a mess, to tell you the truth." He sighed. "Everyone is very . . . supportive, of course, but it all feels . . . I don't know . . . surreal."

I could feel his anxiety and upset. "I thought the service was moving. Very touching." *Platitudes,* I thought, cringing, but I couldn't think of anything else to say.

"Yes." He cleared his throat.

"I'm sorry to trouble you with business at a time like this—" I stopped talking. I knew Bobby was in a hurry, but I felt awful calling him within hours of his wife's funeral about something as prosaic as a key.

"What is it, Josie?" he asked.

"Did you ever find that key?" I asked. "The one for the trunk in the attic?"

"No. I should have called to tell you."

"I hate to ask—but did you think to check her key ring?"

"Yes . . . the police gave me back her . . . anyway . . . the key wasn't there."

"If it's all right with you, I'll go to your house with a bunch of skeleton keys. There's no guarantee, but one of them might work. If not, we'll need to call a locksmith."

"That sounds fine. Thanks, Josie. I know you're being very thorough, and I appreciate it. You have the house key, so if you need to get a locksmith, can you arrange to be there with him? Or bring the trunk back to your place and get it done there?"

"Absolutely," I said. "I'll head over right now."

I walked to the big metal cabinet at the back of the warehouse where we stored our skeleton key collection, pausing en route at Hank's basket. He was still asleep, his breathing deep and rhythmic. *He really is a very handsome boy,* I thought. I watched him for several seconds, then squatted to give him a little underchin rub. He leaned into my hand and began purring, still asleep. As I stroked and petted him, he opened his eyes. He licked my hand, and I smiled. Hank was becoming a friend.

"I've got to go," I whispered. "You be a good boy."

Bobby had seemed genuinely disturbed on the phone, I thought, both unfocused and sad. I stood in front of our skeleton key collection for a long time, trying to decide which ones to bring, finally deciding to take them all. I was white-hot curious about what was inside that trunk, and I didn't want to miss a chance to find out.

As I buckled my seat belt, I looked up. The sky was darkening again. More rain was on the way. Ty pulled into the parking lot. As I watched, he spun his government-issued SUV toward me and stopped short, and my heart lurched. Obviously, something was wrong.

"What's wrong?" I asked as soon as he stepped out of the vehicle.

"Nothing," he replied, smiling, walking toward me. "I'm here to kidnap you."

"You are? Why?"

"I got off early, and I thought maybe I could persuade you to do the same. Then we could go to my place and light a fire and have Cherry Blossoms to greet the weekend."

I grinned. *What a guy,* I thought. Ty's house was a big, angular contemporary, set in a clearing in the forest. He had two fireplaces, a two-sided one in the center of the window-walled great room and another, smaller, stone-faced one in the master bedroom.

"What time is it?" I asked.

He glanced at his wrist. "About one thirty."

"Give me an hour, and you've got a deal. I was just on my way to try to open a trunk in the Jordans' attic." I waggled the tote bag I'd filled with keys. "Wish me luck! I'm hot on the trail of a missing Claire McCardell coat."

He smiled. "What happens if you can't open it?"

"I'll get Eric and Fred to bring it back here and call a locksmith."

"Why don't you just bring it back anyway?"

I nodded and smiled. "I thought about it. I'm impatient. I want to try the keys *now.*"

"You? Impatient?"

I play-punched his arm. "Sarcasm doesn't become you."

He grinned broadly. "Who was being sarcastic? I like it that you're impatient."

"You do? I always thought it was a fault."

He reached out his hand and touched my cheek. "You have no faults. You're perfect."

I touched his fingers with my own and met his eyes. He wasn't joking. "That's sweet," I said, "but we both know that's not true—I'm laden with faults."

"There's foibles and personality quirks and eccentric preferences, and then there's faults. You've got plenty of foibles and lots of personality, and you're pretty darn opinionated when it comes to expressing your preferences, but if you have any faults, I've yet to discover them. For me, you're perfect."

My throat closed as Ty's eyes remained fixed on mine. My lips went dry. "Wow," I said.

He hugged me and I hugged him back, snuggling my cheek

into the soft corduroy of his jacket. After several seconds, I leaned back so I could see his face.

"Ha!" he said. "See what I did? I tricked you into hugging me, and now you're my prisoner. Consider yourself kidnapped. I want us to get settled in front of the fire before the rains come."

"I'd love to, Ty, you know I would, but I can't. Duty calls. Come with me—keep me company."

He thought for a moment. "The Jordans live on Ocean, right? I tell you what—I'll drop you at the house. While you try your keys, I'll get us some kick-ass steaks at Alexander's. We can pick up your car on our way back."

Alexander's was a specialty gourmet shop that carried the best beef on the Seacoast and whose butchers cut prime steaks to order.

"You sure know the way to a girl's heart—Cherry Blossoms and a steak from Alexander's. Let's saddle up, fella."

Ty pulled into the Jordans' driveway.

"See you in a half hour or so," he said.

"I'll be on the lookout!" I waved good-bye and ran around to the front door.

The trunk was in the same position as it had been during my last visit. I tried lifting the lid, just to be certain it really was locked. It was. I sat cross-legged in front of it and began trying keys. Our skeleton key collection included examples of various types, materials, and sizes. Some keys didn't even fit into the lock; others seemed to turn a little, then stopped. Nothing worked.

I replaced the keys in my tote bag and stood up, brushing dust from my backside and glancing around to be certain I wasn't forgetting anything, then made my way down the ladder, switching off the lights at the bottom. The ladder folded up as smoothly and quietly as it had come down.

I'd just stepped out of the sewing room into the upstairs

hallway when I heard glass shatter—one loud crashing sound, then a series of tinklings, followed by cracks and more tinkling. My heart leapt into my throat, then plummeted. I knew those sounds—someone was breaking in. They were clearing away the last bits of glass that clung to the door or window frame, and soon they'd be able to safely reach through and unlock it or climb in.

I was standing in the hallway totally vulnerable. Anyone heading up the stairs couldn't help but see me. Wild thoughts of fleeing had to be quashed. There wasn't time to flee. The best I could do was hide.

From my recent walk-through, I knew that the doors lining the hallway accessed the sunroom, two guest rooms, two bathrooms, the master bedroom suite, a linen closet, and a large storage closet. I looked at the pair of goldfish vases, the side table, and the grandfather clock. *My phone,* I thought. I can call for help. I reached into my tote bag and found my unit. I heard a faint patter of footsteps. The intruder was already inside, walking who knew where. *Move,* I told myself. *Now.*

Without giving myself another second to think, I sidestepped to the grandfather clock while keeping my eyes on the staircase. I slid my hand behind it to reach the mostly hidden alarm panel and pushed the panic button, then darted to the storage closet door and wrenched it open. Inside, I pulled the door almost, but not quite, closed. I stood next to a wooden croquet set, the mallets dangling from notches in the crossbar. Tennis racquets and a badminton set sat on shelves in back of me, relics of happier times. With only the green glow of the display to see by, I texted Ty "911," then tossed the phone back into my bag. *I might need both hands free,* I thought, lowering the bag to the floor. I put an eye to the crack. From my vantage point, I could see the clock's face. It was two forty.

The house phone rang, and I gasped. Instinctively, I stepped back, tripping on my bag and hitting a mallet, creating a domino effect of hammering sounds as each mallet hit the next in line.

I pressed them into my legs and held them steady, then took a deep breath to calm myself.

Probably the security company was calling to ask if the alarm was a mistake. When no one picked up, they'd call the police, and the cavalry would be on its way to the rescue. The phone stopped ringing and the machine clicked on. I could just make out a low rumbling voice, but I couldn't hear any words. I waited, listening. Nothing. Silence that lasted for seconds, then footsteps coming closer. Someone was mounting the stairs. More silence. Fear sent shivers up my neck and spine. The upper hall was carpeted, so someone could be directly on the other side of the door, and I might not know it.

I used my foot to slide my bag into the far corner. I waited, listening. I heard only house sounds—the tiny swish of heat flowing from a radiator; the clicks of a machine cycling on and off, maybe the refrigerator; and the rhythmic ticking of the clock. I put my eye to the crack again. All I saw was the door to the master bedroom and the grandfather clock. It was two forty-two.

Staccato, angry-sounding thuds and thumping exploded somewhere close by. I jumped and nearly stumbled, crashing again into the croquet mallets. I stopped them knocking and placed my palm against the wall to steady myself. I stood, waiting, as the attack grew louder and fiercer.

Do something, I told myself, hating it that I was simply waiting, wanting to control the chaos. My hand touched a mallet. *A mallet would make a good weapon.* I slid one off the crossbar and grasped it firmly, like a baseball bat.

The rhythmic smacks continued, a steady, deadly-sounding assault.

I heard sirens and exhaled. I'd been holding my breath for what felt like hours. Seconds later, as the clock chimed the quarter hour, I heard running feet, followed by a slamming sound. I threw open the door and flew to a street-facing window in one of the guest rooms.

I was too late.

All I saw was a sliver of silver as a car, maybe a sedan, disappeared around the corner.

"I was terrified," I told Ellis. Sitting on the Jordans' floral-patterned sofa next to Ty, I still felt breathless and on edge. Ellis sat across from me on a cranberry-colored club chair. I shrugged. "You should have heard those sounds—someone was attacking something as if they wanted to kill it."

Before he could respond, Detective Brownley appeared in the archway. Ellis turned to face her.

"May I see you for a moment, sir?" she asked, all business.

"Certainly." He walked to join her.

She leaned in close to his ear and semiwhispered. I couldn't hear a word. He nodded and said something that I also couldn't hear. Then she left, and he rejoined me.

"Our initial canvass of the neighborhood hasn't turned up anyone who saw the silver sedan." He glanced at his watch. "It's almost four, so most people are at work." He shrugged. "We'll continue asking, but the closest neighbors offer the best hope, and of the few who were home, no one noticed." He crossed his legs, thinking. "You said you think there's an antique coat in the trunk, and that's why you were here. Is it credible that someone did all this just to get that coat?"

I shrugged. "It seems hard to believe. I mean, Claire McCardell was wonderful designer, but still . . . I'd need to see it, of course, but even if it's in as good condition as the rest of the collection, it's only worth a few hundred dollars."

He pursed his lips for a moment. "Is anything else missing?"

"Not that I'm aware of."

He frowned. "How come you can't say definitively? I mean, you've got the clothes and you've got the list, right?"

"Yes," I said, "but we haven't finished inventorying everything yet. Heck, we've barely begun."

He nodded and leaned back, thinking.

"The phone rang while I was hiding," I said. "Was it the security company?"

He turned his gaze back to me. "Yes. If a panic button is pushed, their protocol has them calling. If they don't get an answer, they leave a generic message requesting a callback. If you don't call them back immediately, they call us." He glanced at Ty. "Ty called, too. Your nine-one-one message got through loud and clear."

"Is there any sign of damage that would account for what I heard?"

He shook his head. "Someone took a whack or thirty at the trunk. The technicians will be here soon to check for fingerprints and so on. Then you and I can look inside."

"A whack or thirty?" I repeated. "You mean like with an ax?"

"Yeah—except I think they probably used a hatchet."

As soon as I reached the top of the attic stairs, I saw the destruction.

"Oh, my God!" I exclaimed.

The leather was ripped every which way all across the trunk's top. Chop marks marred the wooden frame. Whole chunks of wood were missing, strewn across the floor. The escutcheon hung sideways—someone had succeeded in levering out half the nails.

"It wasn't like that when you last saw it?" Ellis asked.

"No, not at all." I turned to face him. In the dim light, the small jagged scar near his right eye that looked bloodred in daylight was hardly visible. "I can't believe it!"

"I'm changing my mind. There may be forensic evidence, and if so, I don't want us to miss it. We'll take the trunk to the station and open it there." He glanced out the window. The rain was steadier now and showed no sign of letting up. "They'll bring tarps." He turned to face me. "Will you come, too? I have a feeling that whatever is inside is something you'll know more about than me."

"Of course. I'm glad to help," I said.

I was also as curious as a cat.

Ty drove me back to my office so I could pick up my car. We agreed he'd go home and I'd join him as soon as I could.

"It won't be the same sitting in front of the fire without you," he said.

"But it'll still be pretty darn good."

He grinned. "Yeah."

I stepped out of the car and waved good-bye backwards as I ran through now-pelting rain into the office. Inside, everyone was getting ready to leave for the day, chatting about weekend plans, the bad weather, and how weird it was that tomorrow wasn't a tag sale day. I glanced at Gretchen's Mickey Mouse clock—it was six minutes after five.

"Were you able to open the trunk?" Gretchen asked.

"No," I replied. "There's a story there, but for another day. You all take off. I'm just going to put the skeleton keys back. I'll close up."

"Or I will," Gretchen said. "I want to put out extra food and water for Hank since we won't be back until Monday."

The wind chimes tinkled as one after another of my staff left.

As Fred slid his tie knot into place, he said, "If it's okay with Hank, I'm planning on coming in for a few hours tomorrow. Tonight, I have a date."

"You do?" Gretchen said, stopping short and turning full around, her gossip antennae on full alert. "Who with?"

I set off toward the supply cabinet, not unhappy that she held the door open, so I could hear about Fred's date, too.

"Sandy Sechrest. From Hitchens. She teaches in the Decorative Arts Department. Do you know her?"

"No. Tell me everything."

"There's not too much to tell. I talked to her yesterday when I began researching some of the fireplace objects, and one thing led to another and I asked her out to dinner."

"Are you telling me you've never even met her?"

"That's why they post faculty photos on college Web sites, isn't it?"

"That's wild!" she said, laughing. "I hope you have a great time. Where are you taking her?"

"Where else but the best restaurant in town—the Blue Dolphin."

"Very nice! I'll expect a full report on Monday!"

"Forget it, Gretchen," he said. "Guys don't kiss and tell."

"How about a high-level update?"

"That I can do!"

They exchanged good-byes, and then I heard the click-clack of Gretchen's heels as she made her way across the concrete to Hank's area. After I replaced the keys, I joined her at Hank's basket. He was awake, and we took turns tossing his mouse and applauding his fetching, then wished him a good weekend and left, umbrellas in hand. I punched the alarm code, and we walked into the parking lot side by side.

"I'll see you on Monday!" she said.

"Bye-bye," I called, turning toward my car.

Before I reached it, I heard a sharp clap, as if someone had slammed two pieces of wood together. It was a distinct sound at odds with the soothing patter of the rain. I looked at Gretchen, and I could tell from her expression that she'd heard it, too. It rang out again, another loud cracking sound, this time less a clap than a strike, like splitting wood.

"What's that noise?" she called.

"I don't know," I said.

I surveyed the forest that surrounded us, the two-lane road that ran along my property's edge, and the stone wall across the way. A third crack shattered the quiet, and Gretchen screamed.

I whirled around in time to see her umbrella spin through the air like a whirling top. She toppled, landing with a thud and made a sound, a gurgle, then a sputter. The umbrella crashed to the ground upside down and collapsed.

Gretchen turned to look at me.

It wasn't until I spotted blood seeping through her jacket that I realized she'd been shot.

CHAPTER FOURTEEN

I tore across the parking lot, dropping to my knees beside Gretchen. She looked bemused more than upset or frightened. *She's in shock,* I thought.

"Don't move," I whispered.

"What happened?" she managed, her voice thin and weak.

"You've been shot."

Her eyes opened wide, but she didn't speak.

"I need to find where you've been hit so I can stop the bleeding," I explained. I unzipped her jacket and saw an elliptical hole in her sweater near the outer edge of her left shoulder. I ripped the sweater to see the wound. Blood oozed from a ragged cut. The bullet seemed to have only grazed her skin. I shoved my hand into my bag, patting around until I found the lightweight fabric tote bag I always carry, just in case I find myself with antique treasures to purchase but no packing materials. It came prefolded into a small square and was perfectly sized for covering the wound. I centered it over the bullet hole and pressed hard.

Gretchen winced. "Ow," she murmured.

"Sorry," I said, keeping the pressure steady. I stuck my left hand inside my tote and felt around for my phone while peering into the trees on the far side of the stone wall. I saw nothing out of place. I saw no flash of color as if someone were running through the woods. There was no glint of metal, at least not enough of one for me to spot it in the dull gray light and driving rain. I turned back to look at Gretchen. Her eyes were closed.

She looked peaceful, as if she were asleep. Without warning, a spasm roiled through her body, and she bit her lip. My fingers touched hard plastic—I'd found my phone.

As I punched 9-1-1, I heard a car start. The engine revved, then quieted. I kept my eyes on the road, but no vehicles passed by. If one had, I knew what I would have seen—a silver sedan.

I called Ty from the Rocky Point police station. I was in Interrogation Room One again, alone this time. As soon as I heard his strong, familiar voice, I began to cry.

"What's going on, Josie?"

"I'm okay," I said through my tears. "I hate crying. I'm sorry."

"There's nothing to be sorry about. Just tell me what's wrong."

I inhaled deeply, twice, then said, "Gretchen's been shot." I told him what happened, then added, "Ellis is calling the hospital right now." As I spoke, he pushed open the door. "He just walked in." I looked at him, but his eyes gave nothing away. "I'm on the phone with Ty. Anything?"

He nodded. "Yes. The doctor says it's a superficial wound. She'll be released shortly."

I felt myself sink farther into the chair. "Thank God," I said. To Ty, I added, "Did you hear that?"

"I did. Let me talk to Ellis, okay?"

"Sure." I handed the police chief the phone. "Ty wants to talk to you."

I listened as the two men spoke. Mostly I heard grunts and affirmations and "Not yet." Ellis handed me the phone.

"How long do you figure I'll be?" I asked, before resuming my conversation.

"I'm guessing maybe an hour or so."

"I'll be there in a little over an hour, I guess," I said. "Maybe longer."

"I'll have food ready and a fire going."

I glanced up and saw that Ellis was watching me, and I felt myself blush. I wanted to tell Ty that I loved him, but instead I said, "Great. I've got to go."

Detective Brownley took my statement, which amounted to a lot of "I don't know," "I can't remember," and "I don't think so" assertions. She video-recorded it, as was their protocol.

After asking me to recount what happened, she leaned back and tapped her pen against the table.

"Can you think of anything that happened today that might account for Gretchen's being shot? I mean, why now? Why today?"

I recalled Gretchen's description of the silver Volvo. *It wasn't boxy like the Volvo,* she'd said.

Something must have shown on my face because the detective asked, "What is it, Josie? What did you just remember?"

I explained.

"Who was there when she made that remark?"

I felt my heart sink. "Becka and Kenna."

I told Detective Brownley the truth, but refused to speculate about which of them was more likely to have shot Gretchen no matter how she tried to worm an opinion out of me.

"I have no idea who'd want to kill Gretchen. It's crazy."

Detective Brownley nodded. She leaned back and tapped her pen. "Which of your staff was there?"

"Almost everyone."

"What can you tell me about them?"

"Nothing."

"Give me one-sentence profiles."

"I don't know anything about anyone's private life. I mean, I know Cara was widowed about ten years ago. She lives with a golden retriever and is close to her grandson. Sasha goes to

Boston a lot for lectures at the Museum of Fine Arts. Fred had a date tonight with a professor from Hitchens. Eric lives with his mother and two dogs and has been dating a girl named Grace for more than a year—but he wasn't in the room." I flipped up my hands. "You see what I mean? I don't know anything relevant about any of them, and I know even less about Becka and Kenna."

"Right—but what do you think?"

"Nothing."

"Tell me about Cara's grandson."

"I don't know anything. I don't even know his name."

"Does any of your staff own a gun?"

"I don't know."

"Where's yours?"

My properly registered Browning 9 mm was in my bedside table, and I told her so.

"Do any of them know how to shoot?"

"I don't know," I repeated like a mantra, thinking of Bobby's Olympic past.

It went on and on, until finally I was rescued when Ellis stuck his head into the room.

"You about done?" he asked Detective Brownley.

"Yes," she said, flipping her notebook closed. "Josie's been very helpful."

"Thanks, Josie," he said, smiling at me.

"I don't know how helpful I've been—all I seemed to say was 'I don't know.'"

"Negatives can be as useful as affirmations," he said.

"I guess."

"Ready to get a look at the contents of the trunk?"

"You bet!" I said, standing, relieved that the interview was over.

Ellis and I walked down the corridor to the entry area, past the long counter where a patrolman I recognized named Darren sat typing into a computer with two fingers, through a closed door that led to another side corridor, and into a medium-sized room that overlooked the rear parking lot. The trunk sat on a metal table. The lid was up. The contents were laid out across three other tables.

"There's the coat!" I said, approaching the table where the gray and lavender coat sat, folded into a neat square, back side up.

"Don't touch—the tech guys haven't finished yet."

"Can you turn it so I can see the label? I want to confirm it's a size two Claire McCardell."

Ellis put on latex gloves and gingerly folded back the collar to expose the label. It read: CLAIRE MCCARDELL, then, on a separate line, CLOTHES BY TOWNLEY. Mystery solved—it was the coat. Another label read: 2.

"That's it. I'm glad to know it's there, but I wonder why Riley kept this coat, and it alone, in the trunk."

"Why do you think?"

"I have no idea. Dr. Walker annotated his list, so I know this coat had belonged to Babs Miller, but so did lots of other pieces."

"Maybe this was the only one she no longer wore."

"Why?" I asked.

"Why do you think?" he said, once again turning the question back to me.

"I don't know."

He nodded. "Do you recognize anything else?" he asked.

"That looks like an Olympic medal," I said.

"It is. It was Babs Miller's."

"Bobby's grandmother?"

"Right. It looks like everything in the trunk belonged to her." He started at one end of the table and called out the objects as he pointed at them, moving from left to right. "Those are her yearbooks from Hitchens University. Those three hold memorabilia from her skating days. The one below contains photos from when she lived in a sorority at Hitchens. The next stack over are scrapbooks from her marriage. From what I can tell, the scrapbooks contain a mixed bag of memorabilia—letters and cards from friends, sorority sisters, Olympic competitors, and her husband, recipes, pressed flowers, and souvenirs . . . you know, theater tickets and Playbills, that sort of thing. That final stack, those are scrapbooks about Bobby. They contain his report cards, letters from camp, newspaper clippings from his Olympic competitions, and so on. From appearances, she was a devoted wife and one proud grandma."

"It's sad, isn't it? Sweet-sad."

"I don't see it that way. I think it's sweet-happy. Obviously collecting all of this gave her pleasure, or she wouldn't have done it."

I nodded. "I guess."

"Does anything here have value?" he asked.

"I can't tell without going through things. Some of the ephemera might."

"Ephemera?" he asked. "I know that word . . ."

"In the antiquing biz, the term refers to perishable objects, like tickets, concert programs, pamphlets, postcards—anything created knowing it would have a short life span. They serve their purpose, then they're yesterday's news."

"Like newspapers," he said, nodding.

"Exactly like newspapers." I looked back at the piles.

"If you were me, what would you do now?"

"That's easy," I said, grinning. "I'd let me examine every-thing."

"I will. The tech guys tell me it's going to take them a day, maybe two, to process everything here. Will you be available to look at things on Monday or Tuesday?"

"Yes, absolutely." I walked over to the trunk. "You said you thought whoever did this used a hatchet."

"Yes. See those indentations? They're small and circular, like someone was trying to punch through with a hammer. Most hatchets have a hammerhead on the other side of the blade."

The frightening-looking marks were everywhere along the top. It was as if someone had been out-of-control enraged and had taken it out on the trunk. Some of the wooden slats that lined the steel frame had been shattered, and dagger-sharp pieces of wood stuck through the leather at ugly angles. In places, the leather had been shredded.

"Why didn't he succeed?" I asked. "I mean, look how the leather is destroyed, just decimated. Do you see how over here it's almost totally stripped away? Why didn't the trunk implode?"

"Steel isn't so easy to hack through."

I nodded, thinking. "Is it even possible to hack through steel?"

He shrugged. "It depends on the tool and the user. Whoever did this wasn't strong enough. Or he got interrupted before he had time to finish. Or his hatchet was too small."

The bits of metal visible through the ripped leather and splintered wood were intact. In fact, as I leaned in closely, I could see that while strike marks were evident, every piece of metal appeared true and level.

"Maybe the tool was adequate," I said, turning to look at him, "but the user wasn't strong enough because he was a she. Maybe this is the work of a woman."

"Who?"

"I have no idea."

He thought about it for several seconds. "It's possible."

"I don't suppose the tool was found tossed into the bushes or something?" I asked.

"Why would you think that?"

"I don't think it—just if it were me, and I'd done that," I said, pointing to the lid, "after breaking and entering, I wouldn't want to be caught with the hatchet in my possession."

"Interesting," he said, avoiding answering my question. "What do you say? You ready to call it a day?"

"Heck, yes," I said. "Ty tells me a fire and food await."

I waited in the corridor while he locked the door, then

tugged on the handle to be certain the bolt had turned. He thanked me again as we headed toward the lobby.

"You're welcome," I replied, "but I wish I could help more."

"You will," he said as if he hadn't a doubt in the world.

"I hope so."

When we reached the lobby he said, "Wait here a sec," and approached the counter. He said something I couldn't hear to Darren. When he rejoined me, his gravitas arrested my attention. His demeanor had shifted from friendly to solemn. "One last thing."

"What?" I asked.

He opened the heavy front door before he answered. We stepped outside and stood under the overhang. It was rainy and raw, the kind of wet cold that gets in your bones and chills you from the inside out. I shivered and hugged myself, waiting for him to speak. He stared out over the parking lot toward the dunes, then turned to me, his eyes caring and concerned.

"When you tell people what happened, you shouldn't mention that you saw a silver car," he said.

My eyes remained fixed on his face. I nodded but didn't speak.

"You going to Ty's?" he asked.

"Yes."

"Good."

A patrol car crawled to a stop in front of the building. Officer Meade, a tall, thin Scandinavian-looking blonde I'd met last fall, was behind the wheel. She nodded at me. I turned to Ellis.

"I've asked Officer Meade to see you get home safely."

"No one knows I saw the car," I said.

"Still."

"You're scaring me," I said, trying for a light tone, wondering whether Wes had already learned that I had seen the getaway car from one of his omnipresent sources.

"Prudence is good. Prudence is smart."

"Okay, then," I said. "Thank you."

The rain slanted under my umbrella, so I ran for my car, and when I was safely inside, latching my seat belt, I started shivering uncontrollably. I looked through the rearview mirror. Quinn Steiner was just turning into the lot, driving a dark blue BMW. As he passed under a high-mounted light, I saw that his expression was sober. When the heat came on, I held my hands to the vent, but it didn't help. I was chilled more from Ellis's words than the weather.

While I'd been talking with Detective Brownley and Chief Hunter, Wes had called three times.

"We gotta talk," he said in his last message. "Call me as soon as you're done at the police station."

Tomorrow, I thought. Before I talked to him, I needed to process all that had happened. By morning, I hoped, I'd regain my usual composure, but right now I felt all trembly inside, and confused and fretful.

"I'll call you tomorrow," I said aloud, but then an idea took root, and within seconds, I changed my mind. *It's all in the emphasis,* I thought. I didn't want to lie, and I didn't think I'd have to. I slipped in my earpiece and called him.

"So, did you get a look at the intruder?" he asked as soon as he heard my voice.

"No," I replied, aiming to sound a bit awkward and embarrassed, as if I didn't want to talk about it, as if I were still scared. "It was so frightening, Wes."

"Tell me what happened from the beginning," said Wes.

"I heard breaking glass and footsteps," I said, "and I pushed the panic button. Five minutes later, I'm being interviewed by the police."

"So you heard footsteps . . . where from?"

"On the steps to the second floor, I thought."

"What did it sound like? Heavy boots? Regular shoes?"

"I don't know, Wes. It sounded terrifying is how it sounded."

Wes sighed. "You're describing how you felt, Josie, not what you heard or saw."

"That's all I can do, because in my memory the footsteps sounded like a monster."

"What about the silver car?"

"What silver car?"

"I spoke to one of the Jordans' neighbors who said the police asked her whether she'd seen a silver car."

"That's even scarier. It sounds like they're checking whether whoever might have been inside was driving the same car as that one Gretchen saw."

"Yeah, that's my point. Why would they go around and ask the neighbors about a silver car if they didn't have a reason to?"

"An excess of caution?"

"Maybe. Fill me in about Gretchen. Is she okay?"

"Yes, thank God. Apparently, the bullet just grazed her shoulder."

"Good. Say hey for me, okay?"

"I will, thanks, Wes," I said, touched.

"Where were you standing when she was shot?"

"Too close. It was horrific, Wes. Petrifying."

"Are you saying you froze?"

I opened my mouth to answer, to recount what it had been like to hear the shots and see bewilderment on Gretchen's face, to tear her sweater so I could press my hand against her bloody flesh. Wes's question was designed to put me on the defensive. It was an effective technique, and I resented it.

"No, I didn't freeze, but I can't talk about that now, Wes. I'm sorry, but I'm too upset. I wasn't going to call you at all until tomorrow, but I wanted to save you from spinning your wheels on what may be a false alarm."

"That's great, Josie, and I appreciate it, but you've got to give me something about Gretchen. I'm on deadline."

"I already gave you something, Wes. You can quote me as saying it was horrific and petrifying. I'll call you tomorrow. 'Bye."

And that, ladies and gentlemen, I thought, as I tossed my phone into my tote bag, *is how you do that.*

I stayed on Ocean Avenue until I came to Main Street, then turned inland and drove through the still-busy town center.

I loved the little village with its well-tended central green and its neat brick-faced shops, businesses, and restaurants. I loved the forsythia and lilac bushes that surrounded the white-washed gazebo where bands played familiar tunes on summer evenings. Across from the central fountain was an old-fashioned ice cream parlor that always stocked my favorite flavor, black cherry. I loved Ellie's, too, a narrow slip of a restaurant tucked between the penny candy shop and an independent bookstore. Zoë and I often met for lunch there. Ellie made a chicken and asparagus crepe with a Mornay sauce that was delicate and rich, and better by far than anything I could make at home.

According to the dashboard clock, it was two minutes to eight. Not too late, I thought, to call Jack and ask about Gretchen. I slipped in my earpiece and got him on his cell phone.

"She's fine," he said. "They didn't even have to put in any stitches."

"What a relief. Is she in pain?"

"No. They gave her something. She says it's no worse than when we were in Hawaii and she tripped on the lava and scraped her knee."

"Was she able to give the police any information about who might have done it?"

"No," he said. He lowered his voice as if Gretchen were nearby and he didn't want her to hear him. "They've assigned a police guard. He's outside right now."

"That's good," I said, thinking it was also terrifying. "Give her my love, will you? Tell her I'll check in tomorrow."

"Will do." He lowered his voice again. "I was going to call you—thanks for recommending Blackmore's. Mr. Blackmore was great. I've picked out the ring."

"Way to go, Jack! I can't wait to see it on her finger." I grinned. "Have you decided when to ask her?"

"The ring's being sized now. It should be done in a few days. I think I'll ask her as soon as I get it."

We ended on a merry note. I couldn't stop smiling. Gretchen was going to be on top of the world. I couldn't wait to begin planning her bridal shower.

As I pulled into Ty's driveway, the question that I'd posed at the police station came back to me like an itch I couldn't reach to scratch. Questions flooded my brain: Why had the intruder tried so desperately to get into the trunk? What was there amid the scrapbooks and souvenirs that he or she was so frantic to get hold of? Had the intruder known that the alarm would be off, or had he or she expected to be able to get into the trunk and out of the house before the police arrived? To me, the most perplexing question of all was, why was the Claire McCardell coat the only garment in the trunk?

CHAPTER FIFTEEN

Ty opened the door and stepped onto the stoop before I rolled to a stop in the driveway. He stood under the porch light watching as I got out of the car.

"Hey, gorgeous," he called.

I smiled. "Boy, are you a sight for sore eyes."

"Come on in out of the cold." He watched me for a moment. "How's Gretchen? Any news?"

"Yeah, she's okay. I just spoke to Jack."

He nodded. "Good. I have news, too."

"You do?" I said. I turned and waved good-bye to Officer Meade as I climbed the steps.

"I made a few calls."

"That sounds mysterious," I said, trying to read his face. I stepped inside. "Yum—I can smell the apple wood."

An old crabapple tree had fallen during a nor'easter last spring, and Ty had spent a lot of last summer splitting logs.

"I'll meet you by the fire," he said as he disappeared into the kitchen.

I shed my coat and boots and slipped on the pink fuzzy slippers I kept under the hall table. In the great room, I sank into the sofa and closed my eyes for a moment, absorbing the fire's warmth and listening to the snaps and cracks as sap erupted. When I opened my eyes, I fell into a kind of stupor. Watching the fire spit pepper-red sparks against the screen was hypnotic. A sense of calmness gradually began to counter the fear and anger and anxiety that had overtaken me from the first moment I'd realized Gretchen had been shot.

Ty entered from the kitchen carrying a brass tray. Two martini glasses and a pitcher filled with frothy Cherry Blossoms sat next to a turkey sandwich.

As soon as he poured, before my first sip, I clinked his glass. "Here's to silver light in the dark of night," I said, quoting my dad's favorite toast.

"To silver light," he said, touching my glass. He turned to face me. "I called in a favor. I wanted to know whether the shooter was aiming at you."

I stared at him, unable to think of what to say.

"From the trajectory, the technicians have no doubt that all three bullets were intended for Gretchen, not you. The police are operating on the theory that the murderer is freaking out because Gretchen's memory seems to be coming back." He shook his head. "Seemingly there's something distinctive about that car."

"Maybe," I said. "Or possibly Gretchen's seen the car before and the killer knows it." Ty's deep brown eyes held steady on mine. "I was in the office when she talked about it—Becka and Kenna were there."

Ty took my hand and squeezed. "The police know that, right?"

"Right."

"Good. Then we don't need to worry about it."

"I don't think I can stop worrying about it."

"Probably not—but in the meantime, you should eat."

"You're so wonderful," I said, touching his cheek.

"If you think I'm wonderful because I made you a turkey sandwich, wait 'til you taste my fresh-made salad. Want some?"

The next day, Saturday, I didn't go into work. With the tag sale canceled, there was no point. I couldn't recall the last Saturday I'd taken off.

The rain had stopped overnight, and the sun was warmer than I'd come to expect. At ten, Ty and I were sitting on his deck sipping coffee and reading the paper when I decided to call Gretchen.

"She's still asleep," Jack said. "She's not in much pain, but she's really tired."

"Poor Gretchen. I'm not surprised, though. Getting shot is a real shock to the system. Tell her I called, will you?"

He said he would, and I hung up wishing I could have spoken to her. *Maybe tomorrow,* I thought.

I picked up the newspaper again. Wes's article was perfect. He reported that I hadn't seen the intruder, and he made no mention of a silver car at all. I felt the weight of fear lighten, just a little. I lowered the paper and stared into the woods. Near the middle of the clearing, a gray rabbit paused as if he could tell I was watching him, then hopped into the forest, disappearing behind a thicket of Boston fern.

"What do you want to do today?" Ty asked.

"Hang out, I guess. Read. Watch a movie. Cook."

"What am I having for dinner?"

I smiled. "Fritz's Glazed Lamb Chops."

"Gotta love Lily!"

In the weeks before my mother's death, she'd written out all her recipes in a leather journal that was my most cherished possession. She'd annotated the recipes with little pen-and-ink illustrations, side comments, and instructions. I recalled the comment in the margin of the page containing this recipe. "This dish came to me through my old friend Lily Rowan who somehow sweet-talked a private chef named Fritz Brenner into giving it to her. Cherish it, Josie!"

"Sounds great," Ty said, breaking into my reverie. "Let's add brunch to the list."

"Great idea!" I said. "I'll take you to Ellie's. You've never been. They make great crepes."

"Sold."

"Tomorrow, I'll grill you those steaks I got from Alexander's."

"A perfect weekend," I said.

Ty parked on the edge of downtown so we'd have an excuse to stroll through the village. As we walked, we admired the just-blossoming deep red azaleas; noticed that the town had already whitewashed the band shell, readying it for the season; and chatted for a while with a man named Noah, a regular customer always in the market for rare wooden planes.

Ty agreed that Ellie's crepes were the best ever, and after we were finished, as I was paying the check, I realized that we hadn't talked about Riley once. He'd filled me in on where he was with his training initiatives—he was on a team charged with designing new curriculum, a huge honor for a relative newcomer—and he was almost done with his annual region-wide checkup on compliance issues. His enthusiasm was exhilarating. He loved his job, and it showed.

Walking to his SUV, I wondered whether Gretchen was ready for another promotion. If she oversaw the tag sales, I could take more Saturdays off. *Food for thought*, I realized, as Ty reached for my hand and smiled down at me.

Just before five, I was driving along Route One on my way to the grocery store when Wes called. I pulled into a strip mall parking lot so I could concentrate.

"You didn't call me back," he said as soon as I picked up.

"I'm fine, Wes. How are you?"

"Good, good, but you need to call me, Josie."

"I was going to," I said. "I've been pretty upset."

"So who do you think shot Gretchen?"

"I have no idea."

"Do you know why she was shot?"

I stared out the window at the passing traffic. *Yes,* I thought, *and I'm scared for her.* "You can't quote this, Wes, even if you get independent confirmation."

"Tell me."

"It looks like Gretchen's starting to remember more about the silver car."

"Really?" he exclaimed. "That's killer news, Josie. Fill me in."

Killer, I thought. I repeated what I'd told the police about Becka and Kenna overhearing Gretchen's comment, then added, "It's a nonlead, though, Wes. Either of them could have told other people."

"Like Bobby."

"Yes," I acknowledged, "like Bobby."

"Or Quinn."

"Or anybody." I glanced at the dash clock. I wanted to get to the store so I could get home and start cooking. I loved to cook, and it always relaxed me. "You said you had news—what?"

"Not on the phone," he said, lowering his voice. "At our dune in fifteen minutes?"

"I'm on my way to Shaw's in Rocky Point. Can you meet me there?"

"Ten minutes, by the front door," he said and hung up.

CHAPTER SIXTEEN

T he bullets were intended for Gretchen," Wes said, thinking he was delivering a bombshell.

"So I heard."

"You did? Who from?"

"I have confidential sources, too."

He looked at me for a moment, then nodded. "Good to know. What else did your source tell you?"

I laughed. "You're incorrigible, Wes!"

"Thanks," he said, grinning. He pulled out his ratty note-paper. "So . . . do you still think Bobby killed Riley?"

My smile faded. I looked around. We stood by my car midway down a close-in row by the main entrance to Shaw's. The parking lot was nearly full. A harassed-looking young mother hurried by, wheeling twins in a tandem stroller. One of the babies was crying. An older couple, holding hands, walked past. A young man, college age, I guessed, jogged into the store.

"I don't know what to think, Wes." I turned to face him. "Have you learned anything more about his playing around?"

He shook his head. "No one else has come forward," he said, his eyes big with news.

"I can see from your eyes that there's more."

"Only a stick of dynamite! Riley found out something huge, I don't know what, the day before she was murdered—*that's* why she changed her will."

"How can you possibly know that?" I asked.

"She called to make the appointment with Max Bixby, her

lawyer, at three o'clock on Monday, the day before she was killed, saying it was urgent. She tried to get in to see him that same day, but he was unavailable."

The implications about the timing were startling, I thought, as I realized that Wes must have gotten Max's receptionist to spill the beans.

"What does Bobby say?"

"According to my police source, he says he hasn't got a clue. Maybe he's telling the truth. It's possible that she didn't confront him until *after* she changed her will, or at all."

"I can see that happening. What about Bobby's alibi? Does he have one?"

"Nope—but for him to be the killer we have to make two assumptions. One, that he knew that Riley was scheduled to speak at Prescott's workshop, and two, that she would be arriving early."

"The first one is, to my mind, a given. I mean, she probably told him about the speaking date when we first booked it. She was so pleased." I sighed, missing her. "Plus, I bet she talked about it over their morning coffee—I would. How can we assume that he knew she'd be arriving early, though?"

"Right after leaving her lawyer's office, Riley made two calls, the first one to a disposable cell phone, the second one to a cell phone on her own plan. The first call lasted ten minutes, from one thirty to one forty; the other one lasted three minutes, from one forty-one to one forty-four. I've dialed both numbers, but no one answers, and the voice mail messages are those generic ones, just a robotic voice listing the number, you know? It gets a little confusing with everyone using cell phones, so let's call the phone Riley called first, the disposable phone, C1, okay? The second call she made went to a phone we can call C2; that's the one on her own plan. Because she called C1 and C2 just before she died, the police were able to get a court order allowing them to review the call logs, and man, oh man, are they glad they did! First, up until that day, the only outgoing calls from C1 were to Ruby, Becka, Riley, and Tamara. Most of the incoming calls were from them, too. So that's got to be Bobby's phone, right? I mean, who else has all those people in common? Some incoming calls were from pay phones and other disposable, untraceable cell phones, but none was from anyone else Bobby was in frequent contact with, like Quinn. About twenty minutes after Riley finished her ten-minute call *to* C1, a call *from* C1 was made to Riley's phone. The call only lasted ten seconds, so I figure the call went directly to voice mail and the caller didn't leave a message. What the caller *did* do is immediately call Prescott's. Your company. That call lasted thirty seconds."

"Someone using the cell phone you're calling C1 called *us*?" I asked, astonished.

"Yup," Wes said, tickled at my reaction. "And the second number Riley called? The one we're calling C2? Guess what? The only calls, and I mean the *only* calls in *or* out, were to or from Riley. So she must have given C2 to someone, right? Only for their private relationship."

"It looks that way, doesn't it?" I said, intrigued. I thought for a moment, then asked, "Why haven't the police asked me about the incoming call from C1?"

"They will. They just got the info a couple of hours ago." He dropped his voice. "Do you think Riley was having an affair, too? Maybe she gave C2 to her lover so she could always reach him."

"No way," I said, appalled at the thought. "Riley never would do that!"

"Of course not," Wes said sarcastically. "Women never screw around."

"I'm not saying that," I protested, but Wes was right. I didn't want the suggestion to be true, so I dismissed it out of hand. I looked at him. "I take it back. You're right. Of course she could have been having an affair."

"So if she had a lover, who is it?"

"I have no idea. Don't misunderstand me, Wes. I don't think there's a chance that she was cheating. I'm simply acknowledging your point—she could have been. Have the police asked Bobby yet?"

"Yes. He says he has no idea why Riley has a second line—referring to C2—and he says that he doesn't know who C1 belongs to."

"Oh, please! Who else but him would make calls to Ruby, Becka, Riley, and Tamara? That would be a heck of a coincidence."

"The police think so, too," Wes said. "So if Riley's call to C1 is really a call to Bobby, then we can assume she told him that she was heading back to Prescott's."

I nodded. "So he'd know she'd be there early. It's not a stretch to imagine her telling him that she just finished meeting with her lawyer, that she was upset and wanted some time to think things through. She would expect that we'd let her in early to relax in private, which is, in fact, exactly what happened."

"Why do you think Bobby called your company?"

"Maybe Riley hung up on him and he tried to call her back. She saw who was calling her from the phone ID and didn't take the call. He called us hoping to speak to her. So what's Bobby's alibi?"

"He says he was in his office, alone."

"There's an emergency exit right there. I mean, he could have left with no one the wiser." I shifted position. "What about yesterday? The day Gretchen was shot?"

Wes grinned. "Bobby says he was driving home—alone."

"That takes care of opportunity," I said. "In terms of means . . . since Riley was killed with her own scarf, I figure that either the murder was not premeditated or that the killer came with a different weapon and used the scarf because it was a better—that is, a less traceable—option."

"That's what I think, too," Wes said, nodding, "and given

that Bobby's a champion biathlon athlete—well, hello!—of course he has access to a gun and knows how to use it."

I paused and looked at Wes. "Except if he had been the shooter, Gretchen would be dead."

"True."

"Unless he's trying some kind of Machiavellian maneuver—since everyone knows he's a crackerjack shot, by missing now he creates reasonable doubt, then when Gretchen is actually killed, no one will think of him as a suspect."

Wes soft-whistled. "Jeez, Josie, that's pretty dark. Do you think that's possible?"

Some people, I thought, *when they have enough to lose, will lie like a grifter, steal like Fagin, and kill like a professional assassin.* I looked up. Wes was waiting for my reply. His expression reflected his youth. With his round eyes and open stance, he seemed, to my eye, absurdly, charmingly, ingenuous. I was about to reply when the reality of what we were discussing hit me like a slap. It was possible, really truly possible, that Bobby had killed his wife.

"Oh, Wes," I said, blinking away an unexpected tear. "It's just so awful to think about!"

"Yeah, but what *do* you think? Is he that diabolical?"

I took in a deep breath. "Yes, I do think it's possible." I paused. "And I know he drives a silver Lexus."

"Right—but while he's the front-runner, don't forget that there are other candidates. Quinn and Kenna might have some kind of financial motive. As for Becka, well, remember the photo of her holding hands with Bobby—and she's one of the people called from C1."

I sighed. "You're right. What does Becka say about that? Won't she say who called her from that number? How about Ruby or Tamara? What do they say?"

"Becka says that she has no memory of receiving any calls from that number. Ruby is refusing to answer questions, insisting that since she was in L.A. taping some insider gossip show, in full view of dozens of people when Riley was killed, she can't possibly be a suspect, and since she has no knowledge of any crime committed by anyone, she's not going to discuss her private life. Tamara's not so reticent. She says it's the number Bobby always used to call her."

I shook my head, horrified. "If it quacks like a duck..." I said.

"Exactly. C1 is Bobby's phone."

"Bobby's lying," I said, disheartened.

"Yeah, but maybe he's only trying to hide that he was screwing around."

"I suppose," I acknowledged. "Does anyone know why Riley had that second phone, the one you're calling C2?"

"Nope."

"How about alibis?" I asked. "Do any of them have one? And could they have known Riley got there early? I mean, are they really suspects?"

Wes nodded. "Let's start with opportunity. Becka and Kenna were students in your class, so we can assume they knew that Riley was scheduled as that night's guest speaker. Maybe one of them arrived early, too, and found Riley there. Becka and Riley were pals, right? So maybe Riley told her about Bobby and that she was going to hang out at your place."

"Did Riley call Becka?"

"Not from her cell phone," Wes said.

"Kenna's office is right across from Bobby's, so if he said something, maybe during that call with Riley—you know, the call she made from her phone to C1—Kenna might have overheard him refer to Riley's plans."

Wes nodded. "Good one, Josie! Then Kenna might have mentioned it to Quinn—from what I hear, although she works for Bobby, she reports to him."

"That's right, she told me so."

"Okay, then...so...at the time Riley was killed, Becka

says she was driving to Prescott's for class, Kenna says she was at her mother's dropping off her kids, and Quinn, like I told you before, says he went to his club to have a drink with a client. His assistant confirms the appointment but says the client, Butch Mavers, had to cancel. Apparently, something came up at the last minute. Mavers left Quinn a voice mail, which he says he didn't get until the next day. He says he hung out at the club for a while, looking at a set of golf clubs the pro shop had on sale, and periodically cruised into the bar and side lounges looking for Mavers, but no one remembers seeing him. The bartender was busy taking care of customers, the golf pro was out giving a lesson, and the in-store clerk was ringing up sales.

"As to when Gretchen was shot, Becka says she was in her office at Hitchens, alone; Kenna says she was at home with her kids nearby, cooking mac and cheese; and Quinn says he was at various shops in the mall choosing a birthday gift for his wife. No one saw Becka, Kenna's kids are too young to be reliable witnesses, and while Quinn did buy a gold bracelet at a department store about a half hour after Gretchen was hit, the timing is iffy. Going by the time stamp on his receipt, he could have shot Gretchen, then hotfooted it to the mall. No one at any other shop remembers seeing him, but unless he did something to stand out, why would they?"

"Alibis are tough," I remarked. "It's hard to prove you're somewhere. What about Tamara?"

"She's out of it. She was working, waitressing, during both events."

"So both Tamara and Ruby are clear, but no one else is."

"Exactly. As to means—according to my police source, Becka says she doesn't know how to shoot, and it looks like that's true. She's got a thing about guns—she hates them—and lots of people know that about her."

"Which only proves that no one would suspect her of shooting someone, not that she didn't do it," I interjected.

"True," Wes acknowledged. "Kenna's brothers all hunt, so, presumably, she knows how to shoot, and it's a safe assumption that she has access to their weapons. Quinn, as we know, is a member of the Rocky Point Gun and Rod Club."

"What about silver cars?" I asked.

"Quinn's wife drives a silver BMW. Kenna's mother drives a silver Taurus. Becka drives a green MG, but her roommate drives a silver Camry. I've looked it up—the most popular car color is silver."

I scanned the parking lot. "I see what you mean. Half the cars here are silver." I thought of my staff—half of them drove silver cars, too. Fred had just bought a new-to-him used silver Audi. Sasha's Prius was gold. Ava drove an old silver Chevy. Eric's 4 × 4 was brown. Cara drove a silver Sonata. I thought of the part-timers' cars, and as near as I could recall, many of them were silver, too.

"Yeah. So considering everything," he said, lowering his tone to a near-whisper, "do you still think Bobby killed her?"

I dropped my gaze to the cracked asphalt. Not wanting to believe something isn't the same thing as not believing it. A horn blared, and I looked up in time to see a middle-aged man behind the wheel shake his fist at a woman who seemed oblivious to the fact that she'd stolen the parking place he'd considered his own.

I thought about Wes's question. Becka, Kenna, and Quinn qualified as killers on paper, as it were, but the question wasn't whether we could build a theoretical case against them. The question was: Did I think it likely that one of them had drawn the scarf around Riley's neck and twisted it, holding the ends taut until she was dead? Did I really think one of them had aimed a gun at Gretchen and pulled the trigger? Or did I think the culprit was the man Riley had cut out of her will the very day she was killed?

I stood, resting my elbows on my car's hood, staring out over the sea of automobiles, thinking. I decided there was no reason to hedge. From where I sat, Bobby looked guilty as all get-out. I turned toward Wes.

"Yes," I said.

"Me, too." He folded up his notepaper, preparing to leave. "Do you have anything for me?"

I weighed asking Wes if he could find out who knew that Bobby never set his house alarm unless he was going out of town. I just couldn't imagine someone giving themselves only a few minutes to break in, get to the attic, force open the trunk, and get out. Whoever did it had to have known that the house was unalarmed.

It came down to trust and confidence. Could I trust Wes to keep a secret? Yes. Did I have confidence that he could ferret out information without revealing his reasons for asking? Yes.

I met his eyes. He was waiting for me to speak. "Who knew that Bobby never set his security alarm unless he was going out of town?"

He narrowed his eyes. "How do you he doesn't?"

"He told me so, through Quinn, when he hired me to appraise everything." I met his gaze. "How can we find out who else knew?"

"Did you see a silver car while you were there?"

"If I say yes and you publish it," I said with a nervous, awkward laugh, "my life might be in as much danger as Gretchen's."

"I won't publish it. Did you?" he asked again.

Trust, I thought. *I trust him.* "Yes," I said.

"Enough to recognize?"

"No. It was a sedan, but that's all I know."

Wes nodded and put away his paper without making any notes. "I'll check who knew about the alarm."

"Thanks."

"You really can trust me, you know?" he said, sounding a little hurt.

"I know—but I needed to think it through."

He nodded. "I'll call as soon as I know something," he said

and jogged toward his car. Wes was always in a hurry. I walked into the store thinking that if Wes could learn who knew about the alarm, we might discover more than an intruder—there was a chance we'd nail a killer.

CHAPTER SEVENTEEN

I was able to speak to Gretchen on Sunday, and it was a huge relief to hear her voice. After thanking me for the call, she told me she didn't want visitors; all she wanted to do was stay in bed.

"I can't explain it—I'm just so sleepy!" she said.

"Nature's great healer, right?"

"I guess . . . Have you heard anything? I mean, do you think the police are making any progress?"

"I don't know, Gretchen. I wish I had news I could share with you."

She sighed. "Yeah. To tell you the truth, I'm a little scared."

"You'd be crazy if you weren't."

"I have police protection, did you know that?" she said, lowering her voice as if she were revealing a secret.

"Jack mentioned it yesterday. I'm so glad they're there."

"Yeah . . . Jack wants me to stay home tomorrow, but I'm planning on coming in."

"Why? That doesn't make any sense, Gretchen! You should stay in bed."

"I hate missing work. I always feel so out of it when I get back."

"Which is admirable, but not when you need rest. Don't come in tomorrow. That's an order."

She giggled. "An order! You're some tough boss."

"You bet your booties I am! I mean it, Gretchen."

"I'll tell you what I told Jack: The doctor said I should play it by ear, that if I was feeling up to going to work on Monday, I could, and if I wasn't, I shouldn't. He said I wouldn't do myself any harm, providing that I didn't lift anything, so my plan is to listen to my body. That's fair, isn't it?"

"You're always so practical and sensible, Gretchen. Jeez—I can't imagine being able to think so logically if I were in your shoes. I think I'd burrow under the covers and refuse to come out."

"No you wouldn't. You'd be at work on time and with a smile on your face."

I was taken aback that she perceived me that way. "Wow, what a nice image. I don't know that it's true, but I sure like the sound of it." I paused for a moment. "I defer to your judgment and withdraw my order. Plus, I know that if you come in, Cara will dote on you. She won't let you lift a thing."

"Except Raspberry Lace Lemon Squares," Gretchen said. "She already called to tell me she's making them, and I definitely plan on lifting several!"

I smiled, oddly heartened by Cara's homey tribute to Gretchen. Cara's Raspberry Lace Lemon Squares involved weaving a home-made raspberry syrup through lemon batter to create an intricate lace pattern. It was a complicated recipe and difficult to make, and she only made a batch on special occasions.

One of the hardest aspects of moving to New Hampshire had been not knowing a soul. I'd arrived a stranger, and it had been an isolating and frightening experience. Now I was part of a community of like-minded people, people I valued and re-spected and admired. It was an enormous comfort to know that when push came to shove, if one of us tumbled off a cliff, we all knew we'd survive the fall because someone who cared for us would be there with a net and someone else would come running up with our favorite treats. After enduring several lonely years, I'd discovered that small kindnesses from friends con-tributed just as much to my overall contentment as big leg-ups, and sometimes more.

"Raspberry Lace Lemon Squares!" I said. "That explains why you want to come into work on Monday—you're afraid we'll snarf them all up before you get back if you don't lay your claim!"

"Busted!" she said, laughing. "And all this time you thought I liked my job! Now you know the truth—I'm a cookie ho!"

"Everyone's a cookie ho when it comes to Cara's baking. Seriously, though, Gretchen, I promise I won't let anyone abscond with your share, so you should feel free to stay home if you need to."

She thanked me, and we chatted until she announced she was ready to drift off again.

After we hung up, I sat for a while longer on Ty's oversized sofa with my feet tucked under me. Through the window, I watched the just unfurling, sun-dappled leaves sway in the gentle spring breeze. Gretchen, I thought, was one of the finest women I knew.

I had to force myself to go to work on Monday morning. Ty left just after six for an all-day strategy session in Manchester, and under normal conditions I would have been at work by seven thirty. Today, though, between the cloudless blue sky and the dazzling sun that had temperatures already approaching seventy, a veritable heat wave for New Hampshire in April, I was fighting a serious case of spring fever. The weatherman said we'd reach a high of seventy-five by the end of the day, and all I wanted to do was put on shorts and a tank top and plant pansies, my favorite spring flowers. Instead, I celebrated spring by finding a pair of lightweight khakis I hadn't worn for eight months, paired them with a short-sleeved blouse, and went for a walk.

I started out along the road, then turned onto an old horse path that wended its way through an ancient forest and marked the edge of the property. A canopy of lawn-green maple leaves kept the path in stippled shadow. Dark purple violets sprouted amid dense patches of moss. Twigs snapped and crackled as I walked. Within a hundred yards or so, I came to the meadow that stretched for acres and abutted a stand of poplar. A stone wall separated it from the path. Every spring as I walked past, I thought of Robert Frost's poem about the ritual of examining his stone walls to see how they survived the ravages of winter, silently agreeing that good fences make good neighbors, that being a good friend meant balancing involvement with respectful distance.

A lot of the time, people have to make their own mistakes. Sometimes emotion overtakes reason and people act stupidly or thoughtlessly. Sometimes people kill for reasons large and small. They kill for revenge. Or avarice. Or envy. Or fear. Why had someone killed Riley?

Despite brutal cold and record-breaking snowfall, I spotted only a few fallen stones, and every one was easy to wedge back into place. I walked the entire length of the wall before turning back.

I felt good, and didn't feel the least bit guilty that I didn't get into work until ten of nine.

Within minutes, Sasha and Ava arrived, both asking if I had an update about Gretchen. Before I even began replying, Fred called to ask the same thing. I put him on speaker so we could all talk at the same time.

"Gretchen hasn't called, so I guess that means she's planning on coming into work. I can't believe it, but there you go."

"Are you sure she should come in?" Sasha asked, concerned.

"No," I said, "but her doctor gave permission."

"Wow," Ava said. "That's amazing."

"Say hey for me," Fred said. "I should be in by ten."

"You got it," I told him, hanging up.

Eric poked his head into the office. "Any news about Gretchen?" he asked.

I repeated what I'd told Fred, and he nodded, his expression glum.

"I think she's doing fine, Eric," I said to reassure him.

He nodded. "Still . . ."

"Yeah," I agreed.

"I changed Hank's water and everything," he said.

I smiled. "That's great, Eric. Thank you."

I had just opened the front office window to let the warm air in when Cara backed into the office, setting the chimes jingling. She was carrying a huge platter of Raspberry Lace Lemon Squares.

"Hi, Josie," she said. "Any news about Gretchen since yesterday?"

I helped her place the platter on the guest table. "No," I said. "Not yet."

The words were barely out of my mouth when Gretchen arrived. She sat in the back of a patrol car with Officer Griffin, whom I'd known for years, at the wheel.

Griff stepped out and looked around, then hustled her into the building.

"You know what to do if you want to leave, right?" he asked her.

"Yes," she said. "Call you." She smiled at him. "Thank you, Griff."

He nodded, touched his cap, and left. He moved his car so he wasn't blocking the entrance but stayed close in.

"Hi!" Gretchen said, including us all, smiling.

She looked as gorgeous as ever with her creamy ivory skin gleaming, her titian hair cascading in graceful waves halfway down her back, and her green eyes radiating joy.

"Thank you all for calling over the weekend. I'm fine, really. I'm not in any pain or anything."

"Gretchen promises to follow doctor's orders," I announced to the group. "Which means not lifting anything and leaving as soon as she feels tired. Right, Gretchen?"

"Absolutely. He told me to listen to my body." She grinned. "Right now, my body is calling for Raspberry Lace Lemon Squares. Let me at 'em!"

I wanted to ask Cara about the call that Wes told me about—the one from the phone he'd labeled C1—but I didn't want to have to field a flurry of questions and comments from everyone else, so I asked her to come upstairs. From the concern apparent in her eyes and the speed with which her smile disappeared, I could tell that she thought she'd done something wrong and was about to be chastised.

"You're doing a great job," I said as we walked across the warehouse. "I just need to talk to you privately for a minute."

"Certainly," she said, her anxiety unmitigated.

"What I'm about to tell you isn't confidential," I explained once we were seated. "In fact, I think it may even be in today's paper. Even so, I didn't want to open up a conversation with everyone and make a big deal out of something that might mean nothing at all. I just have a simple question." I smiled. "At least I hope it's simple. Evidently, Riley made a call just before she died. She called a disposable cell phone, the kind that can't be traced. Within minutes, someone used *that* cell phone to call us on our main number. That's my question to you. On the day Riley died, just before she came inside—that would be around two—who called us? I know it's crazy to think you'd remember a thirty-second call from a week ago, but I thought there might be something about it that stands out."

She nodded. "Yes, I do remember, actually. Someone called and asked if Riley was here. I replied that she wasn't, but that she would be later. I asked if he'd like to leave a message, and he said no."

I crossed my fingers for luck and asked, "Who was it?"

"Oh, dear, I have no idea. I didn't recognize the voice, and we didn't chat. I only recall it because the caller asked for Riley."

I nodded. "I understand. Are you sure it was a man?"

She looked stricken and stared into the distance for several seconds, then shook her head. "I'm so sorry, but I just don't know . . . I think it was a man . . . but I'm not at all certain. The call was so brief, and we were so busy."

I nodded again and stood up, smiling. "Thank you, Cara. The police will probably ask you the same question. It goes without saying, of course, that you should tell them everything you can remember."

"Certainly." She paused at the door. "Gretchen looks well, doesn't she?"

"She sure does—and just wait and see how she looks after she's had her fill of your Raspberry Lace Lemon Squares!"

Her already rosy cheeks grew pink. "Thank you, Josie."

I walked down with her to retrieve the platinum and pearl button we'd logged into lost and found and to talk to Ava.

While Cara prepared the sign-out form for me to sign, I sat at the guest table.

"I'm going to take a crack at tracing the button," I told Ava. "I don't want to duplicate efforts, so as a first step, what did you do?"

Ava's ice-blond hair fell to the side when she leaned over to open a file drawer in her desk. She flipped through some folders, found what she was looking for, and wiggled a single sheet of paper loose.

"Here are my notes," she said, glancing at the paper. "The first thing I did was Google various combinations of 'pearl button' along with the saying on the back, 'Industria et Munus'— adding in 'platinum,' for instance, or just 'button' and the saying. Then I tried Googling the saying by itself. I thought there was a good chance it would lead to a club or an organization, but it didn't. I went to the National Button Society and several regional associations' Web sites—I had no idea there were so many button collectors, nor how many of them collect pearl buttons!—and everyone I spoke to was very kind, but no one was able to help me. There was nothing else to look at, really."

I took the paper when she handed it over and scanned her notes. "Did you look at those letters on the back, *EZK*?"

"No, I assumed they were a person's initials, so I figured it would be hopeless to pursue them."

"Nothing ventured!" I said, thinking that next time I assigned Ava a research task, I'd need to be more explicit about what she should look at. While she'd made a good start, I knew there were lots more avenues of research available. As I climbed the stairs to my office, I made a mental note to tell Sasha and Fred the same thing. When someone was as smart and willing as Ava, it was easy to forget that she was a newbie, and it was our responsibility to mentor her.

I laid the button on my desk. The pearls almost glowed, their sheen was so lustrous. I turned the button over and felt the satiny cool metal, then used my loupe to confirm there were no marks I'd missed. Probably Ava was right about the letters—in all likelihood, they were someone's initials. Still, it was possible they stood for something else, like a company or organization. I Googled *EZK,* and just like that, I learned that there was a sorority named Epsilon Zeta Kappa.

I clicked through to the sorority's Web site, and on the history page, I read that every member used to receive a set of four buttons when she successfully pledged the sorority. I leaned back in my big leather chair, staring at the sentence for several seconds before I read on. The tradition ended in 1941 when the company that made the buttons went out of business. The sorority had posted photos of both the front and the back of the buttons. They'd been placed on a deeply shadowed white satin backdrop. The background and dramatic lighting had no doubt been selected to accentuate the details in the pearl mounts and engravings. It worked—there was no question that the button sitting on my desk was a perfect match. I located the EZK headquarters' phone number on the contact page and dialed. From the area code, I could tell I was calling Florida.

"Zeta Kap, how may I help you?" a friendly voice asked.

Zeta Kap, I repeated silently. A lesson I'd learned in a college communications course came to me. Abbreviations, like acronyms, are one of the ways we distinguish friend from foe—if you recognize my shorthand, you're in my ken.

"I'm not sure who to talk to. I have a question about some buttons you used to award new members," I said.

"Our pearl rosette buttons. Let me connect you to Margo in Member Services."

"Hi, Margo," I said when she came on the line. "I'm an antiques appraiser on a hunt for information about your pearl rosette buttons. I'm hoping you'll answer a few questions."

"Glad to. What would you like to know?"

"Thanks so much! I understand the buttons are no longer made—but what if I needed a replacement?"

"You call and ask me, and I give you Mr. Lossoff's name and number. Nick Lossoff is a button expert. He's been making replacements for members for years."

"Perfect! Do you have his number handy?"

"You bet. Are you ready?"

"Yes," I said. I wrote down Mr. Lossoff's number as Margo called it out. The area code was 212, I noted. New York City. "Are the buttons somehow coded or registered? Like, is there a number that I haven't located that tells you which buttons were given out to which individuals?"

"No. They're all identical."

"Interesting. I bet you get lots of requests for replacements."

"Not as many as we used to. My guess is that the button isn't in style nowadays, so people aren't wearing them as much, and if they're not wearing them, they're not losing them."

"That's logical—and fashion is all about trends, right? I bet they'll come back in style before too long." I paused for a moment, trying to figure out how to ask what I really wanted to know without causing alarm bells to go off in Margo's head.

Don't explain, don't apologize, I thought, silently quoting my dad. He'd spent most of his career in sales, and he said the best way to get people talking was simply to ask questions in a tone that conveyed confidence and competence. "Be polite and be direct," he'd said, "and most people will answer without thinking about why you want the information or whether you have any right to it."

"Did someone call and ask about getting a replacement last week?" I asked, crossing my fingers for luck.

"How did you know?" she asked, sounding impressed, not leery.

"Someone asked me about getting a replacement, and I wondered if she'd gotten in touch with you directly."

"Was it Riley Jordan? She called last Thursday."

I sat forward, my attention riveted. Someone calling herself Riley Jordan called EZK two days *after* Riley had been killed. The button *must* belong to the killer. *The killer must be a woman.* Which meant Bobby *didn't* murder his wife.

"That's her," I said.

"The poor thing. She said she was desperate. Her mom considered the buttons family heirlooms and she'd lost one."

"Thank goodness for Mr. Lossoff!"

"You've got that right!"

I couldn't think of anything else to ask, so I thanked her, and she gave a cheery "Anytime!" and hung up.

I picked up the button and stared at it. It was more than just a magnificent button; it was a tribute from a bygone era and a testimony to a young woman's accomplishment. *With this button,* I thought, *they said you're one of us.*

I turned it over and over, watching the light hit the pearls. *What's the big deal?* I asked myself. If I'd lost it while killing someone, I'd simply deny ever having owed it—destroying the garment it came from, if necessary. Unless people knew I had

the button in my possession and expected me to wear it periodically. Or if I'd borrowed the garment, and it had to be returned. I might think saying I'd lost it would be too risky,
especially once it became known that it had been found near
the scene of a murder. I nodded. It would be more prudent to
simply get a replacement.

I reached for the phone to call Mr. Lossoff, but before I
could do so, Cara buzzed up that Wes was on line one.

"I got some firecracker-hot news about Bobby," Wes said,
jumping in. "The police found a slush fund, an account in a
Swiss bank. Can you believe it? It looks like when Quinn accused Kenna of 'sloppy bookkeeping,' he was being kind. The
forensic accountant the police hired suspects that it's an inten-
tional effort on Bobby's part to hide assets from an investor—
his wife—and he couldn't have done it without Kenna's help."

"Oh, my God, Wes! That's awful."

"Yeah," he said, sounding as if he were salivating at the
thought. "There's more than half a million dollars in the account. That would buy a lot of nachos, baby!"

Nachos? I thought, rolling my eyes. "What does Bobby say?"

"That it's a working capital account, that those monies are
earmarked to fund new ventures. He also says that Riley knew
about it."

"That sounds logical, Wes."

"Maybe—but catch this hot potato! There's only one co-
signer on the account. Want to guess who?"

"Who?" I asked, knowing the answer.

"Kenna."

"That doesn't prove anything. She's his bookkeeper."

"No, but it's plenty suggestive."

"Do you think so? I'm not so sure. What does Kenna say?"

"That she was an employee who did as she was told, that
there's nothing illegal about moving money overseas, and that
if there's something knurly about the account, the cops ought
to talk to Bobby and Quinn, not her."

"Fair points."

"Maybe. What did you learn from Cara about the call from C1?"

"Nothing. She remembers that someone did call and ask for Riley, but she doesn't even know for certain if it was a man or a woman."

"Too bad."

"Yeah. Did you learn who knew that Bobby rarely set his security alarm?"

"You betcha! Becka says Riley talked about the alarm situation years ago, saying she wished Bobby would set it more regularly, but that she'd decided it wasn't a battle worth fighting. That's pretty dumb, isn't it? I mean, what's the point of having a security system if you don't use it? Jeesh! Anyway, neither Kenna nor Quinn admits to knowing anything about it. Bobby says he didn't tell anyone, and he hadn't been aware that Becka knew. I'm still asking around, checking if someone heard someone else mention it, but nothing so far. What else is going on? Anything?"

My eyes took in the button sitting in a circle of golden sunlight. Wes would love to know what I'd discovered. If I told him about the button, he'd pepper me with questions I couldn't answer, demand photos I didn't want to provide, and insist that there was no reason not to publish everything immediately. Until I had more information, there was no point in revealing anything.

"No," I said.

"Okay. Catch ya later!"

I dialed Nick Lossof, the New York City–based button fabricator. A middle-aged man answered the phone with a crisp "Lossoff."

"Hi, Mr. Lossoff," I said. "I'm Josie Prescott, an antiques appraiser from New Hampshire. I'm hoping you can answer a few questions about an EZK sorority button."

"You've got the wrong man, I'm afraid. I'm Tony Lossoff. It was my dad who was the button expert. He died about six weeks ago."

"I'm sorry to hear that," I said. "I hate to trouble you—but by any chance, did someone call you last week about getting a replacement button?"

"Why do you want to know?" he asked, sounding wary.

"The sorority mentioned her call," I said, inventing an excuse for my call on the fly. "It occurred to me, if she's already found a new source, maybe I can save myself some legwork."

"Yeah. Thursday, I think it was. Nancy Patterson, her name was."

Nancy Patterson? I repeated to myself, wondering why she decided not to use Riley's name.

"Were you able to give her a name?" I asked.

"No, but I did give her some suggestions. I said her best shot was to contact one of the fashion design associations and ask them to recommend a button designer, someone with tools and know-how, like my dad."

"Did you mention any association by name?"

"No—oh, and Parsons and FIT. I told her someone at one of those places would for sure be able to help."

Parsons, like FIT, was one of the world's leading colleges devoted to, among other things, fashion design. Both the schools and industry associations were good suggestions, I thought, but I was willing to bet that Nancy didn't call either of them. No way would she risk calling attention to herself by trolling for button designers—her search would be more focused.

"Those are terrific ideas," I said. "I'd love to give her a call and see what she's figured out. You don't happen to have her number, do you?"

"Sorry, no. I didn't ask. I guess I should call the sorority and let them know about Dad."

"A sad task," I said. I thanked him again and hung up.

I knew there was another kind of designer who could handle

the work, a designer who wouldn't think fabricating a jewel-encrusted button was the least bit remarkable—a good thing if I wanted to stay below the radar. A jewelry designer.

I Googled "Nancy Patterson" and wasn't surprised to discover that that there were thousands of women with that name. As far as I could tell, none of them lived in Rocky Point.

I brought up the EZK Web site again and clicked on the members page. Sure enough, Riley Jordan was listed as a member. So was Babs Miller. Nancy Patterson was not. *Why would she have made up a name?* I asked myself.

Maybe she'd been afraid that the sorority would only answer questions from members, and hoped that since the sorority was based in Florida, they'd be unaware of a New Hampshire murder, or, if nothing else, that they wouldn't make the connection until after she was off the phone. It seemed to me to be a risky move. With Bobby's notoriety as a celebrity chef and with the media hype surrounding his relationship with Ruby Bowers, word of Riley's murder had surely spread beyond New Hampshire's borders. Yet it seemed to have worked out as she'd hoped. When I'd spoken to Margo, there'd been no sign that she'd recognized Riley's name as having any significance beyond that of a recent caller who'd asked about a button. Once that conversation was out of the way, the caller probably deemed it prudent to switch to an invented persona, and Nancy Patterson was born.

I turned toward my window. The sky was cloudless and blue. The sun was strong, and the breeze was soft. It was a halcyon spring day. As I looked deep into the forest, seeing lilies of the valley not yet in bud and bushes laden with the pale green leaves of new growth, I considered how I'd go about finding a jewelry designer capable of replicating my button. After several minutes, I turned back to my computer.

I Googled "custom jewelry" and "Rocky Point, NH." The

first listing was Cartier's in New York. The second was Korley's, a branch of a national chain of jewelry stores, located in Fox Run Mall. The third was Zello's, another national chain. It was also located in Fox Run Mall. The fourth was Blackmore's.

I called Chief Hunter, and when Cathy told me he was unavailable, I asked for his voice mail.

"There's something I want to run by you," I said, choosing my words carefully. "I have an idea about how to catch Riley's killer."

CHAPTER EIGHTEEN

Y ou sure know how to get a cop's attention," Ellis
said.

"Well, I guess that's a good thing since I wanted a
quick callback," I replied. "I have an idea, but it's kind of complicated and has a few assumptions built in. Is there any chance
we can get together?"

"Great minds, right? I was about to call and ask if I could
stop by. There's something I want to show you. How's ten
minutes?"

"Perfect." I hung up the phone.

I wondered what he wanted to ask me about. He'd alluded to
the old saw that great minds think alike. True. Of course, it
was equally true that fools rarely differ.

I picked up the button sitting on my desk and tossed it
lightly in my hand. "If only you could talk," I said aloud, "the
tales you'd tell."

"So what's this idea of yours?" Ellis asked, sitting on the yellow
brocade love seat nibbling a Raspberry Lace Lemon Square. He
carried a blue nylon tote bag bearing the Rocky Point police
insignia.

"Normally people can't do anything but ooh and ahh while
eating Cara's cookies," I said, "and here you are acting, I don't
know . . . normal. What are you, superhuman?"

He wiped his fingers on a napkin. "Most people are weak. I, however, am a man of steely discipline and focus."

"I can see that."

"So?"

"What did you want to show me?" I retorted, smiling.

He reached into the bag and pulled out a see-through, jumbo-sized plastic bag containing a gray and lavender coat. I looked at it, then looked at him.

"Is that the Claire McCardell coat from the trunk?" I asked.

"Yes. You know how you wanted to see the label and I was extra careful in opening it up so as not to contaminate any evidence?"

I nodded.

He reached in the bag and pulled out the coat. He stood and held the coat against his chest. The flannel hung beautifully. The lavender piping was smooth and true. The coat featured a classic one-button closure, but the button wasn't standard for a McCardell ready-to-wear garment. I was staring at what appeared to be a twin of the pearl rosette button on my desk.

"Well, shut my mouth," I said.

I turned the button over as far as the thread holding it affixed would allow. The engraving was a match, too.

"So," he said, draping the coat over one of the wing chairs and sitting down, "we now have two buttons to account for, one found shortly after a murder proximate to the scene of the crime, and one on a garment in a trunk Bobby Jordan says belonged to his grandmother, Babs Miller."

I thought for a moment. "According to Dr. Walker's inventory, Riley had several other garments that had belonged to Babs Miller, which we found in her closet. As far as I can see, the only thing that sets this coat apart is the button—which might account for why it's the only garment in the trunk."

Ellis fingered the button, rubbing the pearls, thinking it through.

"Let me tell you what I've learned so far about the buttons," I said. "Sets of four were given to members of a sorority called Epsilon Zeta Kappa up until 1941." I explained how I knew the timeline, then added, "Here's the thing—when I called the sorority and asked how to get a replacement button, the woman I spoke to, Margo, mentioned that a woman named Riley Jordan had called last Thursday and asked the same thing."

He leaned back and looked at me. "Really?" he said, not so much asking a question as expressing surprise. I definitely had his attention, that was for sure.

"Yes, and when I called the button designer Margo referred me to—he's passed away, by the way; I spoke to his son—he told me that a woman had called about getting a replacement, also last Thursday. This time, though, she called herself Nancy Patterson."

"Interesting."

"I thought so, too."

He reached for another cookie and took his time chewing. "We'll need to verify that it was in fact a woman, and not a man trying to sound like a woman," he said, thinking aloud.

"True."

"Was Riley a member of the sorority?"

"Yes."

"I can understand the caller using a member's name in trying to get information from the sorority. Maybe thinking they'd hesitate or refuse to disclose member policies to a nonmember."

"That's what I thought. Except it took me longer to reach that conclusion."

He grinned. "You forget—I'm a man of steely discipline and focus."

"Forgive me, sir."

He waved it away. "Consider yourself forgiven." He finished the cookie. "'Course, Riley's murder's gotten some play in New York because of her husband being a celebrity chef."

"That, and being linked to Ruby Bowers and all."

Ellis leaned back, keeping his eyes on mine. "So the caller decided to use a made-up name."

"A common one, like Nancy Patterson," I agreed, nodding.

"There's got to be a boatload of women named Nancy Patterson."

"Thousands."

"Although it's not a suspiciously common name like Mary Smith."

"Nancy Patterson was a good choice," I agreed.

"Interesting that the killer might be a woman," he remarked, keeping his eyes fixed on mine.

"Not a surprise, though, if the button had been lost during the murder. A man wouldn't wear a button like that."

An idea came to me, and it must have shown on my face, because Ellis said, "What is it, Josie?"

"A man might have been carrying the button in his pocket if he'd bought it at an antiques store to give to his wife on her birthday."

"Who?" he asked.

I met Ellis's eyes. "Quinn. His wife is known for wearing antique jewelry and accessories." A man whose livelihood and social standing depend on his spotless reputation might kill if he thought he was about to be caught with his hand in the cookie jar. A man who, when he realized he'd lost the button, could have run quick like a bunny to the mall for an alternate gift.

"Interesting," Ellis remarked. "Back to this mysterious caller. We might be able to trace her calls if the sorority and Mr. Lossoff give us permission, but it will probably be a bust. Whoever did this knows enough not to call from their home or work phone."

"Right. Probably they used a disposable cell phone, like the one Riley called."

"And you know this how?" he asked, his eyes narrowing and his tone chilly and clipped.

My throat closed and my heart began hammering. It was

hard to remember that while Ellis was a friend, he also was the police chief, and I needed to watch my tongue. I stared at him, my mind racing to come up with an answer that wouldn't involve Wes. He pinned me with eyes. He wasn't giving me any chance to escape his questioning.

"I must have read it somewhere," I replied as if it were no biggy.

"Where?"

"I don't remember."

"When you remember, please let me know," he said, his tone frigid.

"All right."

He stared at me for several seconds longer, then let it go. He reached for his cell phone and hit a preprogrammed button. "Are you certain there's no way to trace individual buttons?" he asked as he placed the unit to his ear.

"Yes. I verified it when I spoke to Margo."

He nodded. He repeated what I'd told him to Detective Brownley, then asked her to call both EZK and Tony Lossoff.

"First," he said, "find out their level of confidence that the woman they spoke to was, in fact, a woman. Second, ask when she called. What time of day. Third, ask if we can check their phone records to discover her number. She called both places Thursday. Once we nail down the time frame, it ought to be easy to spot the number." He flipped the phone closed. "Why do you think the woman calling herself Nancy Patterson cares about replacing the button, anyway? Why wouldn't she just pretend she lost it?"

"I wondered that, too, since after all, that specific button can't be traced to her. I figure she's probably worried that the fact that it's missing at all will make her conspicuous. Maybe she wears whatever garment the button is on periodically, and her workmates have admired it and she's said how much she loves it, and so on. It would be odd if she suddenly stopped wearing it. People would register that she hadn't worn it in a while. People would talk."

He nodded again. "I can see that. It's pretty distinctive. Someone would be certain to notice its absence." He rubbed his nose, thinking. "I'd like your opinion—should we turn photos of the button over to the media and ask them to issue a call for sightings?"

"I don't know. There's a branch of EZK at Hitchens, which means scores, maybe hundreds, of local girls got sets. There have to be hundreds or thousands of buttons knocking around. It seems to me you'd just get a gazillion false leads."

"Chasing down false leads is a big part of our job."

"You'd also alert the killer you know what she's up to."

"Good point." He paused, thinking. "You said you had an idea. What is it?"

"When the woman calling herself Nancy Patterson discovered that the button designer, Nick Lossoff, had died, she asked his son, Tony, for ideas about how she could get a replacement button. He, being a helpful sort, suggested she contact one of the fashion industry associations and two well-known colleges. You're from New York, you know them—Parsons and FIT."

"Sure. Calling someone in a design department—that's a good idea."

"I don't think she'd go that route—too dicey and too open. I don't think she'd call an association, either. It's different calling one man who makes these particular buttons on a regular basis and calling an organization blindly. Probably you'd get transferred a dozen times and have to explain why you're calling time and time again. I'd sure feel conspicuous doing that. What Tony said was that she needed to find a man with tools." I shifted position. "There are no button designers in Rocky Point, and she wouldn't risk leaving the area to go to New York, or anywhere else there's likely to be a professional fashion or costume designer, unless she had another good reason to travel.

That's a lot of ifs. Maybe she ordered a replacement online—but that's risky, too. Talk about leaving a paper trail." I took in a deep breath. "If I were her, I'd want to find someone local who could do the job quickly, before anyone got wind of the missing button."

"What would you do?"

"I'd find a man with tools—a jewelry designer."

"She'd be knowledgeable enough to figure out that a button designer uses the same tools as a jewelry designer?"

"She might. Think of the materials—platinum and pearls. That sounds like jewelry to me." I shrugged. "It seems to me to be worth a shot. If it doesn't pan out, you can always check out the associations and colleges and/or publicize the missing button, like you said."

He nodded. "I agree. Good thinking, Josie. It's definitely worth checking out. I know there are three, maybe four, jewelers at Fox Run Mall alone. Is that where you'd start?"

"No. There's no way a mall jeweler would even consider taking on a specialized project like this. Maybe the caller went there and asked—but I know for sure where she ended up, because there's only one shop in town that could handle the job. Blackmore's."

CHAPTER NINETEEN

P olice Chief Hunter and I walked into Blackmore's Jewelers on the Green in Rocky Point Village less than an hour later, just after noon. Blackmore's had been in business for eighty-seven years and was far and away the finest jewelry store on the coast. A handsome man well beyond retirement age wearing a well-tailored suit approached me as soon as I entered.

"Josie!" he said, extending his hand for a shake and smiling. "It's good to see you."

"You, too, Mr. Blackmore. Have you met Police Chief Hunter yet? He's fairly new in the job, about a year."

"I haven't had the pleasure. Chief," he said, as they shook. "What can I do for you?"

I looked around. The shop exuded a quiet refinement, the kind of place where dickering over a price would seem, well, unseemly. The lighting was subdued, coming mostly from chandeliers, although spotlights illuminated specific cases and displays. The carpet was dark blue and plush. The cherrywood paneling had a luminescent patina.

Two women about Cara's age were examining a gold watch and chatting with a saleswoman young enough to be their granddaughter. A man stood with his hands behind his back peering into a case of jewel-studded bracelets. A woman and a young girl entered the shop just as a man about thirty appeared through a door at the rear marked PRIVATE. I wondered if that was Mr. Blackmore's grandson.

"Josie tells me your jewelry shop is the best around," Ellis said glancing around. "Do you have a minute to talk? I don't want to pull you away from your business."

Mr. Blackmore's eyes narrowed appraisingly as he said, "My grandson can handle everything. I'll be glad to help in any way I can. Please come into my office."

"I wondered if that's who he was," I said.

"I look forward to introducing you when we're not quite so busy," he said, smiling, as he led us past glass cabinets filled with glittering gems.

As we passed his grandson, he pointed to the rear, and the younger man nodded. Mr. Blackmore led us into a large office and stood behind his oversized mahogany desk until we were seated. He waited for one of us to speak.

"I asked Josie to accompany me because an antique is involved in an investigation we're working on," Ellis said. Ellis glanced at me as he spoke, and soon I felt Mr. Blackmore's eyes on me, too. "Please, Josie, would you explain?"

I took the satin case containing the pearl rosette button Hank had found out of my tote bag, shook the button into my hand, and laid it on the old-fashioned desk blotter, the kind with triangular green leather corners and a replaceable pad.

"Am I right that you've been asked to replicate this?" I asked.

He gazed at the button, then raised his eyes to meet mine.

"May I?" he asked.

"Please," I replied, as charmed as ever by his courtly diction and demeanor.

He picked up the button, then switched on his desk lamp and studied both sides in the circle of strong white light, using a loupe. When he was finished, he slid the button toward me, turned off the lamp, and leaned back in his chair.

"Why are you asking?" he asked Ellis.

Ellis paused, perhaps deciding how much to reveal. "I'm hoping you'll keep what I'm about to tell you confidential."

"Certainly," Mr. Blackmore said without hesitation.

"That button was found at a murder site. I think the killer knows she lost it and is trying to get it replaced before she has to explain why it's no longer in her possession."

Mr. Blackmore glanced me for a moment, then turned back to Ellis. "Is this related to the murder of Riley Jordan?" he asked.

"Yes," Ellis replied.

He looked at the button for a moment. "A woman named Nancy Patterson came in last Thursday and asked me to fabricate a button." He pointed. "This button. She had photographs."

"You took the job?" Ellis asked as I returned the button to the satchel.

"That's right. I told her we could do the job, including the engraving."

"Did she tell you why she needed the replacement?" Ellis asked.

Mr. Blackmore nodded. "Yes. She said it was a family treasure, and that her mother would kill her if she ever found out that she lost it."

Chief Hunter rubbed the side of his nose, thinking, the same move he'd done earlier in my office. "That sounds like a young woman."

"Yes . . . relatively young, I think."

I took his assessment with a grain of salt—to a man in his midseventies, like Mr. Blackmore, a thirty-five-year-old woman like Becka or Kenna would look young.

"What does she look like?" Ellis asked.

"She had dark brown hair. I don't know about her eyes—I never saw them. She wore a pink sweater, blue jeans, big sunglasses, and a floppy hat. The hat was made of straw with a big brim and a kind of fringe around the edge, the kind you buy at the beach."

Ellis glanced around. "What about video? You've got to have security here."

Mr. Blackmore shook his head. "My system is old—the tape is on a seventy-two-hour loop. The images from Thursday were wiped out yesterday." He looked embarrassed. "My security company has been after me for years to go digital."

Ellis leaned back and crossed his legs. "This question may sound odd, but how sure are you she was a woman? Could she have been a man playing a woman?"

Mr. Blackmore looked startled. "Oh, no! I'm quite certain. I mean, there was no question at all in my mind."

"Was she big, you know, big-boned?" Ellis asked.

"No, she was rather thin."

"How tall was she?"

"I'm sorry, but I don't remember, which means her height must have been somewhere in the normal range or I would have noticed."

"What about her features? Was there anything remarkable about her nose, for instance?"

"No."

"Her mouth?"

Mr. Blackmore pursed his lips, thinking, then shook his head. "No," he said.

"What color was her skin?"

"White."

"Fair or dark?"

He pursed his lips and shook his head. "I'm not sure."

"How about any tattoos?"

"No."

"Scars or birthmarks?"

"No."

Ellis crossed his ankles and stared at his toes for a moment, then asked, "When did you tell her the new button would be ready?"

"A week, maybe longer."

"Did she leave her phone number?"

"No. She said she would be traveling out of the country and that she'd call me."

Ellis nodded again. "You mentioned photos the woman brought in—do you still have them?"

"Yes, they're attached to the work order." Mr. Blackmore rolled his chair back and stood up. "I'll get them for you."

"Let me," Ellis said, standing quickly. He pulled a latex glove from his side pocket and got an evidence bag from inside his jacket. He smiled. "Just in case there's any forensic evidence."

"Certainly," Mr. Blackmore said, swallowing hard.

Mr. Blackmore walked to a chest-high oak cabinet, the kind with dozens of file drawers used by libraries before computers. Whenever we could get our hands on some of the single- or two-drawer units, we marketed them as recipe boxes. In good condition, they flew out the tag sale door at fifty dollars and up. Mr. Blackmore pointed to a drawer on the left. Ellis pulled it out and placed it on Mr. Blackmore's desk. Mr. Blackmore stared down for a moment, then pointed.

"That's it," he said. "The thick packet in the middle there."

Ellis reached in with his gloved hand and eased the stapled documents out. "Why is it so bulky?" he asked.

"I stapled the photographs to the work order, and the receipt. If I recall correctly, Ms. Patterson paid a thousand dollars as a deposit. We always require a deposit on custom work, and this is an expensive project, what with the matched pearls and platinum."

"Did she charge it?"

Mr. Blackmore shook his head. "No. She paid cash. I remember because she had an envelope in her purse filled with hundred-dollar bills."

"A bank envelope?" Ellis asked.

"No, a plain white, standard number ten envelope. There was no writing on it."

"Do you recall if she touched anything that might not have been cleaned? I'm wondering if we might be able to get some fingerprints. Maybe she dropped her purse, for example, and when she bent down to pick it up, she grabbed a display cabinet leg to steady herself."

Mr. Blackmore shook his head slowly for a moment. "No. I don't remember anything like that."

The two men sat down again. Ellis placed the papers on the desk and used a pen to flip through until he came to the photographs.

"Josie," he asked, "do you recognize these photos?"

"Yes," I replied. "From the background, I can tell they're from EZK's Web site." I pointed. "Do you see the shadows in the white satin?"

Ellis nodded, slipped the packet into his plastic evidence bag, then took off the plastic glove and tossed it into a trash can. "Tell me about the incident from the beginning," he said to Mr. Blackmore. "Did Ms. Patterson call and make an appointment, or did she just show up?"

"She just showed up."

"Isn't that unusual? A young woman walks in out of the blue to order an expensive button? Wouldn't that raise a red flag?"

"Not at all, and frankly, I'm not sure I understand your point. People buy expensive items all the time. Why should it raise a red flag?"

Ellis nodded. "Fair enough. Was there anything about her story or her manner that made you think she wasn't telling the truth?"

"No, not at all." Mr. Blackmore turned to me. "You know what's it like, Josie, when customers come in for the first time. You listen more than you talk as you try to discover if there are any hidden agendas you need to know about in order to close the sale. Do they really want a birthday gift that thrills Mom like they say they do, or do they want a gift that puts their brother to shame?"

"I know just what you mean," I said. I turned to Ellis. "It's not our place to question people's motives."

Mr. Blackmore nodded. "Exactly. I had no reason to doubt Ms. Patterson's story. I still don't."

Ellis nodded. "Then what happened?"

Mr. Blackmore shrugged. "Nothing. She was in here less than ten or fifteen minutes. She told me what she wanted, and I told her I could do it, but that I couldn't price it until I acquired the pearls, although at a minimum, it would be three thousand dollars. She didn't seem concerned with price. She was concerned with speed."

"You haven't heard from her since?"

"No, but she said she'd call early this week just to touch base, to be sure everything was progressing properly."

Ellis tapped a short trill on his chair arm. "I'm going to ask you to come to the station house. I'd like a detective to take you through your interaction with Ms. Patterson again, and I'd like for you to sit with a police artist to see if we can come up with a sketch of what she looks like."

I sat and listened as Mr. Blackmore asked logistical questions—when, how long, where, and the like.

"One more thing," Ellis said as we stood. "I'd like your permission to tap your phone so we can have her voice on file."

"I have no problem with that."

Ellis smiled. "I wish all citizens were as cooperative as you."

"I should have said that I'd have no problem with it so long as you don't share any information with my competitors," he added, smiling and shooting me a glance. "Like Josie."

"Guaranteed."

"I'm not competition! I don't deal in jewelry."

"Still," Mr. Blackmore said.

"No problem," Ellis interjected. "I'll ask the district attorney's office to draft an agreement containing that language."

We walked to the door.

"There's one more thing," Ellis said, pausing. "If and when Ms. Patterson calls, it's crucial that you act naturally, that you don't spook her in any way."

"I can do that," Mr. Blackmore said with conviction. "I'm quite experienced at staying on point."

"Are you sure? It's one of those things that's easier said than done."

"Chief Hunter," Mr. Blackmore said, a look of cynical amusement on his face, "over the years I've spoken to men's mistresses as well as their wives, and women's lovers as well as their husbands, and I've never yet mixed one up. There's no question in my mind that when Ms. Patterson calls, she will have no idea that I'll have grabbed my cell phone to text you about the call."

I grinned at the thought of old-world, proper Morton Blackmore texting.

He noticed my expression. "I tweet, too."

I started laughing. "Maybe you can teach me," I said.

He smiled. "Perhaps we can reach some accommodation. I'll help you develop a social media marketing plan if I can become Prescott's outsourced jewelry expert."

"That's a great idea," I said. Up until now, I'd saved up jewelry that came our way and sold it to trusted experts during my occasional trips to New York. Using Blackmore's would save me the trouble of carting priceless gems to the city, and it would speed up cash flow. "I should have thought of it myself. Consider it done."

He smiled and offered me his hand for a shake. "Thank you, Josie. I won't let you down."

"I know you won't, Mr. Blackmore."

"My grandson is very talented, too. So your appraisals will be in good hands going forward."

"I look forward to working with you both—although I'll have you work with my administrative manager, Gretchen Brock, on the Twitter thing. My brain is full."

Halfway back to my office, I turned to Ellis and said, "I think we should still check the mall jewelry stores."

"Why?" he asked.

"Because while you and Mr. Blackmore were discussing his visit to the police station, I got to thinking. You know how I said Nancy Patterson might have asked about getting the button replaced at one of those stores in the mall, but for sure she ended up at Blackmore's?"

"Yes. You were right."

I grinned. "True, but jewelry stores in major shopping malls don't use old-fashioned security cameras."

CHAPTER TWENTY

E llis punched a button on his dashboard radio unit and stated his name. All I heard was a weird kind of crackling noise, yet from his back-and-forth conversation, I gathered that to him, the staticky-sounding noises were actually words. After a moment, he issued a series of instructions. Police officers were to immediately and simultaneously visit every jewelry store on the coast looking for evidence that a dark-haired, youngish woman wearing a pink sweater, big sunglasses, and a wide-brimmed, floppy straw hat had been there last Thursday. They were to start with Korley's and Zello's. If they got any sightings they were to call him immediately.

I got back to my office just before two. The first thing I did was call Wes.

"I have news," I said.

"About the police deployment?" he asked.

"What deployment?"

"To shopping malls. Do you know what's happening?"

Wes and his police scanner, I thought.

"You've got to promise not to publish anything yet. The police have a solid lead, and I can tell you about it, but we can't risk driving the suspect underground."

"Gotcha. Done."

"Okay, then, here goes. A woman—" I broke off and corrected myself. I wanted to be precise and accurate. "Someone— probably a woman—ordered a replacement button from Blackmore's Jewelers. Have you heard about the button?"

"No—what button?"

I was surprised that Wes's police source hadn't leaked information about the button, then realized that probably his source hadn't considered it significant. After all, until we'd confirmed that a replacement order had, in fact, been placed, it had been pure speculation that the button had been lost by Riley's killer.

I filled Wes in, and as I spoke, I could hear him scribbling. I told him about how Hank had fetched the button, the police's unsuccessful forensic examination, the duplicate button on the gray Claire McCardell coat, the connection to the sorority, my calls to the sorority and Mr. Lossoff, what Margo and Tony had told me about the supposed Riley Jordan and Nancy Patterson, and Nancy Patterson's visit to Blackmore's.

"This is great stuff, Josie! Real juice! So how does this relate to the police fanning out at shopping malls?"

"Blackmore's has an old security system, you know, the kind using actual tape. Her image has been recorded over. I had the thought that maybe the woman, whoever she is, tried a mall jeweler first. Chain stores probably wouldn't take on a project like this—but unless she's an expert, she would have no reason to know that. If she did go to a mall shop, someone might have suggested Blackmore's. Those jewelry stores have up-to-date digital security cameras, which means if she went there, they probably still have her photograph, so we can see what she looks like."

"Wicked good deal, Josie! You ate your Wheaties today, huh? How did Mr. Blackmore describe her?"

I smiled at Wes's compliment, then repeated everything Mr. Blackmore had told us. I crossed my fingers. "I know you stay close to your scanner, Wes. Will you let me know the minute the woman calling herself Nancy Patterson calls Mr. Blackmore?"

"Get me a photo of the button and you got a deal."

I agreed to do so right away, and as we hung up, I thought to myself, *Wes isn't the only one with sources.* I'd just arranged to receive an early alert if and when Nancy Patterson got in touch with Mr. Blackmore.

I called Bobby.

"I think the police have asked you about the coat we found in the attic, right?" I asked. "The gray Claire McCardell?"

"Yes, but I couldn't tell them anything about it—except that Riley wore it a couple of times years ago."

"Why did she stop wearing it, do you know?"

He didn't reply. I could hear him breathing.

"Bobby?" I asked softly.

"She'd hate for me to tell you," he said, his tone matching mine.

I couldn't imagine what could possibly be confidential about a coat.

He sighed, then added, "Maybe some secrets shouldn't survive the grave. It's not like it's any big deal. I mean, it was a huge deal to Riley, but it wasn't to anyone else."

He paused again, and again I waited. I tried to think of something to say or a question I could ask that might nudge him along, but before I could formulate one, he spoke.

"The coat didn't fit her anymore. It's a size two, right? After we got married, Riley gained some weight. At first she just grumped about it a little, then when she couldn't lose it, she got realistic, saying she wasn't a teenager anymore, and wearing a size four was still pretty darn good. To tell you the truth, Josie, I was proud of how she handled her disappointment. I mean, she went from flipping out to philosophical."

He paused, sighing again, and I felt bad for him. Recalling so intimate a conversation must have been difficult. *A measure of love,* I thought, *is secrets kept.*

"In the last year or so," he continued, "she'd gained even more weight. She went from a four to a six, and between you and me, she was not coping well. I didn't notice any change in her body and told her so, but she couldn't hear it. I mean, Jesus, Josie, even if she had gained enough weight that I would have noticed, I truly didn't care—but she did. She told me that she felt fat and out of control. It got to the point where she really seemed to hate herself."

"Poor Riley. I can imagine how hard it must have been for her. To most women, being a size six would be a dream—but not if you were a size two only a few years earlier and felt as if you couldn't stop a downward trend."

"Exactly."

"I did notice the different sizes in the collection. This explains it." I paused. "How are you holding up, Bobby?"

"I'm numb," he replied matter-of-factly. "To tell you the truth, I'm just going through the motions."

"I'm so sorry."

"Yeah . . . well, life goes on, right?"

Not for Riley, I thought.

Wes called just as I was getting ready to leave for the day.

"They got her!" he said in a stage whisper.

I opened my mouth but couldn't find my voice. I felt all tingly, as if I'd touched a live wire. I took a deep breath and tried again.

"Got her?" I managed. "Or her picture?"

"Picture."

"Who is it?"

"No one knows. Isn't that the bomb? According to my police source, they're going to ask you to look at the photo. They've already asked Morton Blackmore, and he's ID'd her." Excitement pulsated in his voice. "Want to see it now?"

"Sure."

"I just sent it," he said.

I stared at my e-mail in-box until the little flag went up, then downloaded the photos. There were three images, all in color.

One showed the woman entering the store. She was wearing a bubblegum-pink sweater, stone-washed, boot-cut, low-rider blue jeans, sunglasses so big they covered her face from brow to cheekbone, and a wide-brimmed straw hat. Another picture showed her standing at the counter. The third showed her leaving.

In every photo she was looking down with her face tilted away from the lens, as if she'd cased the joint and knew where the cameras were. The hat brim and the sunglass frames were both so wide, I couldn't make out any of her features. Her skin was white and unfreckled, but I couldn't tell if the tone was light, like Becka's, or olive, like Kenna's. She seemed to be of average size.

"Wow," I said. "You can't tell much of anything."

"You can tell it's a girl. A woman."

"Yes," I agreed, "but just because it's *not* Bobby or Quinn, that doesn't mean they're eliminated as suspects. Either of them could be in collusion with this woman, whoever she is."

"Fair enough. So who do you think it is—Becka or Kenna?"

I stared at the photo of her leaving the shop. I shook my head. "Whoever she is, she's wearing one heck of a good disguise."

After Wes and I agreed to talk soon, I took the pearl rosette button from the satchel. As I rotated it under the stark white light cast by my desk lamp, I noticed for the first time that the pearls had mirrorlike attributes. I could see a faint reflection of my face in the large center pearl. Looking deep into the shimmering sheen and dull dark spots, I could sense, more than see, my face's shape and features. I moved the pearl a bit, hoping that the image would resolve itself, but it never did. The shadows and shiny spots shifted, but they remained fuzzy and formless, no matter which way I turned it. *Just like the facts of this case,* I thought.

Who was the woman in the security photos? Becka? Kenna? I shivered as if a spider had run up my leg. Whoever she was— was she acting on her own or in concert with someone else? Recalling how nimbly Gretchen's attacker had responded to the mere hint that her memory of the silver car was returning, I could only imagine how she'd react once she knew the police net was drawing close.

CHAPTER TWENTY-ONE

G retchen called in sick first thing Tuesday morning.

"I'm so tired I can barely talk," she said.

"Good—not good, you're exhausted, but good, you're listening to your body. Yesterday was probably too much for you."

"I think it was important for me to come in, to ground myself, you know? To do my routine tasks and to see everyone." She giggled. "Not to mention how crucial it was to my well-being that I eat Cara's cookies. It took its toll, though, that's for sure. So I'm about to crawl back into bed."

"I'll be thinking of you," I said. "Sleep tight!"

I picked up a note Sasha had left asking me to look at a pink Chanel handbag from Riley's collection. From Riley's spreadsheet, we learned she'd bought it at a garage sale in 1997 and thought it dated from the early 1980s.

Sasha's note explained that even though she'd verified authenticity using Riley's own five-point checklist from her book, she still thought something was wrong and wondered if I had any ideas about what it could be. She attached a printout of her research.

According to Sasha's notes, which referenced Riley's checklist: (1) The logo was comprised of two interlocking C's facing away from one another, with the right C overlapping the left C at the top, and the left C overlapping the bottom C on the right. (2) The number on the embossed authenticity card matched the serial number in the bag. (3) The zipper pull featured engraving;

specifically, the word CHANEL was etched on one side and the logo was etched on the other. (4) The logo pattern aligned from top to bottom and from side to side. (5) The stamped MADE IN FRANCE mark was on the inside of the bag, and in the correct color. In authentic Chanel bags, gold stamps match gold hardware, and silver matches silver.

All signs pointed to the bag being authentic, but Sasha's intuition was one of the qualities that made her an excellent antiques appraiser. She had a gift for "smelling" counterfeit anythings.

I removed the black dust bag and picked up the purse. The leather was supple and butter-soft. The hardware gleamed and had heft to it. The lining was soft and smooth. The inner pocket was properly fitted. The stamping was even and true. Suddenly, a fact I couldn't believe I recalled came to me. In the 1980s, all Chanel handbag dust bags were white. Only contemporary bags were sold with black dust bags. The dust bag itself looked right: The lettering was in white, and the logo and company name were properly placed and encircled.

It was possible that the bag itself was genuine but missing its original dust bag. I consulted Riley's spreadsheet. Sure enough, she hadn't listed the dust bag. Probably, when she'd purchased the handbag, the dust bag was missing. She'd somehow procured a contemporary one and used it to protect the bag, but didn't record it because it didn't match.

I e-mailed Sasha, suggesting she call Chanel to verify the serial number and ask if there was any reason for that bag to be sold with a black dust bag, and if not, if there was any way we could acquire a proper white dust bag. It was worth the call to Europe. If Sasha could prove the purse was genuine, we'd value it at close to three thousand dollars, even more with the correct dust bag.

Just before nine, I was downstairs leaving Cara a note about Gretchen when Sasha called to tell me that she'd just made an appointment with Dr. Walker at the New England Museum of Design to discuss how he'd like us to handle a valuation issue. She was going directly there.

"Sounds like a good idea," I said. "What's the valuation issue?"

"Some of the garments have no sales history."

Given that past sales price is one of the primary predictors of future sales price, without a sales history to consult, estimating values becomes more complex. If the collection was going to auction, you could let the market set the price, but these clothes weren't. Accurately valuing the donation was crucial to ensure that Riley's estate received the proper tax benefit and the museum was able to satisfy matching grant requirements.

"Got it," I said.

"If it's all right, I thought I'd call Ava and ask her to meet me there. I remembered what you said about mentoring her. I thought listening to our conversation would be useful for her."

"That's a great idea, Sasha!"

"Thanks. Have you heard from Gretchen?"

"Yes, she called to say she's beat and is going to stay home today and sleep."

"I wondered whether she was pushing herself too hard by coming in yesterday."

"I had the same concern. At least she's going to lie low today."

"True."

I filled her in about the Chanel dust bag, and she said, "I'm really embarrassed, Josie," sounding mortified. "I had Ava consult the checklist. I should have told her to check on the dust bag, too, and to look at the spreadsheet."

"Probably," I agreed, "but we have enough checks and balances built in, so there's no harm done. It's been a long time since any of us has worked with someone as inexperienced as she is."

"I'm sorry," she repeated.

"These things happen," I said, wishing for her own sake

that she wasn't quite so hard on herself. "Give my regards to Dr. Walker, all right?"

She promised that she would. I hung up as Cara walked in. About an hour later, I was upstairs, deep in proofing catalogue copy, when Fred brought up the morning mail, a task normally part of Gretchen's routine.

"Thanks, Fred. I appreciate your pitching in."

He pushed up his glasses. "No prob."

As he left, Hank pranced in carrying a catnip mouse and dropped it at my feet.

"What a good boy!" I told him. "Did you want me to throw this for you?"

I tossed it toward the far corner of the room, and Hank took off like a sprinter. After three more throws, I was growing bored, but he wasn't.

"I need to get back to work, Hank. Come into my lap."

He mewed, letting me know he was disappointed in my priorities, and wandered off.

I flipped through the mail, separating the bills from the ads, until I came to a thick envelope from Max. I tore it open.

The envelope contained photocopies of scholarly articles and printouts from Web sites all having to do with the subject of establishing award-granting criteria in private foundations. Max's cover letter said that he thought I might find them useful as I worked toward establishing parameters for grant giving. I silently thanked him, and decided that there was no time like the present to get started on the process.

I scanned the articles and printouts, then settled in to read them more carefully. Hank came back and jumped into my lap. I petted him as I read. After I was done, I swiveled toward my window and thought about what I'd learned. All of the articles shared one recommendation—grant awards should be carefully aligned to the foundation's mission. I needed to write a mission statement.

I'd already decided to contact Riley's close friends and the vintage fashion experts she respected, like Dr. Walker, to ask if she'd ever mentioned her plans to them, and if so, what she'd said. Bobby, I thought, might be able to help guide me in tracking down friends to talk to. Dr. Walker might know other professionals she'd admired.

I got Bobby at home. He said that Becka was Riley's chief shopping buddy, so probably she was the best person to talk to. When I dialed Becka's office, the departmental secretary answered. Becka wouldn't be in until noon, she said. I glanced at the clock. It was close to ten. I reached Dr. Walker just before his appointment with Sasha, and we scheduled a time on Thursday morning to meet.

I called Max to thank him for sending the information and to update him about my plans.

"Sounds like a great approach," he said. "Is Sister Mary Agnes on your list?"

"No, who's she?"

"One of Riley's closest friends. They went to grammar school together, I think. She's with the Sisters of Repose."

"Which explains Riley's donation to them."

"Yes."

"I'd love to talk to her. Do you have her number?"

He read it off to me. I thanked him again, pushed the button for a new dial tone, and dialed the convent. A woman said she'd get Sister Mary Agnes for me. After several minutes, just as I began to wonder if I'd been disconnected, a pleasant-sounding voice said hello.

"I'm sorry to disturb you, Sister," I said. "I'm Josie Prescott. I got your name from Riley Jordan's lawyer, Max Bixby. I don't know if you're aware that Riley set up an educational foundation. I'm the trustee."

"I know your name, actually. Riley spoke of you very highly."

"Thank you. That's nice to hear. I'm sorry for your loss, Sister. I know you were close to her."

"Thank you," she said.

"I'll tell you why I'm calling—I want to be certain to keep to Riley's vision for the foundation. I was hoping we could talk about it. May I buy you lunch?"

"I'd love it, but only if an early lunch works for you. I'm an administrator at our school, and I'm on study-hall-monitor duty today, starting at one. I could meet around eleven thirty, if that's all right."

"That would be perfect," I said. She suggested the Portsmouth Diner since it was close to the convent, and I agreed.

I stood up, apologizing to Hank for disrupting his sleep, and nodded to myself, pleased that I'd made a good start.

I left early for my appointment with Sister Mary Agnes. I wanted to bring Gretchen some African violets, one of her favorite plants. I stopped in at Rocky Point Floral Impressions and selected a big basket with a purple and white floral ceramic handle and had them fill it with little pots of the violets. I wrote a short note saying only that we missed her and hoped she would be feeling better soon.

The owner, a French woman named Monique, tucked fluffy Spanish moss around the edges and said, "Ooh! So verdant and cheerful! Your friend will smile."

I thanked her, then walked back to my car, lightly swinging the basket. The sun was warm, and the breeze felt fresh. I braced the basket on the backseat and drove to Gretchen's condo. I parked in front of her small fenced-in front yard. My plan was to leave the basket wedged in between her screen door and her front door so as not to disturb her.

As soon as I stepped out, I saw plumes of ugly charcoal gray smoke streaming from the rear of Gretchen's unit. My heart stopped, then began racing. The smell was acrid. I fought rising panic—Gretchen was inside, asleep. I dumped my tote bag onto the passenger seat, grabbed my cell phone, and punched in 9-1-1.

When the emergency operator answered, I told her where I was and what was happening, then tossed the phone onto the seat and bolted toward the condo, leaping over the fence.

"Gretchen!" I screamed as I ran. "Gretchen!"

When I reached the front door, I pressed the doorbell. Chimes sounded. I kept my finger on the bell and placed the flat of my hand against the wood. It was cool. I pounded on the panels with both fists. I tried the knob, but the door was locked.

"Gretchen! Gretchen! Can you hear me?"

I paused to listen. I heard crackling. The fire was well under way.

I pushed through the bushes that fronted the unit, poky bits scratching at my hands and cheeks, reached the closest window, and peered in, cupping my eyes and pushing my nose into the glass. Her dining room table was barely visible through the swirling smoke. I could just make out a bowl of green apples sitting in the middle of the table and an outline of the archway that led to her kitchen. Thin ridges of orange flames waxed and waned along the bottom and sides of the back wall. I stepped back, horrified. Soon her apartment would be fully engulfed.

"Gretchen!" I shouted. "Gretchen!"

I heard sirens.

I elbowed my way back through the bushes, then dashed to the back of her unit. I wrenched open the gate and leapt onto her deck. French doors opened into her den, but I couldn't see in. Smoke was pouring out of a gaping hole in one of the door panes, and I choked. I turned away to breathe in fresher air, but couldn't. The caustic smoke was nearly suffocating. I coughed and gasped until the back of my throat was raw. I turned back to the broken glass. Gretchen must have tried to escape. Realizing that she couldn't make it, she threw something at the glass, perhaps to let fresh air in, or maybe to try to get her neighbors' attention.

The sirens grew louder.

"Gretchen," I said, no longer able to scream.

My eyes burned. I turned my head to the side again, took in a lungful of foul air, then stepped in close enough to jiggle the door handle. The metal was warm to the touch, and the door was locked. Gretchen was in trouble, and I had to get in. I raised my elbow, ready to shatter the glass pane closest to the handle so I could reach in and open the door, then suddenly realized that I wasn't treading on glass shards. The glass had been broken *in,* not out. Gretchen hadn't tried to escape. Someone had thrown something in. I stood, paralyzed with dread.

The sirens blared, one extraloud blast, then stopped, and I ran as fast as I could, which wasn't fast at all, to the front to alert them that Gretchen was inside. I was having trouble breathing. As I rounded the corner I slowed my pace and started waving my arms in big, sweeping motions instead.

"Help!" I called, then choked and fell into a coughing fit.

One of the firefighters, a middle-aged man with jet black hair, charged at me.

"My friend's inside," I managed.

"Just one person?"

"I think so."

He turned on a dime and called something I couldn't hear to a man standing at the truck. The two of them grabbed hatchets, put on their masks, and ran for the front door.

I glanced around the parking lot, feeling helpless. Everywhere I looked there were men in motion. Firefighters rushed from the truck to the condo and back, laying out hoses, turning valves, and sliding their arms into harnesses.

"Are you all right?" a gray-haired woman asked as she approached from somewhere to my left. She looked worried.

"I breathed in some smoke," I managed between coughs. "I'll be okay."

We stood next to one another watching as the hoses came to life. They aimed the spray at the roof. The two firefighters stopped hacking at the front door. One of them jimmied it open, and both men disappeared into the smoke. *They're so brave,* I thought.

"Is Gretchen inside?" the woman asked.

"I think so." My voice cracked, and I felt the ground shift. I began trembling. Tiny gold specks began to shimmer in front of me. *I'm going to faint,* I thought. I stumbled toward a stone wall that surrounded the property and leaned against it. The gray-haired woman followed.

"You need to go to the hospital," she said. "Do you want me to call nine-one-one?"

"No . . . I just need to breathe some fresh air."

The fire chief roared into the lot driving a dark red SUV. "Rocky Point Fire Department" was painted on the sides in black and gold. Almost immediately, Ellis arrived, driving his official police vehicle. The fire chief, taller than Ellis by a head, and rail thin, ran to one of the fire trucks. Ellis pulled to a stop near my car. He took in the scene in one sweeping glance, then jogged toward me.

"Gretchen," I said. I pointed. "That's her unit."

He nodded. "I recognized her address from the nine-one-one call. How come she isn't at work?"

"She called in sick."

"Are you all right?"

"No."

"I'll get an ambulance."

"I don't need medical care. I need Gretchen."

"Wait here," he told me.

Ellis ran to the fire chief, said something, then listened. He made a thirty-second call from his cell, then rejoined us.

"They're checking the apartment now," he said. "I don't think she's here, Josie."

I looked at him, afraid to hope. "Why not?"

"Her police protection isn't here."

I leaned back and tried to smile, but coughed instead. This

time, I couldn't seem to stop. I folded over, hugging myself, and from this angle noticed that my spring-fresh khakis were streaked with soot. I felt dizzy, then sick to my stomach.

Ellis came to me and gently took hold of my arm. "Sit down on the asphalt. An ambulance is on its way. You need oxygen."

"I'm fine," I protested. "I don't need an ambulance."

"Don't argue. Smoke inhalation is tricky."

I sat down. Sitting with my legs straight out, using the wall as a backrest, I felt less woozy. After several seconds, I stopped coughing.

"Gretchen," I said, looking up at him.

"I have a call in. We'll know soon enough."

I nodded, grateful to have his support, knowing that nothing would fall between the cracks with his oversight. I kept my eyes on the front door and prayed.

Ellis asked the gray-haired woman if she'd seen anyone or anything out of the way, but she hadn't.

Two minutes later, both firefighters came out. One ran to his truck to drop his hatchet before taking a place holding one of the hoses. The other man joined the fire chief and began talking. He listened to a question, then shook his head. Ellis walked to join them. He took a call, then came back to me, smiling.

"Gretchen's in Maine," Ellis said, towering over me. I had to tip my head all the way back to see him.

Tears of relief stung my eyes, and I blinked them away. "At Jack's!" I said. "Of course. I should have guessed. He lives in Elliot, just over the border. What a relief! May I talk to her?"

He nodded. "Soon. I'm having her moved someplace safe."

His phone rang, and he strode a few paces away to talk in private. I scrabbled up and walked slowly toward my car. I couldn't remember what I'd done with my phone after I'd called in the fire. I found it under the front seat. I started placing everything back into my tote bag, and as I did, I realized the grim truth— someone was determined to kill Gretchen.

CHAPTER TWENTY-TWO

I sat back down on the asphalt, drained and light-headed, and watched as Gretchen's apartment burned. From where I sat I had a view of the pond. A *quack* caught my attention, and I watched as two ducks, their teal feathers glistening in the sun, dove under water, then surfaced, then dove again.

Moments later, the ambulance arrived. The paramedic, a sturdy-looking young woman with freckles and green eyes, helped me into the back. I lay down on the gurney. She fitted a mask over my nose and mouth, and within seconds I was breathing clean, pure air. She listened to my chest through a stethoscope, took my blood pressure, and monitored my pulse. I felt my trembling quiet, and a few minutes after that, my nausea disappeared entirely. I sat up.

Wes drove into the lot and jerked to a stop. He saw me and ran over, his expression somber.

"What's going on?" he asked.

I couldn't reply without removing my mask. I didn't want to talk to him. I was in shock, and I knew it. I'd gone from terrified that Gretchen might be trapped in an inferno to relieved beyond words at learning she was safe. I'd breathed in deadly smoke. I was petrified, too, scared into immobility. I lay back down and closed my eyes as the paramedic shooed him away. When I opened my eyes again a few moments later, Wes was gone.

She took my vital signs again and told me they were better; a while later, she repeated the process and told me they were good. I removed the mask. She said that if I started wheezing or coughing again, or if I developed a fever, I should get medical care right away. She also recommended that I see my doctor as a precaution. I thanked her, signed a form acknowledging that I'd received services, and stepped out into the sunlight.

Neither Ellis nor Wes was in sight. The fire chief wasn't around either. The firefighters were in the same positions as before, hosing off the roof and shooting streams of water into the interior.

I reached for my phone. It was eleven forty-five. I gasped. Sister Mary Agnes was waiting for me at the diner. I called the restaurant and asked for her. After a shorter-than-expected wait, she came on the line.

"I'm so sorry, Sister," I said. "There's been an emergency. My friend Gretchen, her apartment is on fire."

"Is she hurt?" she asked, her voice strained.

"No—luckily, she wasn't home."

"Thank God. How about you? Were you injured? You sound pretty shaken up."

"That's a good way to describe how I feel. Shaky. I'm okay, though. I'm just sorry to not be there. I guess we ought to reschedule."

"I need to see you," she said. "Forgive me, but it simply can't wait. I don't know what to do. I'm hoping you can help me. I can come to you wherever you are."

"Of course," I replied, bewildered, and gave her the address.

She said she'd be here in five minutes. After the call, I stood staring at the phone, wondering what could possibly have happened.

I called Ty and got his voice mail. I left him a message, trying and failing to keep my overwrought emotions out of my voice as I recited the facts. I was just finishing the call when the gray-haired woman approached me again.

"You look much better," she said.

"Thank you. The oxygen helped."

"Do you know Gretchen?"

"Yes. She works for me. I'm Josie Prescott."

"Oh, you're Josie! I've heard all about you from her. I'm Hilda Carlisle, her neighbor. She loves her job, you know—and you."

I smiled. "That's great to hear. I feel the same about her."

Hilda turned and watched the firefighters. "How did it start? Do they know?"

"If so, they haven't told me."

She clucked and ambled back toward her own unit.

Minutes later, Wes came into view. He'd been at the back of the unit. He headed straight at me. "It looks like arson," he announced in an undervoice, his eyes ablaze. "They think someone threw a Molotov cocktail into the apartment."

I pressed my hands against my lips. The picture Wes's words conjured up was too horrible to contemplate, but now that he'd spoken, I couldn't get the image out of my head. Fill a bottle with something flammable, like gasoline. Stuff a rag inside. Light the rag. Throw the bottle hard enough so it will shatter. *Bam*—it explodes into a fireball—an act of evil.

What on God's earth does Gretchen know?

I sat sidewise on my front seat, my feet on the asphalt. I kept my eyes on the burning building. Wes stood nearby.

"You look like you just walked out of a coal mine," he said. "Were you caught inside?"

"No . . . just the opposite . . . I thought Gretchen was trapped, but the smoke was too thick, and the fire . . ."

"Why are you here?"

"To leave some flowers." I pointed to the basket resting in the back.

"Roll down the window so I can get a good shot," he said. "It'll really add some human interest to the story."

I did as he asked. He wanted to take my picture, too, but I refused.

"And if you sneak a shot, Wes," I warned him, "I'll never talk to you again."

"Okay, okay," he said. "Anything else for me?"

I shook my head, and he ran across the lot to talk to Hilda.

Sister Mary Agnes drove an old blue minivan into the lot. I recognized her immediately as the woman who'd sat next to Bobby at Riley's funeral. She had light brown hair, cut short. She parked in a distant corner, and I walked toward her. Her eyes were big and focused on the still-smoldering building. As I approached her, I glanced over my shoulder. Wes was watching us the way a cat watches a mouse. She turned her attention to me. Her eyes were red, her expression stunned.

"You're Josie?" she asked.

"Yes. You're Sister Mary Agnes?"

She nodded. "Are you all right?"

"Yes," I said softly. "How about you? You've been crying."

She handed me her cell phone. "I don't know what to do," she whispered. "Would you . . . I mean, there's a message." She dug a tissue out of her skirt pocket and patted at the corners of her eyes. She took a deep breath. "Riley trusted you and respected your judgment . . . Would you please listen to it and help me figure out what to do?"

A narrow strip of white adhesive with a phone number written on it had been affixed to the bottom of the unit.

"Is this your phone number?" I asked.

"Yes."

I knew the number. I was holding the phone linked to Riley's account—the one Wes called C2. Riley had called this number shortly before she died. Sister Mary Agnes told me her PIN so I could access the message.

"I wish I could talk to you in person," Riley said, and hearing her voice, I felt as if I'd plunged into a glacial lake. "I just left Max's office. I've told you about him. He's such a decent man." There was a gulping sound. "Bobby's been cheating on me—I've seen photos—disgusting, explicit photos. How could he? How could he do such a thing to me?" Another pause, this one filled with the sounds of sobbing. "I changed my will. I told Max I wasn't leaving his office until it was done. Oh God, I can't believe it! It's just so awful. The bastard. I called Bobby to tell him I was divorcing him, and guess what—he begged for forgiveness." A weak self-deprecating laugh. "He said he'd end the affair immediately, that the other woman meant nothing to him. You're going to think I'm pathetic, and I am. I'm so pathetic I disgust myself. He said he wanted to take me to Crenshaw's this weekend, and I agreed to go, how stupid is that? Bobby promised that if I gave him a second chance, he'd spend the rest of his life making it up to me." More sobbing. "I should have walked away, but I couldn't. I just couldn't. I love him, God help me . . . I love him. Do you think I did the right thing? There's no one else I can talk to about this but you. Call me as soon as you get this message, okay?"

The message ended, and I closed the phone.

"Bobby told the woman he was ending it," Sister Mary Agnes said, "and she killed Riley."

"Maybe," I agreed, handing the phone back. "Regardless, you need to tell the police right away."

"Riley would hate for her dirty laundry to be made public."

"I don't blame her—but you have to do it anyway."

She nodded. "I know."

"Chief Hunter is here. I know him. He's a good man. Discreet. If he can keep it quiet, he will."

"He won't be able to. How could he?"

"Probably he can't."

Chief Hunter came around the corner with the fire chief. I glanced toward Wes. He'd relocated and was standing by my car, and I got his message. I wasn't leaving without giving him the goods. His eyes followed us as I led Sister Mary Agnes to Ellis. The fire chief hurried toward a man steadying a ladder. Wes raised his camera and began snapping photographs.

"Stop it," I mouthed at him and gave him my sternest look. I drew the edge of my hand across my neck, signaling that he was to kill it.

He lowered his camera and narrowed his eyes.

"Ellis," I said. "This is Sister Mary Agnes, one of Riley's oldest friends. I was scheduled to meet with her to discuss the foundation Riley created. En route, she listened to a message on her cell phone. She asked me to listen to it, and I did." I took a deep breath. "You should hear it."

I nodded in the nun's direction, and she handed him the phone. We stood silently as he noted the number and listened to the message.

"Thank you, Sister," he said. "I'll need to keep this phone for a while."

"Of course."

"How do you happen to have it in your possession?"

"Riley gave it to me in case of an emergency. She didn't like the idea of me driving without one."

"And how is it that you just noticed the message today?"

"I only use it when I drive, and I haven't driven since Riley died. I didn't even drive to her funeral. Another sister, knowing how upset I was, drove me there."

Ellis made arrangements for Sister Mary Agnes to come to the police station to give a statement later that day, thanked her again, and slipped the phone into his pocket.

"I need to talk to you, too, Josie."

"Give me one minute, okay?"

"Sure."

"We still need to talk about the foundation," I said as I walked Sister Mary Agnes back to her van.

"I'm glad to discuss it in whatever detail you'd like," she

said, "but I can tell you what Riley wanted very simply. She wanted to help people. People, not things. She loved fashion, but she loved people more."

"I see what you mean—that's why she combined the two." I thought for a moment. "Maybe I'll set up a scholarship program. To cover tuition and rooming expenses for people who want to study fashion." *Like Ava,* I thought.

"Riley would love that."

"There'll be enough money to fund other activities, too. At some point I'll ask your opinion about other options."

"Anytime." She opened her van door, then glanced back toward Gretchen's charred condo. "Do you think the same person who killed Riley set this fire?"

"Yes."

She stared at the building for a moment longer, then turned haunted eyes toward me. "The devil is among us."

Ellis asked me to come to the station house to provide a statement, but I begged off. I needed to clean up, and I had no additional information to give. He didn't push too hard, and at the end of our brief discussion, we agreed that if he had more questions, he'd let me know.

As I opened my car door, Wes tried to get me to comment, but I refused. I was full up with terror and rage and weak from breathing smoke and shock, and I didn't want to think about anything or talk to anyone. I drove straight home.

When I pulled into my driveway, Zoë, tall and model-thin with jet black hair and dark brown eyes, was climbing her porch steps. She held grocery bags in both arms, but managed to grin and waggle her fingers hello. Her grin died away as she took in my sooty face and clothes. She placed the bags on the porch and her hands on her hips. I got out of the car and faced her. She looked me up and down, then up again, then hurried down the steps and cut across the little lawn that separated our houses.

"What happened?" she asked.

A lump closed my throat, and for a moment, I couldn't speak. "Someone set fire to Gretchen's apartment. I got in the way of some smoke."

"Is Gretchen hurt?"

I shook my head. "She wasn't home. No one was hurt, not really. They had me on oxygen for a while." I tried to smile. "Call me crazy, but I thought I'd take a hot shower."

"Good idea. Have you eaten?"

"No. I'm not hungry."

"When you come downstairs from your shower, soup will be simmering on the burner and tea will be in your cup."

I smiled again, a better effort this time. My eyes watered. "You're such a good friend, Zoë."

"Scoot. I have groceries to put away."

When I got downstairs after scrubbing away layers of oily dirt, I found Zoë standing at my range, stirring a pot of her famous hearty beef tomato soup.

She didn't asked me any questions and I didn't volunteer any details. Instead, she sat beside me sipping Earl Grey tea as I consumed two bowls of soup and chatted about little nothings, the Johnny-jump-ups she expected to plant that afternoon, the origami swan she'd almost perfected, and how she and Ellis were talking about taking the kids to the Science Museum in Boston over the weekend.

As I listened to her cheerful chat, the viselike tension that had turned the muscles in my neck and shoulders into twisted steel eased. A faint hint of optimism that the police really would find Riley's killer and that Gretchen really would be safe began to edge out the dark foreboding that had enveloped me like a noxious cloud.

I didn't get back to work until after three. As I approached our front door, I gazed through the window and knew that everyone had heard the bad news. Cara, Sasha, Fred, Eric, and Ava stood in a loose circle, their expressions solemn. They looked up as I walked in.

"You heard about the fire. The good news is that Gretchen wasn't there," I said.

Cara sank into her chair, relief patent on her face. "Oh, thank goodness!"

"The news only talked about the fire and how someone had tried to kill Gretchen last week," Fred said.

"She's really all right?" Sasha asked.

"Yes," I replied. "She's fine. She was at Jack's when the fire started, and now the police have whisked her away to a safe house." I smiled. "It's pretty scary, isn't it?"

Everyone nodded and murmured something.

"Can we talk to her?" Sasha asked.

"I don't know. Cara, why don't you try her cell phone, and if you get her, put her on speaker."

We stood and watched Cara dial.

"It's gone to her voice mail," Cara said.

I felt everyone's eyes on me. I took the receiver. "Hi, Gretchen," I said. "We're all standing in the office. We just wanted to let you know we were thinking about you. We're so glad you're safe. Call when you can. 'Bye!"

Other voices chimed in with good-byes and talk-soons and take-cares, and then I punched the disconnect button. I looked around. Everyone was looking at me waiting for direction.

"I don't know about you guys," I said, smiling, "but I want to get back to work."

Upstairs in my office, I checked messages. Ty had called, concerned. I texted him that I was back at work and okay and that Gretchen was safe. Wes had called three times. I texted him that I had nothing to add at this point. Introducing Sister Mary

Agnes to Wes, which I knew was what he wanted, would be like tossing a minnow into a tank of piranhas.

I scanned my desk seeking out something that would distract me, but nothing fit the bill. Instead, I called Sasha and asked if she and Ava would come up and fill me in about their meeting with Dr. Walker.

Once they were settled, Sasha invited Ava to do the talking.

"Dr. Walker was so incredible," Ava exclaimed. "Sasha explained our dilemma about figuring out value without sales records, and he had all sorts of suggestions. For instance, he talked about something he called 'shared association.' We can add a modicum of allure to the clothing by identifying those garments in Riley's collection that were created by designers who dressed famous people. He gave us an example of Mrs. Wallis Simpson, who became the Duchess of Windsor. Riley owned several Mainbocher dresses, including one in the color known as 'Wallis Blue.'" Ava leaned forward in her chair, her curiosity and intellect a delight to witness. "Mainbocher developed the color to match the duchess's eyes."

"What do you think, Sasha? Is simply owning a dress by a certain designer in a certain color enough to affect value?"

She cocked her head. "It is if buyers care about it, and they do."

"How about the whole concept of shared association? Do you think it's fair play?"

"Oh, yes," she said earnestly. "As long as we keep our notes factual and don't state or imply an actual association, I think it's more than fair—in fact, I think it's appropriate. It provides a three-dimensional view that's highly relevant. The only downside is that it adds layers of research to the job."

I nodded. "I agree on all counts. Let's get cracking!"

As I walked downstairs with them, I asked Ava if she could stay late to help with tonight's workshop. She said she'd love to but couldn't. Sasha said she could and would be glad to.

I thanked her and peeled off toward the back of the warehouse, where we'd sectioned off a section for the vintage clothing I'd bought from Lana.

I wanted to take a look at the handbags. Having seen the variety of sizes, colors, and shapes that had covered Sasha's desk and the floor, it occurred to me that I might be able to find another example or two for the workshop. I reached the area and spotted three clear plastic tubs filled with bags stacked against the wall. I lifted the top one down and opened the lid. A barn-red Clarins Paris shoulder bag caught my eye, and I set it aside. In the second tub, I was tempted by a signature-patterned Chanel shoulder bag, but decided we had enough Chanels as examples. I opened the third tub and gaped—resting near the front was Riley's Louis Vuitton Neverfull tote bag.

I stared at it, recalling Riley's quick visit the day she'd been killed. She'd set her tote bag on the floor next to the jumble of bags near Sasha's desk. After we'd made our lunch date, she'd left. I pictured her walking across the parking lot holding only her car keys. At some point, I'd asked Sasha about the bags, and she'd said Eric was going to pack them up. He must have included Riley's bag along with the others. Why wouldn't he? It wasn't his place to question why this one bag, and it alone, wasn't empty. He might not have even noticed it. It was a bag and it was there.

I reached for the nearest wall phone and called Ellis to report the find, but his phone went to voice mail. I left a message asking him to call me back ASAP, then tried the Rocky Point police station's main number. Cathy told me he was unavailable, and I left another message.

I couldn't take my eyes off of the bag. The side ties hadn't been tightened, and I could see a legal-sized manila envelope bearing Max's firm's name and address preprinted in the upper left-hand corner. The envelope was unsealed, the flap tucked inside.

With Wes in mind, I ran upstairs and grabbed my camera,

then hurried back to the workstation and took some photos. I kept my eyes on it as I debated whether to wait for the police or take a peek myself. Ty would tell me I had to turn it over to the police, immediately and untouched. Ellis would say the same thing. Wes would take a different view. Situational ethics, my dad had taught me, was bull. Right and wrong never depended on the situation, he said, but solely on right and wrong. I sighed. If I didn't hurt any potential forensic evidence that might be present, and if I left everything as I found it, what possible harm could a quick peek do?

Feeling only slightly guilty, I grabbed a pair of long-handled tweezers and some latex gloves, the kind we used to protect our hands when polishing silver or applying polyurethane.

Ellis would be calling soon, and I had work to do before he did.

CHAPTER TWENTY-THREE

K eeping my eyes on Riley's tote bag, I snapped on the gloves and pushed gently at the envelope's sides until a boat-shaped gap appeared at the top. I could see the top of a multipage typed document bound in an old-style blue legal jacket. The heading read LAST WILL AND TESTAMENT OF RILEY JORDAN and below it, stamped in red, was COPY. I jiggled the envelope by tapping the sides with the tweezers. Behind the will were several photocopies of passport pages. At the bottom of the envelope I could just make out a business card.

I used the tweezers to slide each passport page upward until it was almost out of the envelope, so I could look at each one individually. They weren't consecutively numbered. The only thing they seemed to have in common was entry and departure stamps from Honduras. Holding the tweezers with my left hand, I used my right to take photos, then allowed each page to drop back into place. I tweezed out the business card and photographed it as well. The card read:

> **GUS SULLIVAN**
> **Confidential Investigations**
> **603.555.8941**

Riley had hired a private eye, or Max had done so on her behalf. From the area code I knew that Gus Sullivan was local to New Hampshire.

Using my gloved finger, I eased the envelope aside. Something shiny resting on the bottom of the bag caught my eye. Roughly triangular in shape, with two straight edges and one ragged edge, it appeared to be a ripped corner of something, about two inches long at its widest point. I tweezed it out. From the emulsion, I guessed it was part of a photograph, but I couldn't identify the subject matter. The image was shapeless and gray, a shadowy picture of nothing. I snapped a photo.

Cara's voice cackled over the PA system. Chief Hunter, she said, was on line two. I placed the emulsion back in the bottom of the bag where I'd found it, then took the call.

"You sounded as if you had news," Ellis said.

"Big-time," I acknowledged, my eyes fixed on the bag. "You're not going to believe it—I'm having trouble believing it myself. Riley left her tote bag here. She forgot it, the day she died. It got mixed in with other bags and stored. I saw it today while I was looking for something else."

"Someone will be there in ten minutes. I don't need to warn you not to touch anything."

"No, you don't," I said, feeling a sharp stab of guilt.

As soon as I hung up, I glanced at the big clock mounted high up on the far wall. It was nearly four. I called Wes.

"About time you called me back," he grumbled.

"Hi, Wes. How are you?"

"I'm okay, but that's beside the point. Who's that woman, and what did she tell you that made you take her over to Chief Hunter?"

"I have nothing to say about her, Wes. But I do have news. We need to meet."

"What is it?" he said, sounding grumpy.

"It's too hot for the phone," I whispered. "I'm in Durham and have an appointment at five. Is there any way you can meet me somewhere near here?"

Durham, a college town located about ten minutes inland, was home to the New England Museum of Design.

"Do you know the New England Museum of Design? Their building is on Durham Lake. I can meet you in the parking lot in half an hour."

"Done."

When Cara announced that Chief Hunter was here, I stashed my camera in a drawer and used the intercom to ask her to have Fred walk him to the Jordan section. No one was allowed inside our warehouse unescorted, not even a police officer, not even a police chief.

As usual, Ellis's demeanor and countenance revealed only what he wanted me to see, in this case, nothing.

"Which one is it?" he asked.

"That one," I said, pointing.

"I can't stay long," he said, "but I wanted to come myself so I could thank you in person." He looked at me with deceptive innocence. I knew that behind his wide-eyed, open expression lurked a sharp-eyed hawk. "I appreciate your bringing Sister Mary Agnes over to me and calling about the bag."

"Of course," I replied. "Was Sister Mary Agnes any help?"

"Very much so."

"Was this the first time you met her?"

"Why would you think that?" he asked, fencing.

"No reason. Just you didn't seem to know her and vice versa."

He leaned against the workbench, looking relaxed. "Bobby didn't include her on his list of Riley's friends."

"Why not?"

Ellis shrugged. "I assume he just forgot because he has a lot on his mind. Why? What do you assume?"

"Nothing. I just thought you meant he forgot to include her on purpose."

"Maybe he did."

"Because she was Riley's confidante?"

"It's possible."

I nodded. "I can see Bobby conveniently forgetting to mention it. Since she lives in a convent, he might hope that her existence would go unnoticed."

"Do you think she knows more than she's telling?"

"How can I answer that when I don't know what she's told you?"

"Fair enough. Sister Mary Agnes says that she doesn't know anything, that she's deeply shocked, and that Riley's voice mail was the first she heard that there was trouble in paradise."

"I can't imagine her lying."

"I agree. She might want to protect Riley, though," he said.

"From what?"

He shrugged again. "I don't know. I'm just poking around asking questions." He rested his elbows comfortably on the workbench, settling in. I glanced at the time. I had six minutes before I'd need to leave to meet Wes.

"Did Bobby actually call Crenshaw's Resort?" I asked, wondering if he'd answer, and if not, whether Wes would know.

"We're checking that out," he said.

"Any news about the fire at Gretchen's?"

"There's no question that it was arson," he replied, "but no one saw anything relevant, what with most everyone at work and all."

"Is there any forensic evidence?"

"Some. The fire investigator is optimistic that it will lead somewhere."

"That's great news," I said. "I'll keep my fingers crossed."

He stood up, took a jumbo-sized evidence bag out of an inside pocket and shook it gently to unfold it, then eased it over Riley's tote bag. He labeled and sealed it, then started toward the door. I walked alongside him.

"I know you can't tell me where Gretchen is," I said, "but . . . is she okay?"

"She's fine. A little rattled, which is to be expected, but she's fine."

I stood at the door and waved a last good-bye as he drove away. Once he was out of sight, I dashed back to the worktable, grabbed my camera, and ran upstairs. I had one minute before I needed to leave, and I used it to do an online search. That was plenty of time to learn that Gus Sullivan was a licensed private detective who'd been in business for eighteen years. He worked out of Rocky Point and said he specialized in personal, business, and insurance investigations, which seemed to cover all eventualities.

I downloaded the photos I'd just taken, then attached them to an e-mail to Wes. I hit the SEND LATER button, confirmed that I could access it on my BlackBerry, grabbed my tote bag, told Sasha I'd be back by six, and ran for my car.

"Whatcha got?" Wes asked as soon as I was out of my car.

He'd parked on the edge of the lot. Looking through the still mostly winter-bare trees, I could see Durham Lake. Touched by the late afternoon sun, the navy blue water shimmered as if it were covered with gold lace.

"A lot," I said, turning my attention to him. "First, tell me what you've learned about the arson investigation."

Wes half-closed his eyes, and I could tell he was wondering if I was playing him. I kept my expression neutral.

"The investigators are still inside," he said, deciding I had no hidden agenda, "collecting evidence. They found most of the bottle that contained the incendiary device. Believe it or not, they've already identified it. It had been emptied and cleaned, but it's a jar used exclusively by a high-end jelly company—Peterson's. Do you know them?"

"I've never bought their jellies, but I've seen them on the shelf. They're expensive."

"Yeah, no joke. It's like twice the price of most brands. What do you think that means?"

"I have no idea. What do you think?"

"According to my police source, the fire investigator thinks that particular jar was used because the glass is what they're calling 'delicate.'"

I nodded. "Oh, God, Wes, that's awful. They picked the jar because it would shatter easily." I turned toward the lake. Two people, a young man and an older woman, kayaked by, paddling in perfect harmony. "Can the police trace it?"

"To the store that sold it, yes, by the lot number, but since that store sells more of Peterson's than anywhere else in the region, they doubt that will help any. Except for one thing—that lot was delivered last Friday."

I looked back at Wes. "Someone planned this attack over the weekend. After they failed to kill Gretchen by shooting her."

"Looks that way," Wes said, nodding.

"It's horrific." I shook my head. "What else do they have?"

"They've confirmed the fuel—regular unleaded. They're hoping to find some fingerprints, but, you know, you gotta figure the arsonist has heard of fingerprints."

"True."

Wes paused and looked at me straight on, frowning a little. "We're pals, right? I mean, you know you can trust me."

I felt my brow furrow. "Sure," I replied, wondering what he was after.

"Sister Mary Agnes. I know that's the woman you were talking to at Gretchen's condo, and I know she's one of Riley's oldest friends. None of my sources will tell me squat about what she knows. I'm counting on you, Josie. What's so hush-hush?"

I knew that Wes was really a true-blue good guy, hardworking, honest, reliable, and sincere. I hadn't intended to tell him anything about Sister Mary Agnes, but meeting his earnest gaze, I changed my mind. The more I gave Wes, the more I'd get.

"I'll tell you what I know, but only if you promise not to bug her."

"I never bug people!" he protested, sounding hurt.

"Our usual arrangement, Wes."

He sighed, then sighed again, recognizing from my unwavering gaze that I wouldn't budge.

"Okay," he said, resigned. "Deal."

I told him that Sister Mary Agnes's cell phone was the one he called C2, explained how it came into her possession, and revealed Riley's last message.

"This is fab-to-the-max stuff, Josie," he said. He pulled a smudged sheet of lined notebook paper from his pocket and began taking notes.

After I repeated Riley's words, as close to word-for-word as I could get, I took in a deep breath and added, "There's more."

He looked up from his notes, his eyes glittering with anticipation.

"I need you to do some research," I said. "Riley left her tote bag at the warehouse, and it got mixed up with some other bags. Then today, I happened to be looking for something, and I saw it. It's a Louis Vuitton Neverfull bag, you know, the one with the side ties. The ties were loose, and I could see in."

"What did you see?" he asked, waggling his fingers to hurry me up.

I smiled at him. "I took photos."

He grinned and leaned back on his heels and raised his hand for a high-five slap. I tapped his palm with my fingers.

"You know how you told me Bobby has been to Honduras twice in the last six months?"

"What about it?"

"In the tote bag was an envelope from Riley's lawyer, and inside the envelope were photocopies of passport pages showing entrance and departure stamps from Honduras. Since Bobby's trip was out in the open and that resort told you he was with a woman, I'm betting these pages weren't from Bobby's passport."

"Hot petunia, Josie! And you got photos!"

I grimaced at his diction, then told him about Gus Sullivan's card and what I'd learned about him in my quick Google search, as well as the tiny bit of torn paper that I'd concluded had come from a photograph.

"When can I get the photos you took?" he asked, nearly salivating.

"When you promise to research the passport pages and see if you can learn anything about what Gus Sullivan discovered."

"You kidding me? I'm on it like white on rice!"

I dug my BlackBerry out of my bag, found the e-mail I had ready to go, and hit SEND.

"Okay," I said. "You got it."

One minute later, Wes's car jerked out of the lot. He might be a terrible driver, but he was one heck of a savvy investigative journalist. My plan had worked just as I'd intended. Wes would fill me in on everything that Ellis wouldn't even mention. If Wes succeeded as I expected, we'd soon identify Bobby's latest flame—and maybe have the name of Riley's killer.

CHAPTER TWENTY-FOUR

S ince I was already at the museum, I thought I'd see if Dr. Walker was available for a quick hello. I wanted to thank him for seeing Sasha and Ava, and there was no need for me to hurry back. Sasha, I knew, would have everything under control for tonight's workshop.

The New England Museum of Design was comprised of a series of sprawling low buildings connected by enclosed, all-glass breezeways. The contemporary buildings featured shallow, sloping roofs with deep overhangs covering flagstone and river-rock terraces. When it was built, a decade earlier, the innovative and energy-efficient design had won several architectural awards.

Dr. Walker was in and available. A beautiful blonde wearing a micro-miniskirt over purple tights with a slouchy sweater led me from the open reception area through a warren of cubicles to the fashion design wing. When her sweater drooped a certain way I could see she had a tattoo on her left shoulder. The design seemed to include musical notations on a staff. *Her and her boyfriend's song,* I silently wagered, wondering what she'd do if they broke up.

"What's your tattoo?" I asked.

She smiled. "Part of one of Mozart's themes. I'm a harpist, and he's my favorite composer."

I lost my private bet and reminded myself not to jump to conclusions. "Nice," I said.

She stopped at a door labeled DR. WALKER and knocked, then opened it without waiting for an invitation.

"Josie, come in, come in," he said, standing to greet me. "Thanks, Julianna."

I added my thanks to Julianna, and to him for seeing me without an appointment, then paused midstep as I took in the dazzling vista.

Dr. Walker's corner office featured walls of picture windows. The last time I'd been in his office, mid-February, the view had been spectacular—a winter wonderland, where every tree limb had been coated with a layer of white, fluffy snow. Now, in early spring, it was as if a set designer had rolled down a new backdrop. Clusters of pussy willows and stands of tall grasses grew alongside azaleas, just coming into bloom, and mountain laurel, not yet in bud. Beyond the bushes and grasses were stands of maple and birch. A small brown bird with a white belly flew by. A flash of shimmering teal caught my eye. Beyond the still-unfurling leaves trembling in the gentle breeze, a raft of ducks paddled by. Gazing at the bucolic scene, I felt my breathing slow and my muscles relax.

"How do you get any work done in here?" I asked.

"I position my desk so my back is to the window. It's my only hope."

"You're a man of incredible discipline. I don't think I could resist spending most of the day staring out the window. I thought it was spectacular in winter. This is even more beautiful."

"You should see it in autumn." He smiled and gestured toward a red leather chair positioned near his desk, and I sat down.

A knock sounded, and he called, "Come in."

A young man with gel-spiked hair entered and handed Dr. Walker some papers.

"Thanks, Dennis," he said.

Dr. Walker glanced at the documents, then handed a stapled set to me.

"I asked Dennis to photocopy the listing Riley gave me, the one I faxed over to you, in case we want to refer to it."

"Actually, I don't need to see you about the collection. Sasha has that well under control. Thank you for seeing her—and Ava. They said you were very helpful."

"Anytime. Actually, I should be thanking you. Your diligence in researching the collection helps me, too."

I nodded. He was right. "It works out well for both of us." I shifted position. "I'd like to tell you why I made the appointment for Thursday, so you can be thinking about it in advance." I paused. I was still horrified every time I thought of Riley's death. On some level it felt crass to be planning her legacy so soon after her funeral. Intellectually, I knew it wasn't, that the sooner I got the foundation up and running, the sooner we could begin helping people, but that's not how it felt. I mentally shook myself and continued. "As you may know, Riley's will created a foundation dedicated to fashion education. She appointed me as trustee. Max Bixby, Riley's lawyer, tells me that one of my first responsibilities is to establish award parameters. I'm consulting the people she knew best and those professionals in the field she most admired, which, of course, includes you. I'm hoping that on Thursday you can help me determine how to distribute the annual grants."

"How remarkable . . . I hadn't heard. The more I learn about her, the more impressed I am. What a woman." He shook his head a little, communicating shared grief. "I'll be glad to think about it."

"Thank you," I said. I glanced at the papers he'd handed me, his original notes about Riley's collection. As I scanned the detailed descriptions of the Bonnie Cashin day dress, the Tina Leser blue cashmere cardigan sweater, and the Claire McCardell coat with the pearl rosette button, melancholy came over me. "Looking at this list makes me think of Riley. It makes me sad."

He sighed, nodding. "I was very fond of her," he said.

I forced myself to smile and tapped the listing. "At least we know we're doing what Riley wanted. Did Sasha e-mail you a copy of Riley's spreadsheet, the updated list?"

"Yes—although I haven't seen it yet. I haven't mastered e-mail, I'm afraid." He held up his hand. "I know, I know, it's embarrassing. I'm pretty good with a fax machine, but I leave dealing with the computers to my staff. Dennis told me it had arrived, and I've asked him to print it out for me."

I smiled. "You can't be that bad! The listing you faxed us, this one, was created on a computer."

"Yes, using WordPerfect. Once they changed over the computers, oh, eight or nine years ago now, and switched software systems . . . well, let's just say that I'm a Luddite." He shook his head. "I printed out all my documents before the inevitable happened and they got lost. Or rather, before they got lost to me. That's why I faxed it. I had it in my files, thank goodness. God only knows where it is on the computer, or even if it's there after all this time."

"You're too funny," I said, charmed by his self-deprecating humor.

"I'm a dunce, is what I am."

"Hardly."

He walked me to the reception area. I thanked him again and strolled back to my car. A breeze coming from the east chilled me, and I shivered. My wishes for real spring warmth weren't working—it was still cold.

Riley's name wasn't mentioned during the workshop, but her presence was felt. I covered the topics she'd planned to discuss with as much enthusiasm as I could muster, which wasn't much.

The class's mood seemed to match my own. No one asked questions. No one gushed over the examples. No one seemed particularly engaged. I didn't take it personally. It was one of the dreaded "firsts," and had to be endured before we could even begin to feel normal.

Firsts were hard. After my dad's death, I'd fallen into a seemingly bottomless abyss of isolating grief. The first time I had to celebrate my birthday without him, I stayed home alone and wept. His birthday was just as bad. Thanksgiving, my favorite holiday, was worse. Christmas, worse still. Opening my own company, I'd struggled through seemingly endless pangs of wishing he were with me to share in my accomplishment. That first year, each holiday, event, and triumph spent without him crushed my heart. The second year was a tiny bit easier to endure. Now, six years later, while I still missed him every day, I no longer suffered from the shattering shock of loss that had pierced me like a thousand knife cuts. Time might not heal all wounds, but it healed many of them. Over time, I'd learned to cope, and I'd found that I could once again experience joy.

Becka and Kenna sat next to one another in the front row. Kenna, whose frequent smiles were unstoppable, a reflection of her sunny personality, didn't smile once. She'd lost some weight she could ill afford to lose. She looked gaunt. Becka had lost weight, too, and her normally creamy skin appeared parchment-dry and ghostly pale. As I lectured about handbag hardware, I found myself envisioning what they'd each look like in a brown-haired wig, a big-brimmed hat, and oversized sunglasses. They'd look like the security photo. I tried to stay in the present and not speculate.

"I'm sorry not to participate more," Kenna said after the workshop. "I guess I'm just not in the mood."

"Understandable," I said.

"Your lecture was good," Becka said, her tone flat.

"Thanks," I replied, wishing they didn't feel the need to be polite, yet appreciating their efforts.

I was relieved when it was over.

I awoke Wednesday morning to the patter of steady rain. Walking past ancient stands of lilac trees laden with low-hanging, sweet-smelling purple and white clusters of blossoms was one of the pleasures of May, but today it was still April, and it was cold and wet and dreary.

Wes was sitting in his car by Prescott's main entrance when I drove up at eight fifteen. As soon as I stepped inside, he ran to join me. I turned off the alarm and switched on the lights.

"You're here bright and early," I said.

"I've got news."

"Come on in. Let me put some coffee on," I said, leading the way inside.

"Do you have any Coke?"

"Sure," I said, extracting a can from the mini fridge and handing it over. "So what's your news?"

"Are you sure you don't want to sit down?" he asked, grinning. He took a swig of Coke. "Bobby's scheduled a news conference for today at noon. My source tells me he's going to admit to all his tomcatting, and he's going to acknowledge talking to Riley shortly before her death."

The perking sounds and rich coffee aroma were comforting, serving as an odd counterpoint to the anything-but-comfortable implications of Wes's announcement.

"There's more—he expects to be named as a person of interest in her murder."

I stared at him, stunned. "Oh, my God."

"Yeah. Now we're ready to rock and roll!"

"Why would he hold a press conference?"

Wes grinned again. "To control the story."

"That's sick."

"It's smart. It's his only hope. Anyway, I thought you'd be interested."

"I am," I acknowledged.

"If you catch it live, look for me! I'll be up front and in his face."

As I watched him drive out of the lot heading toward Portsmouth, I shook my head, astonished at Bobby's audacity—he hoped to control the story. I poured myself a cup of coffee, then pushed through the door to the warehouse to say hello to Hank, thinking that the only thing I knew for certain was that I was glad I wouldn't have to see it in person.

At noon, I succumbed to curiosity and clicked on the local news station's Web site. I settled back to watch Bobby's live news conference, which they were broadcasting in real time. Quinn was standing near a podium with another man. I recognized him from chamber of commerce breakfasts as a criminal attorney. His name, if I recalled right, was Chuck Something-or-Other.

The camera panned the room. I recognized two national cable TV news reporters and one from a Boston TV station. Wes was sitting in the front row. He had a notebook perched on his thigh. Every seat was filled, and several people stood at the back. I counted seats. The room was set for thirty. I shook my head, amazed that more than thirty reporters, or their employers, were interested enough to attend this news conference. I wondered if Bobby had planned it in a cynical attempt to control the story, as Wes suggested, or whether his motivation was even darker, whether he hoped to milk the publicity for all it was worth.

Bobby entered the room from somewhere on the left and walked to the podium. His chest was blocked by a wall of microphones. Strobe lights flashed. A murmur of anticipation rippled through the crowd. He looked as handsome as ever, and I wondered if he was wearing makeup. Bobby tapped one of the microphones to ensure it was on, and the crowd grew quiet, the kind of quiet that isn't really quiet at all, like still night air in the moments before thunder shatters the silence. Bobby looked out over the crowd and spoke directly into the camera with polished élan. I felt an invisible connection, an inexplicable bond, as if he were speaking only to me.

"I'm Bobby Jordan. My wife, Riley Jordan, was murdered just over a week ago. I asked for this time together so I could tell you the truth, and the truth is that I lied to her, and I lied to the police. My lies had nothing to do with her murder, but regardless, there is no excuse for lying to the police. I am ashamed of what I've done." He took a beat, then continued. "I apologize, and I'm determined to tell the whole truth, here and now. I lied to the police about a disposable cell phone. I lied because I used that phone for private calls I didn't want anyone to know about. The police asked me about it, and I denied owning it." *That explains the phone Wes dubbed C1,* I thought. "I've decided to come forward and publicly admit my terrible lapse in judgment because Riley deserves it. I don't want my irrelevant lies to distract the police from doing a proper investigation. I did terrible things, but I didn't kill my wife." He choked and looked away for two beats, then turned back to face the camera. "I'll answer your questions now."

A cacophony erupted as reporters vied for Bobby's attention. Bobby pointed at a middle-aged man in the front row. As soon as Bobby made his choice, the room quieted.

"Why are you telling the truth now?" the reporter asked with what to my ear sounded like an Italian accent.

"Because I am ashamed," Bobby said, not looking at the reporter, speaking only to the camera. "As a week has passed without the killer being caught, I realize that I need to tell the truth. The police were wasting time trying to learn my secrets, and I wanted their full attention to be on catching the murderer.

My personal shame means nothing. I loved my wife more than life itself."

Bobby's earnest, sound-bite-sized, cliché-riddled comments were tailored for his TV audience, and his frequent use of micropauses added panache to his presentation. I wondered if he'd had media training or if he was a natural.

"Yes, sir," the same reporter said, polite but insistent, "but why *now*? What happened that led you to take this step *today*?"

Bobby tried two more times to spin his confession as a spontaneous and righteous search for justice before finally admitting that the timing had been influenced by a breaking story. A woman reporter outshouted her colleagues to ask if it wasn't true that since a gossip tabloid planned to publish dozens of incriminating text messages he'd sent Tamara, the New York City waitress, essentially he'd had no choice. Yes, he said, looking like a puppy caught gnawing a shoe, ready to hear that he was a bad dog, but not actually contrite.

Ouch, I thought. No wonder Bobby was doing a mea culpa.

Bobby, still standing tall, but with tension tightening the muscles in his neck and jaw, called on Wes next.

"Did Riley catch you in bed with someone?" Wes asked, about as subtle as a steamroller. "Is that why she decided to divorce you?"

"She wasn't going to divorce me."

"Follow-up!" Wes shouted amid the chaotic calls for attention. "I understand she changed her mind and decided to give you a second chance. What is it she learned that made her decide to divorce you in the first place?"

"Riley was a remarkable woman," Bobby said, raising his chin defiantly. "She was good clear through, and she had a generous heart. She learned I'd been unfaithful, but she said she was willing to forgive me. I asked if I could take her away that very weekend so I could begin to prove to her how much I loved her. She agreed. I hung up from Riley and made a reservation at a resort." He shook his head and cast his eyes down for a moment, before once again looking into the camera. "Then she died. She died before I could beg her forgiveness in person."

"Did you speak to her again?" a young woman asked. I recognized her as an on-air reporter from a Portland, Maine, TV station.

"No," he said. "I called Riley back, but her phone went to voice mail. She had a speaking job that night, lecturing on her favorite topic, vintage clothing, and I tried her there, too, but she hadn't arrived yet. While I'm sick that the last conversation I had with my beautiful wife was about my infidelity, I derive some solace from knowing that she was aware of how much I loved her and of how determined I was to save our marriage. I will always be grateful that she was prepared to give me another chance."

"According to the phone logs, you called her back twenty minutes later. Are you saying that making a hotel reservation took that long?" Wes yelled, his baritone carrying over the general shouts.

"No," Bobby replied. "Before I called the resort, I spoke to the woman with whom I'd become involved and ended our relationship."

A thunderous tidal wave of demands to know the other woman's name pounded Bobby. He stood like a bulwark amid thrashing surf. I'd never seen a stonier expression. I listened to him refuse to name her for more than a minute, then clicked off the Web site. I'd had enough.

At four, when I next checked the Web site, they were playing a Web camera interview between Wes and Tamara.

"I don't know who he called," Tamara announced with big eyes and a contemptuous snort, "except that it wasn't me. He broke up with me months ago."

Wes's face appeared, facing the camera. "When asked that question directly," he said, his voice low, "Bobby Jordan refused to answer. There is no record of his calling anyone from his office, his regular cell phone, or the disposable cell phone he used to contact other women with whom he was having illicit affairs. According to a reliable source, the police are currently checking likely pay phones."

I exited the Web site again.

I called Ellis and asked if I could speak to Gretchen. He said no, but that he'd be glad to pass on a message. I asked him to tell her I missed her and was thinking of her, and he assured me that he would. I felt out of touch and disconnected, and my simple message felt inadequate to let her know how much I cared.

I decided to leave for the day, a little earlier than usual. I straightened my desk, placing like items on one another, forming several unified piles. Auction notes topped catalogues, and my accountant's analysis topped Gretchen's revenue reports. I picked up the photocopied inventory that Dr. Walker had handed me earlier, trying to decide where to place it, or whether, since I already had his fax, I should just throw it away, when all at once I realized there was an inexplicable incongruity.

I reread Dr. Walker's description of the Claire McCardell coat. Lavender. Gray. Flannel. Pearl rosette button. I clicked on the spreadsheet Riley had created, the one Ellis had e-mailed us. The coat was there, but no button was mentioned. That was consistent with the other entries—Riley had skipped most details. I found the inventory that Dr. Walker had faxed over. The same coat was listed. It had been typed in the same font, and it was positioned in the same place in the document. On the copy Dr. Walker had given me today, though, the line ended with the reference to the button. On the faxed copy, that space was blank. I held the two documents side by side and compared all of the listings. The two documents were identical, except for this one discrepancy.

I called Dr. Walker and got him. "I have a kind of off-the-wall question," I said. "The copy of Riley's list you gave me when I stopped by—are you positive it's the same one you faxed over? Could there be more than one version floating around?"

"More than one version?" he repeated, bewildered. "No. There's just that one document, the one I printed out years ago. Why?"

I stared at the paper, stunned and horrified. My mouth opened, but no words came. There was only one possible explanation—someone had seen the button listed on the fax and, with malice and calculation, deleted it.

"Thanks, Dr. Walker," I said, ignoring his question. "I'll see you Thursday. 'Bye." I hung up before he could ask me anything else.

I thought back to the day I received the fax. We were all busy. Every time I'd been in the office, the phone had been ringing nonstop.

I closed my eyes and pictured the scene. Bottles of Wite-Out sat on everyone's desk and on the utility shelf near the photocopier—which was out in the open and available for general use. It would be easy enough to take the fax from the machine and go to the restroom, or, as I thought of it, simply to stand with your back to the room, as if you were looking out the window, perhaps, and apply Wite-Out. Two quick swipes and you'd cover up the reference to the button. By the time you walked to the copier, it would be dry. Slip the page into the feeder and hit the copy button. Once you have the replacement page in hand, slide the adulterated page into the paper shredder, and walk the document back to the fax machine for someone else to discover. The entire procedure would take thirty seconds, not more. I opened my eyes.

I remembered the scene well. In addition to my staff, two customers had stopped by that day: Becka and Kenna.

I needed to talk to Wes.

CHAPTER TWENTY-FIVE

I was going to call you," Wes said, his tone urgent and serious. "We need to talk."

Over the phone line, I heard a foghorn, its blare echoing like a death wail. I looked out my window. The rain had stopped, but it was still cloudy.

"It sounds like you're near the ocean," I said. "Can you meet at our dune in ten minutes?"

"Done."

I got there first and clambered up the hill. The sand was wet. Thick fog rolled off the water. The waves were choppy and angled to the shore, a sure sign of a deadly rip tide. If it were summer, unwary or weak swimmers would risk being dragged out to sea.

Wes parked in the breakdown lane and hurried up the dune, climbing sideways.

"Those passport pages you found?" he said as soon as he reached me. "They aren't Bobby's. The dates of travel are right, but the page numbers and stamp placements are off. The pages belong to someone who traveled to Honduras on the same dates as he did."

"Just like we thought. They must be part of the proof Max gave Riley."

"Along with photos, which she tore up and threw away."

"Except that one little piece fell into her tote bag." I paused. "Max won't tell the police anything, right?"

"Right. Gus won't either. Since he was working for Riley's

lawyer, privilege extends to him—and privilege extends beyond death. No matter whether they want to tell the police or not, they can't. Any ideas on how I can trace the passport pages?"

I thought for a moment. "How about looking at people's travel schedules. For instance, was Becka or Kenna out of the country during those times?"

"I checked, but the info is inconclusive. Those dates match Hitchens's vacations—so Becka was off work. She won't talk to me, but according to my police source, she was out of town both times. She says that one time she was visiting friends in L.A., and the other time she was hiking in the Adirondacks, alone. Which might be true. She's done stuff like that before."

"Can't the police check with airlines?" I asked.

"Not without a court order, which they can't get without probable cause. When Judge Gleason refused their application, he accused them of going fishing. He wasn't happy."

"I get his point, I guess. What about Kenna?"

"She says she was in Orlando with her family during the first period—public schools were off, too—but they drove their own RV and stayed with friends along the way, not at campgrounds, so there's no paper trail. The friends the police have spoken to so far refuse to discuss it. During the second period, Kenna says, she was working her regular schedule. Personnel data support it, but since she's in charge of submitting vacation information to the outside company that handles the Blue restaurant chain's payroll, she could say anything she wants." He shrugged. "I haven't found anyone who's contradicting her."

"So we have nothing. Now what?"

"I keep pecking away. I confirmed Bobby's call to that Lake Winnipesauke resort, Crenshaw's. He made the reservation. From the phone log, the police know that his call to Crenshaw's was made from the Blue Dolphin's main line, and that he made it about fifteen minutes after hanging up from Riley on C1, the disposable cell phone."

"He didn't use that phone to call his girlfriend to break up with her, though," I said, thinking aloud.

"No."

"If he has one disposable cell phone, maybe he has others."

"Maybe—but if so, why wouldn't he come clean about it? I mean, it's his own story, you know?" Wes asked.

I stared out over the roiling ocean, ideas flooding my brain. *Lies on top of lies,* I thought, *can create a fictional picture that looks as true to life as if it were real.* I turned to face him. "Maybe it's *all* a lie, Wes. If Bobby *intended* to kill Riley from the start, it's possible that he created a fictional affair so he could pretend to end it at just the right time. I mean, think about it. He could have called Crenshaw's not to set up a romantic weekend, but to create reasonable doubt for a jury. He'd say that since Riley was giving him a second chance, he had no motive for murder."

Wes pursed his lips, thinking. "Except that according to the message Riley left for Sister Mary Agnes, she really was giving him a second chance. And he really did go to Honduras with a woman. And there really was a twenty-minute window between his call from Riley and his attempts to call her back."

I nodded. "You're right. Although taking a girl to Honduras, well, that could have been a fling, not an ongoing affair. As for the lag time between calls—that could have been to give him time to get his ducks in a row before firing off the next salvo in his campaign to get away with murder."

"Good one, Josie!" Wes said.

"Or," I added, ignoring his tasteless compliment, "maybe he didn't break up with her at all. Couldn't the breakup be a hoax?"

Wes nodded and low-whistled. "That'd take a real dog, huh?"

"Yes," I agreed.

"I'll keep digging and get back to you. Anything else for me?"

I shook my head. "No. I have a question, though. Any news about the forensic accounting investigation? Last I heard, the police were looking into Quinn and Kenna."

He nodded. "They're just about done. It looks like there's nothing there. The money Bobby kept overseas is properly listed in his records. It looks like Kenna miscoded an entry or two, but according to the police accountant, that's actually a pretty good record. Most bookkeepers screw up dozens of postings."

"So the only motive we have left is Bobby's infidelities."

"Which doesn't eliminate Kenna," Wes said.

"True," I agreed.

He flashed a grin and walked down the dune. I watched as he drove away, then followed.

I hadn't told Wes about my suspicion that someone had altered Dr. Walker's fax. I needed to think it through and investigate further. I knew what had to be done, but I dreaded it—I couldn't think of anything worse than having to interrogate my staff.

CHAPTER TWENTY-SIX

T hat night I slept fitfully and awoke just before three with the blankets on the floor and the sheets twirled around my ankles. I was numb with cold. Evidently, Thursday was off to a frigid start. I straightened the bedclothes, turned over, and tried to get back to sleep with no luck.

At four o'clock, I gave up, went downstairs, and sent Gretchen an e-mail.

Hi Gretchen,
I miss you! A quick q: Do you remember the faxed inventory we got from Mr. Walker on Friday, the day of Riley's funeral? According to the time stamp, it arrived at 12:37 p.m. Do you know who took it from the machine?
Josie

When I got to work that Thursday morning at seven, Gretchen's reply was waiting for me. I guessed she hadn't been able to sleep well either.

Hi Josie,
Thanks for the messages. I miss you, too!
*   Re: Dr. Walker's fax: I was sitting at my desk, on the phone with I don't recall who, when the fax machine clicked on. I watched the first page kick out, wondering if it was one of the*

asphalt companies' bids, then I got distracted by the call—I don't remember why. There was a lot going on, I remember that for sure . . . a boutique customer came in and Becka and Kenna stopped by. I didn't think about the fax again. Why? Is it missing or something?

I hope to see you soon . . . I'm going nuts not working!
Gretchen

At ten o'clock, once Fred had arrived, I gathered everyone together.

"I have a question that's going to sound a little crazy," I said, forcing a smile, glancing around. "Do you remember the fax we got from Dr. Walker? It listed Riley's vintage clothing collection as of about twelve years ago. It arrived at 12:37 P.M. on Friday, the day of Riley's funeral."

Everyone did.

"Who took it from the machine?"

Sasha looked blank. Fred shrugged. Ava and Cara shook their heads.

"Does anyone remember who brought it to Cara's desk?"

No one recalled.

"I can imagine how odd my questions must seem to you, but please bear with me. Where were you when the fax came in—just after twelve thirty?"

"That's my usual lunchtime," Cara said, "and I know I was in the staff room eating. I remember that day in particular, because I had leftover pot roast—it's my favorite."

"I was with you," Ava said, smiling. "I remember because it smelled incredible."

"That's right. I remember your lunch, too. You'd added avocado to tuna salad. I'd never thought of that—it looked delicious."

I turned to Fred. "How about you?"

"That was the day Mrs. Sheridan stopped by," he said. He pursed his lips, thinking. "At twelve thirty, I was on the loading dock with her fire box. Then I was in the warehouse for a while looking at some fireplace screens, then I was at my desk."

"Did you see the fax at all?" I asked him.

"No. I didn't know that Dr. Walker had sent it in until I heard Sasha and Ava discussing it later that day."

"Sasha?" I asked.

She looked fretful. "I don't remember, and I didn't notice a thing. I'm sorry."

"No problem," I assured her. "What about Kenna and Becka? Does anyone remember what they were doing while they were here? Could they have picked it up?" From everyone's expressions, I could tell that my questions were striking them as increasingly strange. I didn't blame them. They sounded strange to my ear, too. "It's no biggy—I'm just curious."

"Gretchen gave them coffee," Fred said. He pushed up his glasses. "I remember because she made a fresh pot and asked us all if we wanted any." He shrugged. "They sat at the guest table, chatting with whoever wasn't on the phone or working at that moment. Then Kenna wanted to see that purse in the boutique. When they got back, she helped Gretchen retrieve Hank's mouse from under the copier, while Becka stood at the window. That's it, I think."

No one else had anything to add. I thanked them and walked back upstairs. No one remembered much of anything about the fax—why would they? We got faxes all the time, and everyone was busy doing ordinary things: reading, talking on the phone, eating lunch, and chatting with customers. It all sounded logical and reasonable, except that the fact remained that someone had altered the fax.

My money was on Becka.

Upstairs, Hank jumped onto my lap and arranged himself like a comma. As I petted him, I found myself thinking that everything came back to the pearl rosette button. Someone had changed the fax to hide the fact that the McCardell coat had a button on it. Why? The only reason I could think of was that he or she hoped to use that button to replace the one that had been lost during Riley's murder. Margo, the nice woman from EZK, said there wasn't any way to identify individual buttons, but I wondered if there was any way to trace sets. I brought up their Web site and clicked through to the site map. A page called "Legacy" caught my eye.

"Welcome to our heritage," the text at the top began. "You can sort by the date the woman joined EZK, or by her name. If you click on a member's name, her bio opens in a separate window, and all of her relatives are listed. If you know any part of anyone's name, you can search for her by just that part—her married name, for example."

At the bottom of the page, it said, "We do our best to keep up with our sisters! When anyone changes her names for whatever reason, marriage, divorce, business, whatever . . . we track it. Has your name changed? Do you know someone whose name has changed? E-mail us the news!"

Cara buzzed up to tell me that Eric was leaving to go to Rocky Point Nursery to buy some shrubs, that Ava had to leave early to fill in for someone at her waitress job, and that Sasha was going to cover the phone when she went to lunch. I thanked her for the update and turned my attention back to the Web site. I started my search with Kenna.

Kenna Duffy, née Kenna Mitchell, had been a member of EZK when she was at college back in the 1990s. She had no relatives who had ever been a member of the sorority. Becka Dowling had also been a sorority member, and she also didn't have a legacy connection. Riley, I knew, had been a member, and I learned that she didn't have a legacy connection, either. Even though Quinn had apparently been eliminated as a suspect, I checked him out, too, just in case. He didn't seem to have any female sorority sisters. Nor, I confirmed, did his wife have any connection to the sorority. It looked like the only person connected to Riley who'd received a set of buttons was Bobby's grandmother, Babs Miller. According to the entry, she'd joined the sorority in 1938.

I called Bobby and got him at the Blue Dolphin.

"Your grandmother was a sorority girl—Zeta Kap. Every girl got a set of four buttons, pearl rosette buttons. Assuming the button on the gray coat is one of them, do you know where the others are?"

He paused, thinking. "I don't remember Riley using any of the others—but to tell you the truth, I didn't know that she'd used this one, or that my grandmother had."

"I understand," I said. "I didn't see them in the house. Do you have any idea where they are now?"

"The police told me the pearls are real," he said, and I wondered if he was trying to change the subject.

"I hadn't heard, but I'm not surprised," I replied, following his lead. "The setting is platinum."

"Then probably, Riley put them in my safe. She kept all her jewelry there. In a box. You know the kind of box I mean. It's specially designed with hooks and little compartments."

"In your safe where? At work?"

"Yeah. In Kenna's office."

I recalled seeing it. When I'd stopped by, I'd paused for a moment to say hello to Kenna. I'd noticed that there was a safe in back of her, and that it was big and solid-looking. "Can you check and see if the buttons are there?"

"Now?"

"Would you mind?" I asked.

"No problem. Hold on."

I listened to the Blue Dolphin's on-hold message describing the week's specials—baked stuffed lobster and buckets of little-necks, the first of the season. I started salivating.

"The jewelry box is there," Bobby said. "Right where it should be."

"And the buttons?"

"Right—they're there, too."

"How many of them?"

"Two."

One on the McCardell coat. Two in Riley's jewelry box. Where was the fourth button?

"So one is missing—and you don't know where it is?"

He paused again, maybe thinking it through, like me, and wondering if any of the suspects besides him had a connection to the sorority.

"I have no idea," he said. "Maybe Riley gave it to someone."

I couldn't imagine Riley, known for valuing tradition and heritage, giving away one of Babs Miller's buttons. The bottom line was that either Bobby didn't know where the missing button was, or he wasn't telling. Either way, I had no leverage to make him come clean, and I couldn't see how I could get any.

Kenna's eliminated as a suspect, though, I thought. With the safe located behind her desk, if she'd needed to replace a button, all she would have had to do was take it. *Or not.* If it were me, I'd be too scared. As far as I knew, she and Bobby were the only people who had unfettered access to the safe. Talk about raising a red flag. If anyone came looking for Babs Miller's buttons—like me—Kenna would have turned a spotlight on herself. I shook my head. No way was Kenna involved.

Tracking the button had been a good idea, but from what I could tell, it was just another dead end.

Cara buzzed up to tell me that Wes was on line two. I thanked her and punched the blinking button.

"Nancy Patterson just called Blackmore's to see if the button is ready," Wes said. "He told her to come in at noon tomorrow."

I heard myself inhale sharply and felt my pulse spike. "Did anyone recognize her voice?" I asked, knowing the police were listening in.

"No." He lowered his voice. "The police are already at the

shop, setting up their cameras and planning their on-site surveillance." Before I could comment, he added, "There's more. Go to our Web site. We just uploaded an interview."

I brought up the *Seacoast Star*'s Web site and saw a frozen image of Wes standing in front of a blue backdrop featuring his newspaper's logo. My cursor hovered over the triangular PLAY button.

"Is your paper moving into TV?"

"Nah. We're just adding a little multimedia content to the Web site, you know? Go ahead, play it."

I clicked the PLAY button.

"Nancy Patterson," Wes said into an unseen camera. "A common name. A name that has come up in connection with the Riley Jordan murder investigation, possibly as a made-up identity. According to the police, a woman named Nancy Patterson bought a gun on Thursday from a Maine dealer—the day before Gretchen Brock was shot and two days after Riley Jordan's murder. Here's what Roland LeBlanc told me just hours ago."

The video went black, then came up showing a parking lot and part of a log building.

"What did you see?" Wes asked a man standing next to him.

"I didn't wait on her myself," Roland said with the laconic delivery and downeast twang of a native Mainer. "My boss did."

"Did you see her?"

"Ayup."

"What did she look like?"

"Don't know. She wore a big straw hat and sunglasses. Couldn't see her face."

"What did she buy?"

"Don't rightly know," Roland said. "The police took the receipts."

"Where is your boss now?"

"Fishing. He took his boat out for a couple of days."

"According to official reports," Wes said into the camera, "the Coast Guard is searching likely coves along the Maine coast for an eighteen-foot boat named *Gone Fishing*. If you spot it, you're asked to call them immediately."

Wes's image faded away and was replaced by an 800 number running along the bottom like a banner.

"A woman bought a gun on Thursday?" I said into the phone.

"Amazing, huh? She bought it around 7:00 P.M. The store stays open until eight on Thursdays. No security cameras, can you believe that? At a gun shop? My sources tell me she bought a rifle, but I don't know which model yet."

"It's so frightening, Wes," I whispered.

"Yeah," he agreed sounding not the least bit scared. "Catch ya later."

I could tell from Wes's high-energy sign-off that he felt exhilarated, not upset at all. I, on the other had, felt seriously shaken. I tried to imagine how the woman calling herself Nancy Patterson was feeling. Was she calm and controlled, planning the alibi she'd use to cover her trip to Blackmore's the next day? Was she sitting with Bobby, coldly calculating their next moves? I considered the timeline.

For whatever reason, Riley got suspicious that the rumors about Bobby's infidelity were true.

She asked Max for help.

Max hired Gus.

Gus took compromising photos and e-mailed them to Max.

Max called Riley, probably on Monday, the day she called his office wanting an immediate appointment.

As soon as Max told her he had news, she would have asked him to forward the photos to her so she could look at them right away, and privately. She saw them, freaked out, and picked up the phone to schedule an appointment. She must have been heartsick, beside herself, and ready to act.

When she saw Max on Tuesday, he would have handed her printouts of the photos. Sickened by them, she probably tore them to bits, and one tiny piece accidentally fluttered into her tote bag.

I shook my head. It couldn't have happened that way. If it had, the police, having commandeered Riley's computer, would have found the photos. I considered alternatives until a possible explanation came to me.

At Prescott's, we deal in huge graphic files all the time. Sometimes it's a hassle since many e-mail systems don't allow large files to be sent or delivered. Our solution is to create private pages on our Web site where we post the images. By uploading photographs to a Web site, and giving its unique URL only to the people we want to be able to access it, we make it easy for clients with limited e-mail capacity to see the images. If they can access a Web site, they can view the photos.

I wondered if Gus had done something similar. In addition to hidden pages on a Web site, he could use an online photo scrapbook or an FTP site. Whichever option he chose, I bet he did what we do: e-mailed the instructions; otherwise customers have no way of finding the location or knowing the password.

I called Ellis and got him at his desk at the police station.

"I know you're going to tell me it's none of my business, but I had an idea I wanted to pass on. Am I correct that you didn't find any photographs in Riley's possession, ones she might have looked at just before she died? Like in the glove compartment of her car?"

"What are you asking, Josie?"

I bit my lip. There was no way around it. I had to reveal what I'd seen. "While I was waiting for you to come and pick up Riley's tote bag, I peeked inside. The side ties weren't pulled tight, so I could see in without touching anything. I noticed a bit of ragged emulsion, and it got me thinking about photos and why she might have ripped them up."

"I'm listening," he said.

"If Max showed her photos of Bobby and another woman, for example, it wouldn't surprise me to learn she'd destroyed them. I figure that a little piece fell into her bag and she didn't even notice it."

"And if she had?"

"After the initial shock wore off, I bet she wanted to see the photos again. That would be my reaction. It's like poking your tongue at a tooth that's aching. It hurts and you don't want to do it, but you can't resist. The point is that almost all photography nowadays is digital, and some of the files are too big for some personal e-mail systems and most smart phones. Assuming I'm right, if whoever Riley hired to take them uploaded them to a Web site for convenient viewing, they probably e-mailed instructions on how to access the site. If the e-mail simply said to go to this Web site, whoever you have reviewing Riley's e-mails might not have realized its significance."

"This is good thinking, Josie. Thanks. I'll follow up right away."

As soon as he found the photos, he'd know the killer's identity. Now was the time to call in a favor. I needed Wes's police source to tell him who it was immediately. I called him, and his phone went directly to voice mail.

"Call me, Wes," I said. "It's urgent. I have news."

I couldn't concentrate.

I had the itchy sense that something significant was happening or that it was about to happen. Things were closing in. Something was going to break long before noon tomorrow.

Becka.

It has to be her, I thought.

CHAPTER TWENTY-SEVEN

After staring at the phone for fifteen minutes waiting for Wes to call me back, I got up and paced, walking from my desk to the cabinet containing my rooster collection and back. Back and forth. Back and forth, over and over again.

I wanted to be there when the killer realized the jig was up.

I stood near one of the guest chairs and dialed Becka's number at Hitchens University. Her direct line went to voice mail. I didn't leave a message. I called the English Department, and the secretary told me Becka had called in sick. I tried her home number and got her answering machine. Her cell phone went to voice mail.

I pushed the button for a new dial tone and called Wes again.

"I was just about to call you," he said. "I was in an interview before, so my phone was off. What's up?"

"Where's Becka? Do you know?"

"She's not at work?"

"No. They said she's out sick, but she doesn't answer at home or on her cell."

"Maybe she's sleeping," he said, not understanding my urgency. "Why do you want her?"

I repeated the idea I'd passed on to Ellis, then added, "It's got to be Becka, and I want to be there when she's brought in for questioning. How can we learn where she is?"

"I've got an idea," he said. "I'll call you right back."

I continued to pace, thinking. It all came back to the button.

A pearl rosette button Hank found. Finding its history had been easy. Margo was helpful. The sorority's Web site was impressive.

"Oh, wow," I said aloud.

I stood in the middle of the carpet. Implications ricocheted in my brain, boom, boom, boom. Riley's Burberry trench coat had been buttoned to the neck. Riley decided to give Bobby a second chance. The fax Dr. Walker sent had been altered. Hitchens's vacations aligned with Bobby's trips to Honduras.

How could I not have known? I asked myself. *I didn't want to know,* I answered. *That explains why the police haven't been able to find the phone Bobby used to break up with his mistress. He told her in person.* I sank onto the love seat, my mouth open, my heart racing. Or he hadn't told her at all. I couldn't believe it. I couldn't stand it. I felt sick.

I knew who'd killed Riley—and I knew why.

Seconds later, I gave myself a mental shake, grabbed my tote bag, and ran for the stairs.

As I dashed by Cara, I called, "I'll be back."

I dialed Wes as soon as I was on the road.

"Meet me at the Blue Dolphin," I said. "Bring a camera. Stay out of sight."

I parked in the city lot on Market Street and jogged across the street, entering the alley that ran behind the Blue Dolphin on the far end. As I rounded the corner, a man wheeling a dolly came into sight. I slowed my pace to give him time to reach the street. As soon as he'd turned onto Bow Street, I scooted up the alley and stepped behind a copper tub filled with pansies and tall grasses at the Ceres Street end. By leaning to the right I had an unobstructed view of the front door. I watched Ellis drive up in his SUV and park at the curb. A Portsmouth patrol car rolled to a stop just behind him. Two men, one in uniform, one in plainclothes, stepped out of the Portsmouth police vehicle. Ellis and Detective Brownley joined them on the sidewalk. Ellis said something, and the man in the suit nodded, then the four of them strode inside.

Within minutes, I heard a rustling in the tub to my left and turned, expecting to see a squirrel or a bird. It was Wes.

"You picked a good spot," Wes said, "assuming what we're supposed to see happens out front."

"It will."

"What do you know?"

"I figured out who they're after. Given the timing, I'm certain the arrest will occur here."

"You know who it is?" he asked.

"Yes."

"Who?"

A toddler ambled past the alley opening, catching my attention. A young woman wearing a lightweight red anorak, his mother, I assumed, followed close behind. From her doting smile and the way she matched his unhurried pace, I could tell she wasn't the least bit bored or impatient. The little boy was talking to himself, or maybe to an imaginary friend. Cars passed, a Mini, then a Camry. A Mercedes pulled into a parking place near the Bow Street Emporium. An older woman with silvery gray hair got out, dropped a quarter in the meter, and ran into Hot Buns, a new bakery known for its rich desserts.

"Who is it, Josie?" Wes asked again.

I shook my head. He'd learn soon enough.

He didn't push. We stood and watched and waited. The screams, when they began about ten minutes later, were shrill and sustained, reaching a crescendo just as the Blue Dolphin's door flew open and Ellis appeared. I glanced at Wes. He held a palm-sized video camera aimed at the front door.

"Resisting won't do any good," Ellis said, his voice calm.

Detective Brownley appeared on Ellis's right, followed by

the uniformed Portsmouth police officer. "Come on, ma'am," she said to someone inside.

In tandem, they took a step onto the sidewalk, then another, and just like that, they eased their prisoner onto the street.

Ava.

She tugged and yanked and kicked, her thick-soled white waitress shoes nearly connecting with Detective Brownley's shin. Ava looked so young.

"Stop it!" she screeched. "You don't understand! It was a mistake! Stop it!"

I stepped out from behind the pot, and as soon as she saw me, she stopped flailing.

"Josie," she shouted. "Help!"

"Ava," I said.

"It was an accident."

I didn't respond. I couldn't think of anything to say.

"It was an accident," she repeated, seeming to gather strength as she spoke. "It was all a mistake."

A slight scuffing sound alerted me that Wes, still hidden behind the copper tub, had shifted position.

Ellis caught Detective Brownley's eye and patted the air, signaling that they should hold steady. Detective Brownley nodded, indicating that she got the message. The Portsmouth detective stepped outside, saw what was happening, and paused under the shell-shaped overhang. Ellis looked at me and lowered and raised his chin one time, a mini-nod. I got the message, too. If I could keep Ava talking, he wanted me to do so.

"What was a mistake?" I asked her.

"Really, Josie," she said, her chest heaving, "it wasn't my fault."

I nodded. "Tell me what happened."

"Riley was upset about me and Bobby," she said, sounding ingenuous, as if Riley's reaction was irrational or had caught her unawares.

"Really?" I asked.

She paused, and her expression changed. There was none of the ingenue in her now; she was all viper. She raised her chin. "So she said. I think it was all pride and insecurity, myself. I told her the truth—the only reason Bobby stayed with her was for her money. She didn't want to hear it, but it was true."

I could tell that she was sincere, and that made it even worse.

"Bobby loved me," she said, "but he needed Riley's money."

"You don't care about money, do you?" I said.

"Not a bit. All I care about is Bobby."

"Is that what you told Riley in the parking lot?" I asked, aware that to a stranger listening in, it would sound as if we were having a normal conversation.

"Yes, exactly. Riley had learned about Bobby and me from her lawyer. To tell you the truth, I was glad it was out in the open. I was tired of living a lie. I knew Bobby would be upset, though. We talked about his leaving Riley all the time, for months. He told me not to be shortsighted, that a little patience now would pay off later, big-time." She snorted, an ugly, derisive sound. "Riley told me to leave him alone. As if. She was delusional, that's all, just delusional, and I told her so. Riley said that Bobby had promised to break up with me, that he was taking her to Crenshaw's that very weekend. I told her Bobby was playing her, that he would do and say whatever was necessary to keep her money. I showed her my button. I told her Bobby gave it to me because he loved me, but she still didn't believe me."

"Did you tell Bobby that you'd had the run-in with her?"

She nodded. "Yes. Right away. I went straight to the Blue Dolphin." She smiled, remembering. "Bobby told me not to worry about anything, that he'd smooth it out with her, no problem."

The snake, I thought. *How could he?* I glanced at Ellis, and he nodded.

"When did you get the button, anyway?" I asked, trying for a neutral tone, hoping Ava would mistake my horror and dismay for empathy.

"Christmas Eve. When Bobby gave it to me, he said it was a token of his love."

"You must have been over the moon," I said.

Her eyes lit up like a Christmas tree. "I was *way* over the moon!"

"What happened next?" I asked.

"Gretchen came and joined the conversation. I said something about McCardell's use of closures, something . . . I don't remember. Whatever it was, it was lame, and I knew that sooner or later, Gretchen would realize it." She paused and shook her head. "I'm sorry about Gretchen, Josie, I really am—but at that point, I had to do everything I could to minimize risk. That was the first time I'd ever shot a gun. The recoil really hurt my shoulder."

Good, I thought, hoping her shoulder was still sore.

She continued talking. "After that, I decided that my best hope, and realistically my only option, was to do nothing."

"You didn't do nothing, though. You burned her condo down."

"That was later, after her memory of the car started coming back." She met my eyes, and I could feel her intensity as if it were heat. "I had no choice, Josie. I couldn't risk it."

I was revolted and infuriated in equal measures. I felt my lip raise into a snarl. I wanted to strike out at her or walk away. Instead, I glanced at Ellis. He nodded, encouraging me to continue. I looked at Ava and saw no guile. Evidently, she thought her attempts at killing Gretchen were logical and understandable, and, knowing me to be a reasonable woman, she was certain I'd agree.

"How did you get the gun?" I asked.

Ava made an "Oh, please" noise. "My roommate's from Maine," she said, "so I know what their driver's licenses look like. Photoshop did the rest. I figured that the license didn't have to be good enough to fool an expert; it only had to be good enough to fool a salesman who'd be way more focused on earning a commission than he would be on my ID." She shrugged again. "I was right. It was easy."

"Why did you use the name Nancy Patterson?"

"I thought it was pretty, and I knew it was fairly common."

She selected a name for her killer persona because she thought it was pretty, I thought.

"Why did you use Riley's name when you called the sorority about getting a replacement button?"

"I was afraid they would only give out information to members," she replied.

As suspected. "Did you have any trouble tracing the button to the sorority?"

"No. I only pretended." She paused, then added, "I didn't want to lie to you, Josie. I'm sorry that I had to."

"I understand," I said. "Why did you alter Dr. Walker's fax?"

"That was such an opportunity! When I saw that a pearl rosette button was on one of Bobby's grandmother's coats, it was the answer to a prayer. I knew that if I could get my hands on the coat, I could remove the button, and that would be far less risky than ordering a replacement—and as long as the fax didn't show a button, no one would ever know. I went through every garment in the collection looking for that coat. Do you remember? You came in while I was looking."

"Right," I said, recalling how frightened I'd been listening to the little rustlings. "You were listening to your iPod, so you didn't hear me call your name." I paused. "Did Bobby know you'd lost the button?"

"Yes . . . I had to tell him. I knew he'd wonder if he saw I wasn't wearing it. I said I lost it at work, but since the police seemed to think that it might have been worn by the killer, I was afraid to tell."

"And he believed you."

Her eyes opened wide. "Of course."

Wow, I thought, wondering if it was true and deciding it probably was. There's no fool like an old fool except a fool in love. I recalled how I'd known something was off with Bobby the day I'd stopped by the Blue Dolphin to offer my condolences. Apparently, what I'd witnessed was the age-old battle between mind and heart: Bobby had wanted to believe Ava, but inklings of doubt had begun to edge out blind trust.

Ellis interrupted my speculation by waggling his fingers at me.

I took a breath as I pushed thoughts of Bobby aside. "Was it hard to do—change the fax, I mean?" I asked.

"Not at all. Everyone was busy. No one noticed."

"When you discovered that the coat wasn't among Riley's collection, what did you do?"

"I ordered the replacement from Blackstone's. I went to a mall jeweler first, thinking they'd be less likely to remember me, but they don't do custom work. I'd heard you recommend Blackstone's to Jack."

"Then you heard that I thought the coat was in the trunk in the attic."

"Right, and I knew I had to get the trunk open before you did."

"You used the hatchet."

"I tried so hard." Tears welled in her eyes, and her handcuffed hands curled into fists.

"What about Bobby? You couldn't just take the button from his grandmother's coat, could you?"

"He wouldn't care." She seemed to read skepticism in my expression, because she added, "Bobby adores me, Josie. He'd never question my motives."

"What about Ruby Bowers? Didn't it bother you that he was seeing her, too?"

"Ruby and Bobby? What a joke!" She paused, looking at me. "I'm not lying, Josie. Ruby was nothing to him but a ticket to the big time. Bobby and I . . . we're so close. We're soul mates."

I felt my stomach clench. *Soul mates,* I thought, disgusted. I swallowed and forced myself to continue.

"Where did you meet Bobby, anyway?" I asked.

"Here. It was my first day on the job. We both knew right away."

I needed to ask about her killing Riley, but I didn't know if I could bear to listen to her sick rationalizations. She was waiting for me to comment, and from her expression, I could tell she expected me to share her joy.

"Why did you go to the tag sale room to talk to Riley? I mean, you knew how upset she was, and you knew Bobby wasn't ready to get off the gravy train. What made you do it?"

She nodded, eager to explain. "I'd thought of a way for her to save face. She could use Bobby's move to New York as an excuse for their breakup. I told her lots of people break up because they grow apart, that there was no shame in it. I begged her to leave her money in the business. I said that just because their marriage was ending didn't mean the restaurants weren't a good investment."

"What did she say?"

"She laughed at me. She told me I was pathetic. Can you believe it? *Me*. She told me *I* was pathetic. Ha."

"That must have been horrible to hear."

"It was beyond humiliating. It was unendurable. Riley taunted me on purpose, then swatted at me as if I were a gnat." She paused again. "What could I do? I had no choice."

"What did you do?"

"I pushed back."

"What happened then?" I asked.

She looked off into the distance, and I thought I'd lost her, but from her tone as she continued talking, I could tell she was back in the tag sale room with Riley.

"She grabbed my necklace," she said.

"Did it break?" I asked.

"Yes." She looked back at me. "That's when the button fell off. I'd looped it through a silver chain." She smiled, a sad, small smile. "I can't believe I lost it. When I put it on, I swore I'd never take it off."

"What happened after Riley tore your necklace?"

Ava kept her eyes on me, and I could tell she was daring me to dispute her version of the event. Her gaze was searing. "I didn't mean to kill her . . . you know that, right?"

"Right," I said, only because in order to keep her talking, I had to. I felt no guilt fibbing to her.

"If she'd agreed to give Bobby up, none of this would have happened," she said. "It was her own fault."

I nodded, hoping she'd believe that acknowledgment implied agreement.

"It was so easy," she said, "and quick. I grabbed the ends of her scarf, twisted them, and pulled. She was dead in less than a minute."

"You killed her."

"I had to."

"No, you didn't."

She raised her chin. "You're right. I wanted to . . . but that doesn't change the facts—it was her own fault."

I was out of questions. I couldn't stand to talk to her anymore. I'd been right about what happened to Riley, but I took no pride in that because I'd been wrong about who'd done it. I felt awful that I'd misjudged Becka and Kenna so completely.

I was also crushed by Ava's betrayal. I'd trusted her. I'd planned to hire her full-time. I felt like a fool. I hadn't watched my back, and now I was paying the emotional price. I looked at Ellis and shook my head, one shake.

Ellis stepped forward. "Let's go," he said to Ava.

Ava jumped, startled. It was as if she'd forgotten she was in police custody.

"No!" she protested. "I'm not done."

They ignored her protests, and within seconds, Detective Brownley had her in the back of Ellis's SUV.

Just before the detective closed the door, Ava leaned out and called, "Tell Bobby where I am, will you, Josie? Thank you!"

Her words echoed in my mind long after the door was shut behind her and the car had pulled away from the curb.

How, I wondered, *could I have been so wrong about her?* It was as if up were down and back were front. *If I couldn't trust my judgment,* I thought, *I might as well pack it in.*

"You okay?" Wes asked, stepping out from behind the tub.

I shook my head, keeping my eyes on the place the car had been. "No."

"How did you know it was her?"

I didn't reply.

Wes stepped in front of me, blocking my view. I looked up and met his eyes. He waited for me to speak. He must have recognized my upset, because when he spoke again, his voice was different, softer and more compassionate.

"Want a cup of coffee or something?" he asked.

I nodded, wanting to sit down, wanting warmth. Wes led the way to Hot Buns. It felt good to follow along and not to think.

As soon as he pushed open the bakery door, I felt some of my tension drop away. The place was redolent of fresh-baked cinnamon buns, and the scent reminded me of my mother's kitchen on Fridays, her regular baking day. Cinnamon was the smell of comfort, the aroma of love.

Most of the bakery's business was takeout, and there were only two tables. Both were empty. I chose the one farthest from the counter, and I let Wes wait on me.

I'd known what was coming, but I was shocked nevertheless. That Ava was soulless was the only way to explain her matter-of-fact recitation of murder, arson, and attempted murder. Soullessness accounted for the way she'd blamed her victims, too. I had no context, not yet, for the fact that I'd welcomed her into my world. I'd taken a monster under my wing.

"How did you know it was Ava?" Wes asked, after he'd placed a pot of Earl Grey tea and an apple croissant in front of me.

"Never overlook the obvious," I said. "When I had an easy time tracing the button, and Ava said she hadn't been able to get to first base with it, the obvious conclusion was that she was lying. When the police couldn't find the phone Bobby used to break up with his mistress, the obvious conclusion was that he did it in person—or that he didn't do it."

"You think he didn't break up with her for real?" Wes asked, sounding shocked.

I shrugged. "You heard her. It sounded true to me."

Wes soft-whistled. "Not nice."

"He's not even close to nice, Wes. He's a creep. A louse. A rat. He's a jerk."

"So you figured out Ava killed Riley and tried to kill Gretchen just because she screwed up researching the button and there was a chance Bobby didn't break up with her?"

"Those, plus two other things: The trips to Honduras oc-curred during Hitchens vacations—and Ava is a grad student at Hitchens. Also, in Ava's first interview with the police, right after Riley's body was discovered, she said she'd admired Riley's McCardell jacket that afternoon in the parking lot, but she couldn't possibly have seen it then. Riley's trench coat was buttoned to the neck, and she wore a scarf—the scarf Ava used to kill her. She had to have seen Riley without her coat on, and that could only have happened later in the day."

"Which cooks Ava's goose, for sure. What's going to hap-pen to Bobby, do you think?"

I finished my tea and pushed back my chair. "My guess? Nothing. He'll hold another press conference and throw her under the bus."

"You're probably right," Wes agreed.

"If he does, I want to be there. Can you get me in?"

Wes grinned. "You bet."

CHAPTER TWENTY-EIGHT

W es called at eight the next morning. Bobby had scheduled a news conference for noon, and Wes had snared me a press pass.

Due to the incredible wave of media interest, the news conference was being held in the Sheraton's Grand Ballroom. I got there early and sat in the last row, by the exit. I hoped to be practically invisible. All the major news and Hollywood gossip organizations were represented, along with specialty publications like *New York City Restaurateur.* By noon, there was standing room only.

At ten after, Bobby entered the room from a service door without his entourage and walked to the podium. He scanned the room and waited for people to quiet down. He looked older than he had the last time I'd seen him, and worried.

"I'll read a brief statement," he said, "then answer your questions. I asked you all here today because I know your readers and viewers and listeners have questions. They are as shocked at Ms. Marlow's assertions as I am, and they want to know the truth about my role in this tragedy. I want to set the record straight as to what I did and didn't do."

He took a deep breath, then continued.

"After listening to nonstop rumors that I was unfaithful, Riley decided to find out for herself if they were true. Through her attorney, she hired a private detective to investigate. He succeeded in finding evidence of my wrongdoing. Riley saw the evidence and instructed her lawyer to immediately file for divorce and change her will. Then she called me."

He cleared his throat.

"Getting caught was a real wake-up call. I knew I didn't want to lose Riley, and I told her so. I begged her to forgive me, to give me another chance. I promised her that I'd change, and she agreed."

Bobby paused, and I could see rock-hard muscles pulsing in his neck and jaw.

"Make no mistake, Riley was a saint. I am the sinner. Riley agreed to forgive me."

He cleared his throat again.

"I immediately ended my relationship with the young woman I'd been seeing, Ava Marlow. I would now like to anticipate some of your questions. First, I didn't tell the police about Ava because I was in shock from losing my beloved wife. It never occurred to me that a woman I perceived as sweet and kind could possibly be capable of murder." He raised a hand as if he expected a barrage of questions. "I know, I know . . . some of you are thinking it's impossible that I was that stupid—but it's true. I was exactly that stupid when it came to Ava. I believed what she told me. Now, of course, I see the truth. Ava isn't sweet, she's manipulative and narcissistic. She would do anything to achieve her ambition."

He paused and inhaled deeply.

"Second, I suspect you're wondering why I gave Ava my grandmother's button. I could have told you that I did it simply because it was handy, but the truth is more complicated than that. I wanted the gift to mean something special to her. That I didn't properly value my family heirloom is another thing of which I am deeply ashamed." He paused to sip water. "I'll take your questions now."

As Bobby answered the reporters' questions, I observed him closely. His eyes reflected his jumbled emotions. I could see his thoughts and feelings as clearly as if the words "mortified," "horrified," "shocked," and "crushed" were tattooed across his forehead. Ava was right—she and Bobby hadn't been having a casual fling; he'd fallen as deeply in love with her as she had with him. I almost felt sorry for him. Almost, but not quite, because from the way he spoke to the camera, not the audience, I could tell that the tattoo artist would have inked the word "calculating," too.

Bobby kept his cool throughout the hour-long ordeal. As far as I could tell, he wasn't purposefully evasive. He stated that he hadn't seen or spoken to Ava since her arrest and had no intention of ever seeing her again. He had no idea whether she was cooperating with the authorities or not. While his protestations of ignorance, shame, and embarrassment seemed genuine, I remained skeptical that his motives were pure. Bobby was a good talker with a lot at stake. Regardless of the truth of the matter, from what I could see, his apparent candor was working its magic. Even Wes, as hard-nosed a reporter as I'd ever met, was nodding as he scribbled notes.

"I didn't want to believe it," Bobby said, responding to a question about whether he'd thought that Ava was capable of murder. "Frankly, I'm still struggling to believe it."

When the pace of questioning slowed and I sensed an end in sight, I stood up. I hated being the center of attention, but there were questions that needed to be asked. Bobby looked at me, confused, and I could tell that he hadn't known I was in the room.

"Why didn't you tell the police that you gave Ava one of your grandmother's buttons?" I asked.

Several reporters skewed around in their chairs to see who was talking, then turned back to listen to Bobby's answer.

"It was a private gift," he said, narrowing his eyes. "I didn't see the need to tell them."

"Why not? As soon as they told you that a button had been found at the murder scene, you must have known it was hers."

"That's not true. I still don't know it's hers. Thousands of buttons were produced. None can be traced to an individual."

"Fair enough," I said, "but she told you she lost it at Prescott's, in the room where your wife was murdered, right? And you still didn't tell the police?"

He paused for a moment to sip his water. "That's correct."

Questions exploded from all directions.

"When did she lose it?" a man on my left shouted.

"She said it must have happened on the Thursday or Friday before Riley was killed. She thought it probably fell off while she was dusting the undersides of tables and chairs at her job."

"What's the big deal? Why didn't she just tell the police about it?" another man asked.

"She said she was scared—and that she wanted to protect me. She told me that she was a terrible liar, that if she tried to make something up about where she got the button, they'd know she was lying for sure." He paused, his expression a combination of awkward embarrassment and pride. "You don't need to tell me I fell for the oldest line in the book. I already know it. All I can say is that every man wants to believe the woman he loves is a lousy liar—me included."

"So you loved her?" a woman sitting next to Wes called out.

He exhaled loudly. "Yes."

"Do you still?" the same woman asked.

He raised his chin. "No," he said, his tone defiant.

"When did she tell you she'd lost the button?" Wes called.

"The Thursday after Riley died," Bobby replied.

"What about Ruby Bowers?" I shouted, still standing. "How is it you became involved with her if you were in love with Ava?"

The room quieted.

"I'm not going to say anything about Ruby except that she's a beautiful woman and a good friend."

"You said you broke up with Ava as soon as you hung up from Riley. Did you call her?"

"No . . . I told her in person."

"Where?"

"Outside the Blue Dolphin. She ran into Riley in the parking lot as she was leaving for her lunch break. They spoke briefly, and from there, she came directly to see me. We stood near the river and talked."

"Did you really end your affair? Or did you just tell her that you needed to be discreet for a while?"

"I told her I wasn't going to end my marriage."

"That doesn't answer my question."

He took in a deep breath and pulled back his shoulders, a warrior readying himself for battle. "I hope I would have had the strength to stop seeing her."

Another reporter, a woman standing in the back, asked what Ava said, exactly, when they met by the river, and I realized that I didn't care what Ava said, exactly. I made my way through the crowd to the exit. My questions had been answered. I'd wanted to see him, to get an in-person sense of the man behind the words, and I had. Now I just wanted to get out of there.

I called Wes around three and asked if we could meet.

"Sure," he said. "Whatcha got?"

"Questions."

"I'm near your office. I'll be there in ten, okay?"

"I'll meet you in the parking lot," I said.

"Ava's lawyer won't let her say another word," Wes said. "He's really hot that the police let her talk to you, and he's certain that her confession will be ruled inadmissible."

"Really?" I said, upset at the thought. "Do you think he's right?"

"Beats me, but I don't think it matters. There's so much

evidence against her that even if her confession is thrown out, they've got her." He ticked off the evidence on his fingers. "The police have the photos Gus took, and they're pretty explicit. Based on the photos, not the confession, they got a court order to search her apartment." He tapped a second finger. "They have her passport in hand, and it matches the passport pages showing the trips to Honduras that were found in Riley's possession."

Wes paused, then said in a different tone, "Aren't you curious how that detective got hold of her passport?"

"Yes. Do you know?"

"The police think he cozied up to Ava's roommate and got into the apartment that way."

"Heck of a way to earn a living," I said.

"Anyway . . ." A third finger went up. "A police artist took her passport photo and added dark hair, a straw hat, and big sunglasses. Both Mr. Blackmore and the Maine gun dealer identified her as the woman they knew as Nancy Patterson. Also, the gun dealer kept a copy of her driver's license, and the police found the original in her apartment." Wes raised two more fingers, one for the fake license and one for his next point. "Several employees from the Honduran resort have identified her as the woman they knew as Mrs. Jordan." He brought up his left hand to mark his sixth point. "They found the hatchet in her car. It had been cleaned with bleach, so there was no trace of the leather on the trunk or any other forensic evidence, but they expect to be able to prove the strike marks on the trunk are an exact match to the blade and hammerhead." He raised a seventh finger. "Last but not least, there's a red-light camera on the service road leading from your place to the interstate. Guess what? They've got photos showing Ava driving away in her silver Chevy both after Riley's murder and after Gretchen was shot."

That must be the same camera that nabbed Fred for running a red light, I thought.

"Why didn't they check it before?" I asked.

"The light's brand-new, and it's in Portsmouth, not Rocky Point. The Rocky Point police didn't know about it, and it never occurred to the Portsmouth police to check until after Ava was in custody. Then someone had a bright idea."

"Do you know why the police didn't search for silver cars as soon as Gretchen reported seeing one?"

"They did. They pulled together a list of all silver cars registered within a fifty-mile radius of Rocky Point."

I nodded. "Which means Ava's name didn't come up because she's a student and her car is registered at her parent's address in Michigan."

"Exactly. Students don't have to transfer their registrations."

"I still can't believe it, Wes," I said, shaking my head.

"She snookered you good, huh?"

"I'm not sure I like your word choice, but yes, she did."

"Happens to the best of us," he said, alarmingly unconcerned. "Anything else?"

I shook my head.

He opened his car door, then paused. "Do you think Bobby's apology was sincere?" he asked.

"I don't know."

"I thought it had a ring of truth."

"If Bobby was so in love with Ava, how come he got involved with Ruby?"

"Maybe he didn't."

"I told you about Ruby's phone message."

"You've got a point there—that was definitely hubba hubba hottie stuff. Maybe he's one of those guys . . . You know what I'm talking about. You read about them every day. They can't say no, or at least they don't say no. Of course, even if that's what was going on, that doesn't mean he wasn't for real in love with Ava or that he isn't genuinely sorry now."

"That sounds right. I think Bobby truly loved Ava and is

actually sorry about how things turned out. I also think those guys get very experienced at fixing things."

"You mean they lie?" Wes asked.

"I mean they say whatever is necessary to extricate themselves from whatever situation they find themselves in. Sometimes they lie. Sometimes they apologize. Sometimes they probably even mean it—at least at the moment they're saying it."

Wes nodded slowly, thinking it through. "Do you think Bobby will always cheat?"

I shrugged. "Over the years, I've discovered that leopards rarely change their spots."

"Well, sometimes they do."

Wes was young, in his twenties. *He'll learn,* I thought. "I don't mean to sound cynical, but that hasn't been my experience."

"So you think he's a goner from the world of celebrity bad boys?"

"Oh, no, not at all. He sounded sincere, and the world likes good-looking, successful go-getters who take responsibility for their mistakes. I can almost guarantee you that he'll recover his golden-haired-boy image, and that he'll do it in nothing flat."

Wes nodded. "I can see that." He started to step into his car, then paused again. He grinned. "You called him out good, huh?"

I smiled. "That's one tiny ray of sunshine in a pretty bleak landscape."

I watched Wes drive away, then walked slowly back toward the office, thinking about Ava and Bobby and truth.

I wanted to talk to Ty, but he was in a closed-door meeting and unavailable until six. I thought about calling Zoë, but she would be busy with after-school child care. My instinct was to get back to work, but I knew that wasn't what I needed right now. I needed joy. I needed an antidote to Ava's betrayal and Bobby's conveniently timed contrition. I needed to be around people I could trust.

As I reached the door, a marked police car pulled into the lot. Griff was driving. He stopped near where I was standing, stepped out, and opened the back door. I leaned down, trying to see who was inside the vehicle, but before I could, Gretchen leapt out, ran around the car, and flew into my arms. I hugged her, then hugged her again. She waved good-bye to Griff, and he drove off.

"I'm back!" she shouted, spinning around like a ballerina. "My shoulder's fine, and with Ava in custody, I'm free! I didn't want to wait until tomorrow to get back to work, and the police said it was okay, so I had them drive me directly here!"

"It's so wonderful to see you!" I hugged her again. "I was just thinking that I needed some good news. Are you really okay?"

"You mean, given that one of my favorite customers was strangled at my place of employment and her murderer tried to kill me—twice—and succeeded in shooting me and burning down my home—you mean, given all that, you're wondering if I'm really okay?"

I grasped her forearm. "That's exactly what I mean," I said, looking into her shining green eyes.

She grinned. "Yes," she said. "I am."

"Thank God."

"I'm sad about Riley and I'm beyond shocked about Ava, but I'm just so darn happy to be safe and alive and free!"

She jumped up in a spontaneous expression of delight, whipping her arms over her head, sending her spring-flower-patterned skirt twirling.

When she landed, she shouted, "Yippee!"

I giggled and jumped a little myself. Her happiness was contagious.

"Can you and Jack come to dinner tonight? I want to invite everyone to a celebration party. We can celebrate Riley's life as we celebrate your emancipation."

"Yes! We accept with pleasure." She jumped again, giggling. "Maybe Fred will bring Sandy, that girl he took out the other day. I want to meet her."

CHAPTER TWENTY-NINE

I made a reservation for fourteen at the best Italian restaurant in Rocky Point, Notaro's.

Fred brought Sandy, the Hitchens professor he'd just begun to date. Eric brought Grace, his girlfriend of more than a year. Sasha brought her roommate, Jenn. Cara brought her grandson, Patrick, a cutie. Ellis brought Zoë, a last-minute coup he managed to achieve when Cathy, the police civilian admin, overheard him say that she couldn't find anyone to watch the kids and offered to babysit. I brought Ty.

We met at the restaurant at seven, and at seven fifteen, when Jack still wasn't there, Gretchen began to fret. As people were settling in at the long rectangular table in the private, wood-paneled room, she took me aside.

"He told me he'd be here before me," she whispered. "Do you think something happened, like a car accident or something?"

"No. Probably he just got delayed for some reason. I'm sure he'll be here in a sec."

She took her seat in the middle of the table and glanced at the empty chair next to her.

"Does everyone know everyone else?" I asked, but before anyone could reply, horns sounded.

Trumpets, I realized, followed by trombones. I looked over my shoulder in time to see four men in tuxedos enter our private room and arrange themselves in a loose semicircle against the far wall. They were playing Henry Purcell's "Trumpet Voluntary," one of my favorite ceremonial music pieces, from miniature sheet music clipped to the end of their instruments. I knew the group, Academy Brass. I'd hired them occasionally to play at auction previews.

Jack walked into the room and stopped halfway to the table. He kept his eyes on Gretchen and smiled. She stood up. He dropped to one knee, extracted a Blackmore's jewelry box from his pocket, and opened it. Nestled on the white velvet lining was an emerald-cut diamond ring. In the soft golden light cast by the chandeliers, it sent out rainbows like a prism.

"I love you, Gretchen," he said. "I want to spend the rest of my life with you. Please . . . will you marry me?"

"Oh, Jack," Gretchen whispered. She pressed her fingers into her cheekbones. Her eyes filled with tears. Time stood still.

"Will you, Gretchen?" he asked again.

I held my breath.

"Yes!" she said. She ran around the table, reaching him just as he stood. "Yes! Yes!"

He slipped the ring on her finger and gathered her into his arms.

I smiled and stood up and began applauding. "Wow!" I said.

Ty put his arm around me and drew me close. I leaned my head on his shoulder. Soon everyone was standing and applauding. Fred whistled. Cara was crying. Gretchen was flushed. Jack was grinning.

The musicians segued into Jean-Joseph Mouret's joyous "Rondeau." Gretchen and Jack turned to face the quartet and listened to the end of the song. When it was finished, the bass trombonist stepped forward and smiled at them.

"Congratulations," he said, then the four men filed out.

"Can you believe this?" Gretchen asked as she and Jack walked back to the table.

"Yes!" I said. "Let me see the ring." The sparkles were dazzling. "It's magnificent, Jack."

Jack raised Gretchen's hand to his lips and kissed it, then pressed it against his chest, holding it to his heart. "So's Gretchen."

She kissed his cheek. She looked radiant.

It was an evening of toasts—to their engagement; to Gretchen's safe return to work; to Riley's legacy helping children, providing scholarships, and preserving fashion; and by me, to us all, to our health and happiness. The last toast was my dad's, "To silver light in the dark of night."

At the end of the evening, as Ty and I walked hand in hand to the car amid the sounds of crickets and katydids, I repeated Wes's question about whether Bobby's apology and promise to Riley to change were sincere, summarizing Wes's perspective, and adding my leopards-don't-change-spots metaphor.

"How about you?" I asked. "What do you think?"

"I think you're right on all counts." He laughed and paused under one of the floodlights that lined the parking lot. He pulled me close. "If nothing else, Bobby knows a romantic spot when he sees it. I did some training at Crenshaw's a couple of years ago. It's spectacular. Every ground-floor room in the main chalet has a private walled-in outdoor area with a hot tub."

"That sounds heavenly!" I said, leaning in against him, my cheek resting against the soft cotton of his denim shirt. I could hear his heart beating.

"Maybe we should go."

I leaned back and pretend-pouted. "What do you mean, maybe?"

He laughed again. "How's Memorial Day?"

"How's tomorrow?"

He kissed me and I kissed him back.

"Tomorrow works," he said. "Can you really get away?"

"Yes. Can you?"

"Yes."

We kissed again, a long one this time, and then we walked arm in arm to the car.

As some things end, others begin, I thought. Gretchen and Jack's life as a married couple was about to begin. The people Riley would touch through the scholarships her foundation would award and the scientific research she'd fund represented new beginnings, too. Earlier in the day, I'd hoped for some moments of joy, and my wish had come true.

ACKNOWLEDGMENTS

Special thanks go to Leslie Hindman, who, with her team at Leslie Hindman Auctioneers, continues to appraise antiques for me to write about. Please note that any errors are mine alone.

As a former Mystery Writers of America/New York chapter president and the chair of the Wolfe Pack's literary awards, I've been fortunate to meet and work alongside dozens of talented writers and dedicated readers. Thank you all for your support. For my pals in the Wolfe Pack and fans of Rex Stout's Nero Wolfe stories everywhere, I've added my usual allotment of Wolfean trivia to this book.

Thank you to Jo-Ann Maude, Katie Longhurst, Christine de los Reyes, and Carol Novak. Thank you also to Dan and Linda Chessman, Marci and James Gleason, John and Mona Gleason, Linda and Ren Plastina, Rona and Ken Foster, and Liz Weiner and Bob Farrar. Thanks also to Harry Rinker for his invaluable assistance about antiques.

Independent booksellers have been invaluable in helping me introduce Josie to their customers—thank you all. I want to acknowledge my special friends at these independent bookshops: Partners and Crime, Front Street Books, the Poisoned Pen, Well Red Coyote, Clues Unlimited, Mostly Books, Mysteries to Die For, Book'em Mysteries, Mystery Bookstore, Legends, Book Carnival, Mysterious Galaxy, San Francisco Mystery Bookstore, M is for Mystery, Murder by the Book in Houston, where David Thompson will be forever missed, Murder by the Book in Denver, Murder by the Book in Portland, Schuler

Books, the Regulator, McIntyre's, Quail Ridge Books, Book Cove, Remember the Alibi Mystery Bookstore, Centuries & Sleuths, Mystery Lovers Bookshop, the Mystery Company, the Mysterious Bookshop, Partners in Crime, Booked for Murder, Aunt Agatha's, Foul Play, Windows a Bookshop, Murder by the Beach, Books & Books, Moore Books, The Bookstore in the Grove, Uncle Edgar's Mystery Bookstore, Seattle Mystery Bookstore, Park Road Books, and Once Upon a Crime.

Manhattan's Black Orchid Bookstore is still sorely missed; I remain grateful to Bonnie Claeson and Joe Guglielmelli for helping launch Josie.

Many chain bookstores have been incredibly supportive as well—thank you to those many booksellers who've gone out of their way to become familiar with Josie. Special thanks go to my friend Dianne Defonce at the Border's in Fairfield, Connecticut.

Thanks also to Nili L. Olay and Gene C. Gill of the Jane Austen Society of North America, Linda Landigran of *Alfred Hitchcock Mystery Magazine*, Barbara Floyd of *The Country Register*, Aldon James of the National Arts Club, and Wilda W. Williams of *Library Journal*. Many thanks also to Molly Weston and Jen Forbus.

Special thanks to my librarian friends David S. Ferriero, Doris Ann Norris, Sally Fellows, Mary Russell, Denise Van Zanten, Mary Callahan Boone, Cynde Bloom Lahey, Cyndi Rademacher, Eleanor Ratterman, Jane Murphy, Jennifer Vido, Judith Abner, Karen Kiley, Lesa Holstine, Monique Flasch, Susie Schachte, Virginia Sanchez, Maxine Bleiweis, Cindy Clark, Linda Avellar, Heidi Fowler, Georgia Owens, Eva Perry, Mary J. Etter, Paul Schroeder, Tracy J. Wright, Kristi Calhoun Belesca, Paulette Sullivan, Frances Mendelsohn, Deborah Hirsch, and Heather Caines.

Thank you to my literary agent emerita, Denise Marcil, and my much-appreciated literary agent, Cristina Concepcion of

Don Congdon Associates, Inc. Special thanks go to Michael Congdon, Katie Kotchman, and Katie Grimm as well.

My editor, Minotaur Books' executive editor, Hope Dellon, continues to provide insightful feedback about the manuscript, helping me write stories that ring true. Special thanks also go to Laura Bourgeois, assistant editor, for her thoughtful comments. I'm indebted to them, and to the entire Minotaur Books' team. Thank you also to those I work with most often, Andy Martin, Hector DeJean, Sarah Melnyk, and Talia Ross, as well as those behind the scene, including my copy editor, India Cooper, and my cover designer, David Baldeosingh Rotstein.